Edward and the Island

By Charles Martin
&
Will Weinke

A work of fiction

Edited by Emily Jerman
Cover images and design by Nicole Moan .

Note to the reader:

Many will believe this to be merely a long metaphor on the human condition; the rest will dismiss it as silly fantasy and a melodramatic argument against the possibility of a utopian civilization. They will assume, understandably, that my yarn is nothing more than a whimsical, albeit blasphemous, comedy.

Those few who realize the gravity, the staggering implications of my firsthand account of the afterlife, and even more troubling, of God, will call me insane or a presumptuous liar!

To that, I say I have imparted on this author nothing less than the future of the 'Blessed' who will be chosen to enter Paradise. Call me what you will. Deny my story as lunacy or vile misinformation, but I have not altered one moment of my experience of the afterlife.

Then, the question of all questions:

How did I return from Heaven?

That is an answer for another book. Instead, I will only complicate the question by admitting that I not only returned from Paradise, but the story that unfolds in these pages happened well after Judgment Day, after the last flickers of life were extinguished from this planet and the universe was discarded like a failed math equation.

This story is of an experiment conducted well after the death of humanity, once your Earth, your Sun, the entirety of your known universe existed only in the memories of the Blessed, the damned and all those in-between.

—Bali

chapter i

Edward Smitherson died on June 23, 2001. It had been a balmy afternoon in his retirement village in North Carolina. A maple, rosewood and mahogany chess board was populated with abandoned blood red and ivory chess pieces. The red king had been trapped after his bishops, a knight, five pawns and his beloved queen were all struck from the battlefield. The ivory forces were engulfing the blood king. At the cusp of utter defeat and certain exile to a small island state, the blood king was granted a reprieve when Edward failed to rise from his recliner.

Typical of those immune to the shock of mortality, Edward's neighbors joked that the proud, retired pastor died as an act of defiance. Edward would rather shrug off his last days on Earth than face his first loss since arriving at the retirement village four years prior.

In Edward's few clear moments before death, he did not think of his doomed blood king, the dirty dishes in the sink, the half-full laundry hamper or the fact that he had no heirs to claim what few riches he left behind.

Instead, Edward thought only of the afterlife. He managed a grin and replayed the faces that had populated the pews for his thirty years at a small Episcopal church.

He also feared, as he had all his life, that he would be discovered as a latent homosexual. That, regretfully, was the last thought of his human existence.

The massive stroke did not give Edward long to fret. He died quickly and the pain subsided as death neared. It was an easy passage as Edward felt lifted and overwhelmed by a warm tide. Briefly, he tried to mark, remember and categorize the wellspring of glorious sensations, but they were too numerous, too vast and too thrilling. Instead, he dissolved. He dissolved and was weightless.

Heaven embraced Edward, and within its bosom, he thrived. He quickly lost any sense of himself and abandoned any concept of time. The confusions of the flesh were gone and Edward was, at long last, at peace with himself.

Because of Edward's euphoria, he was understandably confused by the heavy tug of flesh weighing down his soul once again. Initially, he feared what had felt like centuries of bliss was merely a dream. He feared he would return to his weathered, flawed body. He was terrified of returning to his retirement home, to his dirty dishes, to the hopeless plight of his blood king.

I'd witnessed the process many times before—the jittery eyes and the small spasms as the equilibrium adjusts to gravity again. It was like waking from a warm, vivid dream into a cold, lonely reality.

So, how long was Edward's glorious dream? That is hard to quantify, time has so little value in heaven. He was there for many, many perfect years and should have been there for many more. I don't believe that the human soul was designed to leave Heaven, and yet, there was Edward's soul, trapped again inside his body.

At Edward's death, he'd been a tall, thin and wrinkled man with sun splotches, a neatly trimmed beard and gray hair that receded to form a "U" on his head. His jaw was stern, his smile was slight and clever, and his eyes were thin and patient. He had been a stoic man with fixed determination—not unlike the painted icons that hung on his church's walls.

At this moment of reanimation, his familiar aged and withered body was replaced by the small, bony frame of a nine-year-old. It was the body that preceded the blossoming of adulthood, the jolting cocktail of hormones and the heavy burdens of maturity. His hair was again a full mop of light-brown curls, his arms and legs were lithe matchsticks and his face was swept with constellations of freckles. He wore the same tan shorts and blue button-up shirt we all wore in this new world.

The cabin of the small luxury jet rattled as it passed through turbulence. Edward's head jerked, but his eyes were still shut tight. I glanced over at a short, dark-skinned boy with a mushroom shaped haircut. His name was Jay; he was the only other human in the cabin. Jay's eyes were wide, lush circles of emerald green. His eye color was so vibrant that it struck many as inhuman.

Jay was lounging across three seats with his head propped up on an armrest and his legs stretched out. His tongue stuck out contemplatively as he picked at the rip he'd worn into the seat.

People often thought we were twins, but we weren't. His nose was long, thin and hooked slightly and mine was wide and flat. I had one of his shining green eyes, but the other was a pale blue, which made me seem even more unnatural.

Then, there was the vast divide between his boyish temperament and my—and I say this with all modesty—more adult mind-set.

Jay's fidgety nature could be exhausting to even the most patient, and I was the one who had to rein him in when he got over-stimulated. I often served as a buffer between Jay and the children, as well as Jay and God.

We all had our parts to play in this new land, but I often tired of my unofficial role as Jay's voice of reason. The long plane trips were especially hard on Jay, thus even harder on me. It was a small price, though.

Jay's attention turned to a travel-size Etch A Sketch. He curled up in the seat and worked the knobs furiously as he chuckled to himself.

"He's waking up," I mumbled.

Jay sat up and looked over the seat towards Edward, who was twitching and shifting. Jay lowered back down and showed me the Etch A Sketch. It said "BALI = TOOL!"

I sighed and grabbed a small black organizer from underneath my seat. I opened it, slid out a pen and flipped to a page with "Edward" written on the top. A mug shot of Edward as an adult was stapled to the top of the page. I checked my watch.

11:38.

"Hurry up," Jay sang. "It doesn't count if you don't write it down."

I ignored Jay as I scribbled a few notes on Edward's condition, replaced the pen, closed the organizer and left it on my seat. I moved to a seat next to the former pastor.

"Edward," I whispered, nudging his shoulder.

His head wavered and he leaned away from me. His body swayed in the seat, then his eyelids slit and widened. He blinked in rapid flutters, wiped away the moist glaze over his eyes with his forearm and looked up at me.

"Hello," I grinned as Edward's confused eyes swept over me. "Welcome back to the physical plane."

"Plane—ha, ha," Jay snickered mockingly.

Edward's mouth moved and a grumble seeped out. The words were indiscernible. Jay slid off his seat, tossed the Etch A Sketch to the floor and climbed down the aisle, using the armrests as stepping stools. He was playing "Hot Lava," the child's game of not touching the ground to avoid burning up in the imaginary lava.

"Take your time, Edward," I said. "It will take time to adjust. My name is Bali; my high-strung companion is Jay. We are taking you to another realm; it is something like Earth."

Edward mumbled again. He grimaced, took a deep breath and tried again.

"Why?" Edward managed.

"Because God wants you to, Edward," Jay answered, his voice flat, almost apathetic. Jay swung around a seatback and landed on the cushion of another seat.

"It's not a punishment, Edward," I added. "It's a reward; God has created something special for select humans who have made it to Paradise."

Edward took a deep breath. His brow crinkled as he thought.

"What's it like?" he said, clearly.

Jay flipped up into a headstand on the cushion, his feet dangling over the back of the seat.

"It's cool," he grimaced as his face turned a brownish red. "It's a surprise, though; we'll be there soon. We're picking up people right now, kinda like a chauffeur service, you know? This is the last load—everyone else is there waiting for us."

Edward sat back against the seat. He closed his eyes, rubbed his eyelids and then stretched. He gripped the back of the seat in front of him. He tugged himself up, but his feet stumbled and tripped as they searched for the ground. He looked down at the floor of the cabin, and then at his legs.

"You have a child's body," I said.

He looked at his feet, his small stubby fingers, the carpet of freckles on his forearms. His breath caught, his eyes reddened.

"Why?"

"Because God wanted you to," Jay sighed.

Before we go further, I want it to be known that Jay might seem cold and callous, and perhaps so do I, but we both shared an affinity for the children chosen to go to God's new world. The Island was a difficult transition for everyone, but its affect on Jay was particularly acute.

Edward began blinking away tears.

"Gah," Jay sighed, rolling his eyes. Jay started to walk to the other side of the plane, but then, remembering the hot lava, jumped back up to a seat. He kicked my organizer off the seat.

"Hey, watch it!" I growled.

"Oh, sorry, sir!" Jay snapped. He grabbed my organizer, pretended to clean it, then held it reverently as he brought it to me. I jerked it out of his hands.

"You're welcome, gah!" Jay shrugged.

"Just be more careful."

"Yessir!"

Jay jumped back up onto the seats and climbed to the front of the cabin. I examined my organizer, rubbed the brown footprint off the front and opened it to make sure no pages were torn.

"Will I ever go back?" Edward asked. The tears were still fighting through his eyelids and sliding down his cheek.

"I'm not sure," I answered, just as Jay fell over the back of a chair, his foot banging against the ceiling and turning on the flight attendant button. I sighed and then looked back at Edward.

"God is certain you will enjoy your new home," I whispered. "He designed it specifically with humans in mind."

Edward studied me. His tears had stopped and been replaced by red veins webbed through the whites in his eyes. He nodded and looked away, sucking hard through his nostrils. He slid over to the window seat and craned his head to look down.

Below the plane was an immense blanket of tumbling reds, whites and pinks. If Edward looked closely enough, he would see thin lines, like threads turning and weaving in and around each other. The mass moved slowly, like clouds, but without vapor— just millions of tiny threads sliding around in the quilt.

"Is that Heaven?" he asked.

"Yes."

"Why?" he mumbled, not wanting an answer.

I sat back in my seat and kept my eyes on Edward. Though I watched the boy with pity, I was also curious. These moments of adjustment were markedly different from one soul to the next. Some cried, some were angry, some were curious.

Edward was morose, almost defeated.

"Here's the other one," Jay called from the front seat.

I stood and made my way to the first row. I knew to expect a stunningly handsome boy, but was still struck when I saw the tall, tan-skinned boy with sun-bleached hair. The boy's name was Tommy Humphries and he possessed the kind of beauty that was either a key to the universe and anything he could ever want from it, or a debilitating burden. For Tommy, unfortunately, it was both.

He'd lived nearly his entire life on a beach, first with the relative stability of two parents who thought of themselves as artists, but were little more than drug-addled nomads. Tommy's father finally disappeared when Tommy was seven, just as the other nomads that dropped in and out of his parents' lives began to notice that the boy was growing up tall, golden haired and frequently unsupervised.

His mother packed up, left southern California and settled with Tommy in Hawaii in a large house on the beach owned by an older man who Tommy avoided whenever possible. Tommy spent many nights on the beach, which prepared him for when the police invaded the mansion. Tommy's mother snatched him out of bed, fled out the back door and they slept under a pier.

Tommy and his mother spent the next decade making homes out of tents, vans or whatever shelter they could find. Tommy grew more handsome with each passing year and his mother increasingly depended on his blue eyes, square jaw and burgeoning sex appeal to keep the pair fed and clothed.

Tommy's mother died of a drug overdose when he was eighteen and he did his best to follow her example until he finally hit bottom and got clean at thirty. He covered his arms and chest with religious tattoos, including a large and rather gruesome crucifixion piece on his back. He began working to save other children being dragged into the same world that nearly consumed him. Tommy died at 32 of a gunshot wound.

"Okay, keep an eye on him," I said, looking over at Jay who was standing on his head again. "Jay! Keep an eye on him!"

"Okay!"

Edward was still staring out the window, crying again. I sat down next to him, opened my organizer and turned to Tommy's page.

11:43.

"Do you want to try standing up again?" I asked Edward as I closed my organizer.

Edward rubbed his eyes, then nodded without looking at me. I slid my hand around his elbow. He clutched onto his armrests and eased his feet to the ground. He pushed himself up, one hand on the seat back and the other grabbing my forearm. He shuffled out to the aisle, grabbed the seats on either side of the aisle and made his way to the back of the plane. His feet dragged and trembled, but his body memory was returning. He turned and went back the other way. With each step, his body seemed to strengthen, to become more comfortable in this new skin. By the time he reached the front row of seats, he was confident enough to walk on his own.

Some found joy in relearning the movements of the body. Some did not, and I was not surprised that Edward, who'd struggled so deeply with the desires of the flesh, was not happy to be returning to bodily form. I hoped that this time would be easier.

Edward wavered and fell against the door to the cockpit, sliding against it until he landed on his knees. He rested his forehead against the egg-white plastic, took a deep breath and forced himself up onto his feet again. I walked up to him and put my hand on his shoulder, but he jerked his shoulder away.

He sighed.

"I'm sorry," he muttered.

"That's fine. I know it's frustrating, but your muscles, your balance and gravity itself all works here exactly as it did on Earth. Your body knows what to do; you just have to reassert control over it again."

Edward nodded, looking back at me with a timid smile.

"So, are we all kids again?" he asked.

"Yes," I answered. "We are going to a place we call the Island. All the souls there have the same minds they died with, minus any dementia or deterioration. God will also be there, but He will not be a child."

"God? I'll be able to see him?" Edward asked, a weak smile forming.

"Yes, He's taken on a body, but He won't be a child. He will be the only adult."

Edward chuckled to himself. He rested his head against the wall.

"Do you think I will enjoy it?" he asked.

"Yes."

I hate answering that question.

"So, if we're all kids, who's flying the plane?"

I put my arms around his shoulder and helped him away from the wall. I opened the cockpit door and Edward struggled inside. Both pilot seats were empty. I eased Edward's weight off me and then walked to one seat. I jabbed my finger above the headrest.

There was a sudden "Hrmph!" as light shimmered around the seat.

I glanced back at Edward with a grin.

"They're angels."

Edward's head cocked as he looked at the shimmering light. The light faded and the seat was empty again. A smile surfaced on Edward's face, this one wide and curious.

"You never know where they are unless you run into one," I said. "They are God's chaperones. They ensure that human curiosity doesn't get the better of your judgment."

Edward watched the seats, his eyes narrow and searching.

"Hrmph!" the angel grunted as I felt a dull thud against my chest. I jerked away and backed up against Edward.

"Okay, we're going," I grinned as I held Edward's elbow. "They don't exactly share God's love of humanity. Let me introduce you to one of your cohorts."

I turned Edward towards Tommy, who still slept but was beginning to twitch.

"He'll be waking soon," I said. "The two of you will be companions and responsible for each other. His name is Tommy."

It would take a person who knew Edward well to notice the shift, the muscles in his jaw tightening, his back arching slightly. If anything, one might think that Edward was struck dumb by the boy's attractiveness, but I knew better.

Sometimes, two souls who knew each other on Earth would find each other on the Island, and it was chalked up to coincidence. Though Tommy had been twenty-two years old when Edward met him, Edward recognized his face. Tommy would not recognize Edward; Edward had been a much older man, hidden behind a web of wrinkles.

I made a mental note to record the "coincidence" in my organizer.

Edward continued to stare down at Tommy. Edward's face paled and he seemed suddenly older. Jay stood up on the seat and leaned closer to Edward.

"Hey," Jay whispered.

Edward jerked his eyes off Tommy and toward Jay.

"Not going to throw up, are you?" Jay smirked.

chapter ii

Questions abound, I am sure. Perhaps the more learned of you readers have queries about metaphysics, religious theory or philosophy. Perhaps the more opinionated of you are screaming "blasphemy" or have already abandoned the story altogether.

To be blunt, these matters are a mere trifle. I am here to tell the story. Physics and religious paradigms are simply not my area of expertise and I therefore choose to not get bogged down by them. But, if those questions are answered in the telling of this story, so much the better.

Sixty-one souls stared at me. Sixty-one men and women plucked out of the fabric of Heaven; given fresh, young bodies and brought to the Island. The children were of all shades and ethnicities, from all manner of societies and across denominational divides. The only unifying factor was their connection to Christianity and that they spoke Americanized English. God felt it was easier that way.

There were thirty females, thirty-one males and all wore button down-blue polo shirts and khaki shorts. They'd seen the Island on the way in. At first, it looked like a rock amid the sea of colors, an oasis amid Heaven.

On the Island, a vast forest of trees near the landing strip led to the base of a wide, naked mountain that climbed up into a veil of clouds. A distant orange star hung in the deep blue sky, similar to the sun that had warmed their skin in their previous lives. The sky reflected the hue of their former world, but without the immense systems of clouds that would drift across the horizon like weary nomads.

Their new sky was perfect and uncluttered, thus less interesting to me. At times, though, when God was feeling more artistic, He might dream up distant storm systems that would tumble along the sky. The rains would never reach the Island, though, and the clouds seemed more a cruel tease, an unfulfilled promise.

If the souls could have broken free of the Island, soared out into the ether and swept across Heaven's expanse, they would have seen the blue sky shift to a warm purple, and eventually they would have found themselves in complete and infinite darkness.

At the precipice between light and dark, they would see a small veil of shimmering luminosity that stood just before the darkness. It was just a few hundred miles wide where light made its final, and most breathtaking, attempt to illuminate the universe. As you passed through this shroud that hid the light from the darkness, every color in God's spectrum would sparkle and drift like ghostly waves in a mirage.

The darkness beyond scared me, as it scared everyone, including God.

That vibrant curtain that stood before it, though, that was my favorite place in all of His creation. It saddened me that so few attempted to see it for fear of falling through into the nightmare beyond.

These souls, these sixty-one strangers, were limited to the awe of this Island, God's new Eden. The center of the Island was dominated by an expansive lake, a large silvery disc of calm water with a shore on the near and far sides of the Island. Each shoreline was backed by a forest, and along the sides of the lake, slivers of forested levees prevented the waters from spilling out into the patchwork of souls below.

If the children were still looking as the plane dipped towards the Island's airstrip, they could see a small cluster of cabins nestled between the shoreline and the trees. That was to be their new home.

The plane came to a rest next to a cliff at the edge of the Island. Beyond that, the land gave way to a long drop into the blanket of souls. After deboarding, the children were gathered into lines and sat down to wait.

They stared at the wall of trees between them and their cabins. They rarely talked, but many smiled nervously as they had when they waited to meet old men in malls dressed as Santa Claus.

Edward's eyes trailed to Tommy often, but always jerked away when Tommy glanced back at him. Several girls within the group also played the same nervous game with Tommy and Tommy began the process of building a wall around himself. They could look, there was nothing he could do about that, but if they wanted anything more from him, it would cost them. Even

Christianity couldn't unlatch his instinct for perceiving affection as a bargaining chip. Nothing was free.

The souls had arrived at different times—some just touching down, some hours ago who wasted away the time staring at a slim trail cut out of the forest. The trail was dark, weeds grew up through the ground, and it curved downhill, so the children were only given a shallow view into their future.

The cliff behind the landing strip was the most accessible spot on the Island where the children could watch Heaven below. All other edges of the Island were sealed off by an impenetrable wall of trees, rock and vegetation, or lay on the far side of the lake. God wanted the children to be immersed into His new world, and they couldn't do that if their eyes continually strayed back to Heaven.

There was a light, ever-present breeze that wafted across the Island. God never let any rain fall on the land, yet the trees never parched and the lake never dried up.

A rustle from the trail seized the group's attention. They could see something approaching. A human figure emerged from the trees. I checked my watch, noted the time and wrote it in my notebook.

Humans often assumed that when they finally saw God, He would be large, looming, probably with a long, flowing beard or perhaps a halo hovering above His head. Regardless, they thought there would be no mistaking Him.

This particular group of sixty-one did not recognize God as He emerged from the shadows of the forest.

He seemed tall to them, but only because He was in an adult's body. He wore dark aviator glasses; His belly hung just over His belt and it bobbed as He walked. His skin was a pasty white. His hair was dark brown and cut jaggedly short, as if He'd cut it himself and styled it without a mirror. His aviator glasses were the kind that darkened in the sunlight, and then would clear up once He went inside. The shades didn't improve His appearance.

Not much He ever did improved His appearance. Instead, His awkward attempts at replicating human fashion and style would always, improbably, make Him look a little worse.

The children anticipated meeting God with a sense of awe, but when they saw Him, they mistook Him for a man. A simple, forgettable, middle-aged man.

He stopped in front of the group and looked them over, with neither approval or disapproval. He pointed at each, counting them in His head. When He was satisfied they were all there, He reached into His back pocket. A crumpled piece of paper emerged in His fist. He unfolded it, held it out and tilted His head up slightly so He could read the words through the bifocals in His aviator glasses.

"Why did the papa banana marry the mama banana?" God asked.

The children glanced at each other, and then at me, to which I could only shrug.

"Because," God read, then cleared His throat. "He found her a-peel-ing."

Jay laughed high and shrill like a jackal. Once the children caught on that it was a joke, they forced respectful laughs. A few of them blushed out of embarrassment for the poor man. A tall and husky black child named Ossie was the last to stop chuckling. He shook his head and covered his eyes. He was the only one brave enough to laugh at the absurdity of the joke. God noticed Ossie and frowned.

"A-peel-ing," God repeated, just above a whisper. He folded the paper, shoved it back into His pocket and removed His glasses. His eyes had no irises and were just pools of soft pink.

The children tried not to stare.

"Hello, my name is God."

He seemed to mentally count the children again, making sure that they all did understand that He was, in fact, God. He'd had problems with that before.

The children's faces gave them away. After a long minute of silence, Ossie chuckled again, but abruptly stopped when Jay slapped him in the back of the head.

"That's all," God mumbled, then turned away to return to the forest.

The children looked around at each other, then to me. Again, all I could do was shrug.

"Um, excuse me?" Edward called, raising his hand. A few of the children hushed him, but Edward stood and stepped out from the group. Jay jogged to block his way.

God turned around, looked at Jay, then me.

"What is it Edward?" I asked.

"Um, well," he stammered, looking from me to God. "Can I ask a question to … Him?"

"What is it?" God asked curtly while taking off His glasses, huffing on the lenses and buffing them with His shirt.

"Why am I here?" Edward asked.

"Because I want you here."

"Yes, and thank you, but why?" Edward furthered. "Will I ever return to Heaven?"

God frowned and put on his aviator glasses.

"Sit back down," Jay hissed, then turned and walked to God.

"He's the pastor," Jay whispered, just loud enough for everyone to hear.

"The pastor?" God asked.

"You know," Jay said, holding his hand out limp. "The pastor."

"Oh," God grunted. "What's his name?"

"Edward Smitherson," I answered.

"Be patient, Edward," God answered. He turned away and walked into the forest.

Edward maintained his composure, much to my surprise, but no one could miss the devastation in his slumped shoulders, his downcast eyes and bitter frown. Tommy moved closer, nudged Edward in the shoulder and gave him a nod of approval. Edward smiled weakly.

I jotted some notes on the conversation in my organizer, closed it and then walked to the group.

"Now that we got that over with," I called, clapping my hand against the organizer.

I let the statement linger, not really expecting a laugh, but hoping. Even Ossie couldn't muster a response. They were all still too confused. So much had changed for them in such a short time.

"Let's check out your living quarters, shall we?"

I started the procession into the forest. It was a long process, especially as the children began gathering the courage to talk. There were so many questions, so many things for them to look at, so many colors and scents they'd forgotten about. The pine needles were always a surprise to them, the rich smell and the sharp sting against their skin. The winds would rattle the needles together, and those who grew up with those trees in their living room at Christmas would pause and listen. Maybe it was the memories that slowed them down so much. Those memories melt in Heaven, but they never completely disappear.

God still didn't understand why.

Edward trailed towards the end, eyes fixed on the dirt path. He kicked over a rock, then craned his neck down to look under brush. At first, I thought he was sulking, but when I slowed and let the others pass, I realized he was looking for something.

"Where are the bugs?" Edward asked, still examining the ground.

"There are no bugs here, Edward. God thought they would just be annoyances and distractions."

Edward glanced up at me, his face twisted as he thought.

"What do the animals eat?"

"There are no animals either," I said.

"Wait," a thin brunette girl said. Her face, with a long beak nose and small eyes, was designed for eyeglasses, but there were no glasses in Heaven either. Well, aside from God's of course, and I assumed He just wore them to keep from freaking out the children with his iris-less eyes.

The beak-nosed girl was named Sophia. She'd been a nun in the past life, but her life of devotion had been far from serene and peaceful. I could still see the suffering in her hardened smile and eyes that never quite met mine.

"Did you say there are no animals here?" Sophia asked.

"Correct."

The group stopped and began looking through the woods. Like most, they'd assumed life was around them, but at that moment realized they didn't hear the birdcalls, the rattle of insect wings, the snakes and rodents rustling through the leaves.

"Why not?" Sophia asked.

"God doesn't want to have them here, okay?" Jay called from down the path. "Now, hurry up!"

The group continued studying the trees and the woodland floor as they followed Jay down the path.

"What are we going to eat?" Edward whispered to me.

"The food will be provided to you."

"It's not going to be powdered eggs and generic cereal like they used to serve at camp, is it?" Ossie chuckled.

"Umm …," I smiled, opening my organizer. I flipped to the week's menu. "For your first breakfast, it looks like we will be dining on a delectable entree of rehydrated gravy and biscuits accompanied by something that very much resembles bacon."

Tommy grunted and shook his head.

"Really?" Ossie asked, rolling his eyes and showing his big, toothy smile, then jabbing two thumbs up in the air. "Awesome!"

Jay stopped, swiveled around and glared back at the group.

"If any of you have a problem with our food, you can just not eat!"

Everybody's eyes dropped to the ground, except for Ossie's.

"Powdered eggs and fake gravy are my favorites, sir!" Ossie snapped, holding his thumbs up higher.

Jay's eyes narrowed.

"I'm watching you," Jay sneered.

The path wound through the trees and finally reached the clearing. Jay turned and waved everyone to him. The group all gazed out at the landscape as they emerged from the woods. The mountain caught their eyes first. Now that they saw it from the ground, they could better grasp its massive size. It was impossible to tell from the ground that it was actually a volcano which hadn't erupted since it had spewed out the molten rock that formed the Island. The tree line surrounded the base of the volcano, and a few hardy trees managed to sprout farther up the volcano's face. The top of the volcano's cone was draped in clouds.

"How soon until we can get our feet wet?" Tommy asked as he stared out at the vast, crystal-clear lake wrapping around the other side of the volcano. It stretched out across the Island, disappearing on the far lip of the Island into a hazy fog.

"Soon," I said. "After everyone is settled in."

Edward watched the fog intently. The wall of trees seemed to give way just as the mist overtook the land, but the mist was too thick to see what lay within it. The trees picked up again on the other side of the fog.

The far bank of the lake was miles away. It could be seen, but not much detail could be discerned with the naked eye. The lake itself was so clear it was like a window. The water was never too cold; there was a mild current with small, gentle waves licking at the shore.

Children thought the lake was perfect, but it reminded me of a lake in Eastern Europe where I'd seen many, many bad things. There was a lurking evil about the still, blue waters that repulsed me. Jay didn't swim in the lake either, but for different reasons.

The Island would be the ideal playground for geologists, chemists or physicists because of the differences from Earth, but God considered them to be troublemakers and felt they were best left in heaven.

There were explorers though, and the more adventurous souls would promise to explore the entire land. Night after night, they would circle the lake and push deeper into the forest before being called back to the campground. Some would want to go past the volcano and find a way through the trees and around the lake.

No one ever made it farther than the volcano, though. And the other side, where the trees disappeared into fog — no one ever made it past that either.

The trail finally opened up enough to see the campground, made up of cabins, larger cheap, fabricated buildings and a short pier. The trail led right into the heart of the camp, with a tetherball pole, basketball court, three sand volleyball pits, and a gazebo where Jay would bore all the children with his stories and lectures that lost all relevance in this new world.

Farther down the shoreline there was a small boathouse and on the other end of the camp was Cabin One, where God stayed. It was small and modest; he spent very little time there.

"This is it?" a stern-faced boy with thick shoulders asked. "It really is a church camp?"

"You were a Boy Scout once," Jay said. "You should feel right at home here."

The boy, named Billy Rose, only grunted. He was once a Boy Scout, then an Eagle Scout, then a Marine. He temporarily survived a Japanese POW camp, but the damage from his time in enemy hands would kill him a decade later. Even in this new world, I could see the ghosts from that camp haunting him.

Billy was not alone in his disappointment — the others were trying to smile and appear eager but instead were just confused.

"Spectacular," Ossie grinned, then chuckled to himself.

"Okay, gather around," Jay called. "I am sure many of you have had the camp experience, for better or worse, so you already know the drill. There are scheduled activities, such as arts and crafts, sports, swimming, lessons, lunch, breakfast, dinner, blah, blah, blah. We will provide you with weekly schedules and if you use your structured time wisely, that will leave about half your day to do with what you please. You are not allowed to take boats out across the lake; we have one boat, and it is for official use only. You may swim, but stay near the shoreline. There are angels throughout the area, so if you do something wrong, we will know. Any questions?"

"Where's the library?" Tommy asked.

"There is no library," Jay answered. "There is a Bible you can check out."

"Hmm," Tommy responded, his face automatically falling blank and unreadable.

Tommy had no interest in reading the Bible again. He had studied it extensively in rehab, but was strangely repelled by it now, as if opening the pages would somehow drag him back in time to those long, painful days and perhaps even beyond.

I'd noticed many times that such reflexes from Earthly lives are the first to return. There appears to be some part of the soul that never truly forgets. That little puzzle was something of an irritant to God, even if He wouldn't admit it.

"All you need to know is in the Bible," Jay said with a labored sigh. "It may not be as fun to read as your comic books and *Mad* magazines, but it's got all the answers. Any other questions?"

"What part of the Bible are we supposed to read?" Edward asked. "I've studied it. I've read it in Greek and Aramaic. There is no mention of anything remotely like this."

"Maybe you should read it again" Jay snapped.

"This is something separate from Heaven," I said. "I know it is a little confusing, but the same rules of morality apply, your relationship with God may be more immediate, but you should treat him with the same reverence as on Earth."

Edward frowned and stared at his feet.

"Any other questions?" Jay asked the others.

"Are there pool tables or ping pong?" someone from the back asked.

"No."

"What about motorcycles or bikes?"

"No."

"What about horses?"

"There are no animals on the Island; why would there be horses?" Jay snorted.

"What about television?" Ossie smirked, glancing at Edward, who grinned.

"No!"

"Video games?"

"No!"

"What about the Spice Channel?" Tommy asked innocently.

"What's the Spice Channel?" Jay asked.

"That would be an adult channel, sir," Ossie beamed.

"No!" Jay growled. "No, why would we have that in Heaven?"

"'Cause it's Heaven," Tommy responded with a shrug.

"No!" Jay snapped. "There's no television at all!"

He rubbed his eyes and shook his head as the group stifled laughs.

"ESPN?" Tommy asked.

"No!" Jay shouted, turning his back on the group and walking away.

I moved to Jay's place and let the children laugh until it was out of their system.

"Okay, ladies and gentlemen," I began, watching Jay storm off down the trail. "This might not be the luxurious getaway you saw in the brochure, but I may be able to secure some amenities to make your stay a little brighter."

"Like what?" Ossie asked. "'Cause, to be honest, I'm just not sure I want to live in a world without VH1."

"That's a bit of a tall order," I answered, opening my organizer. I flipped to a page labeled "Contraband." "I can get some secular books. I've already got binoculars on their way. Before you start deluging me with ridiculous demands, I won't be able to take orders for at least two to three days. In the meantime, enjoy yourselves as much as possible."

Tommy raised his hand.

"Before you ask, Tommy, I cannot and will not get the Spice Channel."

Tommy stomped his foot and the group laughed, the girls a little harder than the boys. I was glad to see them relax finally. I flipped to another page and wrote a few notes, then waved them to follow me toward the campground.

"I don't get it, what's the Spice Channel?" Edward asked Tommy as I led them down the hill. It was the first time Edward had actually talked to Tommy, and he was still worried Tommy would recognize him.

"Porn, man," Tommy gasped, slugging Edward in the shoulder. "You've never heard of it? Where were you during adolescence?"

"I think it was after my time," Edward chuckled. "We were still looking at Sears catalogs."

I hung back and followed Edward and Tommy. They talked quietly. Edward was still uncomfortable, but as he realized Tommy wasn't going to recognize him, he relaxed and let himself fall into Tommy's trance.

It was a cruel thing God was doing to Edward.

Edward's eyes suddenly veered off into the woods behind us. I followed his gaze, and sitting in a tree was a red cardinal. It wasn't chirping; it just sat on the branch looking back at us. I jogged up to Edward, who was pointing it out to Tommy. I grabbed Edward's hand and moved it down.

"Don't draw attention to it," I whispered.

"I thought there weren't any animals here?" Edward asked, still looking at the cardinal.

"It came from across the lake," I answered. "It needs to find its way back there, or it won't be around much longer."

I made a note of it in my organizer.

"Are you going to tell God?" Tommy asked.

"No, God doesn't read this. It's just for my records."

"Records for what?" Edward asked.

"I'm writing my memoirs," I smirked, then shooed them down the trail. I glanced back towards the bird, but it was already gone.

******

Unlike everyone else on the Island, I volunteered to come. Once, I'd heard about the plan, I just couldn't resist. God's plans were always curiously suspect, considering He was omniscient. It often made me wonder what it truly meant to be omniscient, and the best I could figure was that if He did know everything, it didn't mean He was skilled at formulating plans.

C.S. Lewis had theorized that time had no meaning for God, that he knew everything that would happen and had happened, and for Him, it was all one eternal moment. If that was true, it would certainly explain why He seemed so absent-minded. Albert Einstein was undoubtedly a genius, but I wouldn't have put him in charge of my travel agenda.

But then I consider the possibility that I am selling God short, that He knows exactly what he is doing. He understands that He is designing scenarios that cannot end as planned, and He enjoys watching them implode. For a challenge. For the entertainment. Eternity is a really long time, even in Heaven.

Jay and I divided the cabins in hopes of coming up with the best chemistry between the campers. You don't want the quiet ones with the loud ones, the weak kids with the bullies and the gung-ho campers with the slackers. There was always a small group of children whose attitudes would define the entire tone of the campground. The challenge was finding those trendsetters and ensuring they bought into the spirit of the Island.

We would then sit back and watch, along with the angels, along with God. There was one cabin that we would all be watching.

"Which one do you think is going to be first?" Jay asked, following my gaze towards Edward, Tommy, Ossie, Billy and a black-haired boy named Simon Roma. The group talked and laughed as they walked into their cabin, Cabin Five.

"First? Are we betting, sir?"

"No," Jay snorted indignantly. "No, we don't gamble here. But I want to see if you're better at reading them than me."

I shook my head with a grin.

"I am, and you already know that I am."

"Whatever," Jay huffed. "So, who's it going to be?"

"Are we talking about just Cabin Five, or the whole camp?"

"The first will come from Cabin Five," Jay said. "You know that; I know that. That's why we put them together."

"Oh, is that why?" I mumbled, looking over at a small, quiet boy named Petrov who was slowly returning from the shore. I'd noticed he'd wandered off from the group earlier and decided to let him go.

"Petrov!" I called, then pointing over to the cabin that housed Edward's group. "That one's yours!"

Petrov nodded and ambled towards Cabin Five, his head ducked, his hands jammed into his pockets and his eyes on the ground.

"What about Petrov?" I whispered.

"No way," Jay replied.

"Hmm."

"I'm betting on Ossie," Jay smirked.

"I thought we weren't betting."

Jay rolled his eyes. "We're not, it's just an expression, gah!"

I nodded my head and watched the cabin. I could see Ossie through the window, smiling, talking. He was the most talkative of the group by far and the first one who seemed to be enjoying the experience, though possibly not how God intended.

I opened my organizer and flipped to Ossie's page. He was in his nineties when he died, but the mugshot on the page showed that he'd kept his handsome face all the way into the grave. In old age, he'd had a few wrinkles, but not nearly as many as a man that old should have.

"Why Ossie?" I asked, flipping the page over and skimming over a typed profile on the back.

"Really? Do you have to ask?"

"I suppose not," I replied, slapping my organizer shut. "Well, you're right; it'll probably be someone from their cabin. I doubt it'll be Simon—he'll get into a lot of trouble, but I think he'll enjoy the challenge. Billy's got issues he needs to deal with, but I think he'll do pretty well here. Edward is the one to watch. He won't be the first, but I don't think it'll be long for him, sadly."

"Ossie'll be first; just wait and see," Jay said.

I shrugged and watched Petrov. He finally reached the door and just stood in front of it, staring at the doorknob and listening to others inside.

"Go ahead, Petrov," I called. "It's okay."

Petrov glanced back, nodded his head and then opened the door.

"You're sure it won't be Petrov?" I asked.

"Guarantee it!"

"Okay, then it's a bet."

Inside the cabin, Edward slid his fingers along the wooden desk, drawing his name in the dust. Light poured in from the windows, glimmering against the particles swirling in the air. There were three sets of bunk beds with bare mattresses on them. Each bunk had two footlockers in front of it. There was one desk, one chair and everything was covered in light gray dust.

"Charming," Edward mumbled as he lifted up the tip of his fingers to look at the dust he had collected.

"There's no light switch," Billy the Marine said. "How are we supposed to see at night?"

"I don't think they want us to," Tommy ventured. "The nighttime is when we tend to do most of our sinning, so maybe it's a preventative measure."

Billy looked at the window, and then walked to the bunk across from it. He flipped open a footlocker in front of it and found blankets, a pillow and sheets.

"Dibs on the top bunk," Billy said.

Simon took the cue and jerked past Edward and climbed up to another top bunk. Simon was a short boy, even shorter than Petrov, but with baby fat in his cheeks and a devious glint in his eyes. As he rolled onto the mattress, dust swirled up around. He coughed as he waved it away.

Ossie, the tallest of the children, was the only one who could leap up onto his bed. As he landed, the mattress bowed under his weight and creaked.

"That's my bed, son!" Billy snapped, watching the bed sag down.

Ossie groaned, and then rolled off the bed and landed on the ground. He slumped down and moved to the other top bunk, but Tommy beat him to it. Tommy climbed quickly and grinned down at Ossie. Ossie sighed and then walked to the bottom bunk under Billy.

Two bottom bunks were left, one beneath Tommy and the other beneath Simon. Edward's mind whirled. He finally shuffled nervously toward Tommy. Left with no other option, Petrov sat stiffly on the bunk under Simon.

"I gotta warn you, Eddie," Tommy called as he laid back on the bed. "I drink a lot of water at night and I'm a real deep sleeper."

The others laughed, and Edward smiled. No one had called him 'Eddie' before.

"Nothing a roll of Saran Wrap can't fix," Edward grinned, sitting down on the mattress and brushing the dust off the mattress.

Simon jumped down from his bed and walked to the window to survey the campground outside. Simon had been a manager of a rent-a-car franchise and an amateur magician. He'd married three times in his life, and had ultimately died alone without any children to carry on his name.

He had always wanted to become a Vegas performer, but instead devolved into a small-time con man before handing his life over to Christianity and to the rental car industry. He never fully retired from magic, though. Instead, he had volunteered his time at children's hospitals, and was known as "Simon Roma: The Magic Tomato."

I opened the door and stepped inside. Edward slid off his bed and stood up, as if I'd caught him at something. Simon didn't acknowledge me as he searched the camp.

I carried a Bible along with my organizer. I wedged the Bible in my armpit as I wrote down the campers' sleeping arrangements.

"Looking for angels?" I asked.

"Yeah," Simon answered. "What do they look like?"

I walked over to Ossie's bottom bunk and he scooted over to let me sit next to him. The dust puffed up.

"It's hard to say," I said, waving the dust away from my face. "The only time you can see the angels is when they get touched, and then they only shimmer like sunlight on water. You can hear them when they talk but you won't really understand them."

Simon frowned and looked back out the window.

"Are they watching us now?" Billy asked from the bunk above me.

"Why?" I asked, craning my head to look at him. "What are you planning on doing?"

"Considering my options," Billy smirked, then motioned at my organizer. "You going to narc me out if I do?"

"Perhaps," I grinned.

"So, what are you writing in there?" Simon asked.

"Just details, things that I want to be able to remember," I answered. "There are a lot of details I have to record to keep the campground organized and functioning properly. I write everything down to keep it straight."

Simon grunted skeptically.

"I guess that's the campgrounds only Bible?" Edward asked.

I nodded and then flipped the Bible to him and he lunged to catch it like it would shatter if it hit the floor.

"I thought you'd be interested in looking it over."

Edward opened it and looked over the table of contents, checking over the chapters.

"So, this is the official version of the Bible, all the translations are correct?"

I shrugged.

"It's the one God let me bring into the campground, so I guess so."

Edward's eyebrows crunched together and he looked at me with exasperation. I shrugged again. He slumped down on the bed, rubbed his eyes and then flipped the Bible open.

I leaned back on the bed, resting my head against the wall. I looked over the room, recognizing the fear and uncertainty in some of their faces. On the bottom bunk next to me, Petrov's pale, thin face was ducked away. He had been a Russian icon painter as well as a successful secular artist. I'd hoped putting him with the others in Cabin Five would help him open up. He'd been quiet all his life and likely wouldn't change here without help.

"They might be watching," I said, keeping my eyes on Petrov. "The angels, I mean. You're not being judged anymore, though. Don't go out of your way to defy God, Jay or myself and you will be fine."

"What do we get in trouble for?" Simon asked from the window.

"Essentially the same as while you were on Earth: stealing, lying, cheating. You're too young for sex, so you don't have to worry about that."

"But that's the best part!" Ossie gasped.

Simon and Billy laughed, Tommy grunted and watched the window and Edward eventually chuckled without looking up from the Bible. Petrov continued to stare at his hands.

"You know when you're doing something wrong," I continued. "Don't try to trick God and the rest is easy."

"Why did he choose us to come here?" Tommy asked, looking directly at me.

I sighed, glanced at the open door and motioned for Simon to close it. I stood up from the bed and faced the group.

"I don't know," I whispered as the door closed. "None of us really knows why God is doing this. Perhaps he's taking another crack at an Earth, and this is his testing ground? Whatever his reasoning, my advice is to do your best to enjoy your stay. You may return to Heaven in a couple of days or maybe not for several years."

"Maybe not ever?" Edward asked. He lowered the Bible and glared up at me, red lines forming in the whites of his eyes, his face flushed. I shrugged, letting him shoot his resentment out at me. I don't mind taking the blame if it makes it easier on them.

"Wow," Ossie mumbled. "That's just awful."

"If I had better answers for you, gentlemen," I shrugged, "believe me, I'd tell you."

"So who are you?" Tommy asked. "A camp counselor or something ridiculous like that?"

"My name is Bali," I answered. "I'm not really a counselor, but I do assist God, to whatever degree I can. Essentially, I help keep track of the details on the Island. Jay and I work together a lot."

"Is Jay your friend?" Tommy asked, sitting up on his bed and letting his legs dangle down.

"Ehh."

"Why are Jay and the Big Man such dicks?" Tommy asked.

The cabin went silent. I paled slightly and waited for an angel, but none came.

"Don't use expletives, Tommy," I finally whispered. "God does frown on crude language, especially when it is directed at Him."

"Okay, whatever, but answer my question," Tommy said. "Why did we get treated like that the second we stepped off the plane? If they don't want us here, why are we here? I mean, if it's just me, if I'm the asshole here, I'll shut up."

"No, you're not," I sighed. "And please, no cussing."

Tommy grunted and then nodded his head.

"God does want you here," I said. "I just—He's difficult to read, but you will get used to Him. Same with Jay. Just don't take it personally."

"Okay," Tommy grumbled under his breath as he laid back on his bed.

"So if you're the scribe," Billy said, "what does Jay do?"

"You know, he's explained it to me, God's explained it to me, but I'm not really sure I understand it," I said. "God seems to think he needs to be here, so I give Jay small tasks to make him feel useful. I think maybe Jay's true purpose is to be God's confidant."

"Why doesn't He talk to you?" Ossie asked.

"I'm a nag, always pestering Him about something the Island needs."

"Will God talk to us?" Edward asked.

"Maybe, not sure," I shrugged. "I guess that might be why He brought you here in the first place."

Edward gave a slim smile, then returned his focus to the Bible.

I walked to the door and opened it, glancing out of the cabin and then back at the group.

"Okay, take as much time as you want; explore the camp," I said. "You might dust off this cabin and beat your mattresses outside. There are some towels in your footlocker and more at the mess hall if you need them.

We eat in a few hours. Whenever you hear the bell, that means it's time to return to camp, okay?"

The group mumbled unenthusiastically. Edward used his shoulder to rub a tear off his cheek while he read.

"We're pairing you up," I continued. "Just like you chose your beds—Ossie and Billy, Petrov and Simon, Edward and Tommy. You're responsible for your companion, so keep each other accountable or at least cover each other's excuses."

A few in the group chuckled and I waved before closing the door on them. They began talking again as soon as I walked away. They were probably still searching for angels and trying to figure out what it was they were supposed to be doing there.

chapter iii

Night had fallen, but the children were not sleeping. Instead, they stared blankly out into the darkness, remembering the world that no longer existed, longing for the friends and family that occupied their richest memories and envying the souls still wound in the fabric of Heaven.

No one had left their cabin. God had announced there would be no dinner, against my firm objections. No one seemed to miss eating, because no one asked.

There were few artificial lights in the campground — just a light post by the basketball court, a floodlight behind the mess hall and a lamp in God's house. Those all flicked off precisely at 9 p.m. The children lounged on their bunks as the weight of the physical plane began to settle in their minds. The silence kept them awake.

God, in an effort to ease their transition, had placed a large, silver disc of a moon high above the horizon to make the Island more like Earth, but it wasn't nearly enough.

The trees rustled as the wind swept along the cabins and the lake lapped at the shore, but there was no real life around the campground. Without the chirps of courting crickets, the mournful howls of distant wolves or even the ever-present white noise of human society bustling around them, the children were only left with memories.

Voices surfaced over the breeze and Billy looked out the window to see children from other cabins venturing out into the night. He slid off his bed, pulled on his shoes and opened the front door.

He took in a deep breath of the damp air, then exhaled the dust from the cabin. A lazy breeze was soaked with the sharp tang of pine needles. He began walking, with no particular direction, no particular purpose. The cabins reminded him more of the Marine Corps than the Boy Scouts, except there was no structure, no urgency. That was part of what kept him awake — if there was nothing for him to wake up for, why sleep at all? He was also not ready to fall asleep and face the nightmares again.

Edward sat beneath the darkened light post by the basketball goal, now reading the Bible by moonlight. Edward looked up just enough to see Billy, wave and then bury his nose back into the pages.

A few children wandered the campground while others played a lethargic game of tetherball. For a moment, Billy considered joining them but instead walked on toward the lake.

Surveying the water, Billy wondering if he would know an angel if he saw one. As his eyes followed the waves toward the shoreline, he saw a figure sitting with feet just out of reach of the waves.

"Evening," Billy called. The figure looked over at him. It was the thin, brown-haired girl with a beaked nose.

"Good evening," she replied, her voice weary and tired.

She looked back at the water. Billy considered leaving her alone, but he couldn't stand the thought of returning to the cabin.

"Mind if I join you?" he asked.

She studied him for a few moments, a slim smile emerged and, finally, she shrugged. It wasn't much of an invitation, but Billy had never been easily dissuaded.

"Sophia, right?"

"Yes."

"I'm Billy. Those cabins were driving me crazy; I had to get out."

She smiled, polite and distant, then let her eyes trail back out across the water. He sat down on the sand a foot away from her, not wanting to make her uncomfortable, and began searching his mind for conversation.

He strained to see all the way across the lake but could only make out the blur of trees stained by the silver of the moonlight. The breeze cooled as it passed along the water, the pine smell replaced by the scent of algae. It made him want to find a rod and reel and head to the pier, but he guessed fish fell into the "no animals" category. He then wondered if killing a fish would be wrong up here if the fish were around to be caught at all. He didn't buy the bullshit that Christians should be vegetarians.

Billy was anxious to find out what the angels did when they caught a kid screwing up. He hoped that some other kid would be the first to get in trouble so Billy could see the severity of God's wrath. That would help him gauge the cost/benefit of bending the campground rules.

"I miss the animals," Sophia whispered.

Billy nodded, not sure if she wanted him to answer. He guessed probably not.

"I keep on thinking I hear bullfrogs out there," she continued, eyes fixed on the dark waters.

"Maybe you do," Billy whispered, looking around and then leaning toward her. "Don't tell anyone, but one of the guys in our cabin said he saw a cardinal earlier. That creepy kid who writes everything we do down in his notebook …"

"Bali?"

"Yeah, him. He said the cardinal was from across the lake, but not to tell anyone about it. Birds are not supposed to come over to this side."

Sophia looked over at Billy, her eyes steady and skeptical. A slight grin curled up at the side of his mouth.

"Really?"

"That's what they said," Billy shrugged. "Who knows, though?"

"Why wouldn't they let them over here?" Sophia whispered.

Billy wasn't sure if she wanted an answer, so he didn't give one. They sat in silence. After a few minutes, Billy thought he heard a long croak, so he leaned over close and nudged her.

"Just heard one," he whispered. "You want to go out looking for them, see if we can find one?"

Sophia shook her head.

46

"Suit yourself."

He leaned back, holding himself up with his elbows. Footsteps drew his attention from the water to someone approaching from behind. Tommy passed by them and walked down to the water. He was barefoot, and walked into the gentle waves until the cold water reached his knees.

"Hey, Tommy," Billy called.

"Hey," Tommy replied without looking back.

Tommy leaned down and lowered his hands to the waves, letting the waves reach up and cover his fingers.

"He's having trouble adjusting," Billy whispered. "Not sure what I think of him yet, hard to trust someone that looks like that. When you're ugly like I am, you learn to work for everything you get, but pretty people tend to be pretty worthless."

Sophia laughed politely and looked away.

"He seems all right, though," Billy tacked on. "We'll see how it goes."

Sophia didn't respond and Billy could feel her interest fading.

"I heard you were a nun," Billy ventured. "I've never actually met a nun face to face."

Sophia arched her back and folded her arms across her chest. Her eyes fell to the sand.

"I'm not a nun anymore."

Billy could sense he was in dangerous waters, and he was annoyed at how everything was a landmine with the girl. Undeterred, he forged on.

"Well, I guess I'm not a Marine anymore," he chuckled. "But it doesn't quite feel that way yet. I still feel like I've got somewhere to be, something to do and someone to yell at me 'cause I'm not doing it fast enough."

Sophia smiled but didn't laugh. That was good enough for Billy.

"Hey, guys!" a voice called behind them. Jay was standing near the mess hall and was watching them. "Can you come over here?"

Tommy didn't look back at Jay.

"You come over here!" Billy replied. "We're comfortable."

"Please!" Jay said.

Billy considered ignoring him, but when Sophia began shifting to stand up, he hopped to his feet and offered her his hand. Sophia didn't take it, didn't even look at it. Billy wasn't sure if she had noticed his gesture.

Sophia pushed herself off the ground and dusted off her shorts.

"You coming, Tommy?" Billy asked.

Tommy grunted, shook the water off his hands and trudged back to the shore.

"What do you need?" Billy called to Jay as he led Sophia away from the shore.

Jay was transfixed by the waves, not in admiration, but more trepidation. It seemed to Billy that Jay was waiting for something frightening to emerge from the water.

He broke off his gaze and looked over to Billy and Sophia.

"We don't mind you coming out for walks at night, but you do have to get some sleep," Jay said.

Billy and Sophia nodded. Tommy was already walking back to the cabin. Edward had stood up from where he was reading and jogged to meet Tommy. Jay turned and quickly made his way back into the camp.

"Well," Billy said. "Thanks for letting me sit with you."

"It was nice," Sophia said, dipping her head.

"Are you going to be out here tomorrow night?" Billy asked, and Sophia nodded. "Mind if I join you again?"

Sophia lifted her head and met his eyes, her mouth twisting into a skeptical grin.

"Nothing inappropriate, ma'am," Billy said, raising his hands as if he were proving he wasn't carrying a weapon.

"Okay," Sophia answered with a playful smirk.

She ducked her head and walked back toward the female end of the camp. Billy grinned and turned toward Cabin Five. Ossie, Simon and Petrov watched from the front porch. Ossie and Simon began clapping as Petrov smiled weakly.

"Nice work, playa," Simon chirped.

Billy glanced back at Sophia. She'd heard the comment and was clearly ignoring it. He jogged quickly back to the cabin.

"You've been here less than one day," Ossie called to him. "Well done, sir!"

"Shut up and get inside!" Billy growled as he reached the cabin. He grabbed Simon by the collar and shoved him through the door. Ossie dodged Billy and jumped inside, laughing. Petrov smiled and followed Ossie. Billy glanced back toward Sophia, but she'd already disappeared into Cabin Eight.

"Goddammit," Billy grumbled.

"Uh, oh," Simon sang. "Someone's got a potty mouth. Angels gonna get 'im."

chapter iv

Edward woke the moment the sunshine reached the cabin window, but he remained nestled inside the scratchy white sheets as he held the Bible open so the sunlight reached the pages. He wasn't reading the book front-to-back, but skipping around, looking for clues, returning to any portions that might seem relevant. He quickly decided that "Revelations" was totally useless, the prophets of the Old Testament weren't that applicable and now he was pouring over the Gospels to see if any of the Messiah's parables might offer a hint.

The others still slept heavily, their bedsprings creaking as they rolled, their mouths agape and rumbling as they snored.

Edward had noticed Billy jerking awake a few times in the night, sitting up straight and staring around the cabin. Before Edward could say anything to him, Billy would settle back into his sheets, grumble and finally begin snoring again.

The human mind is a fascinating thing, a complex machine more like a computer than an internal organ. It is capable of storing massive amounts of information

— memories — but the brain needs time to categorize, save, discard and arrange those memories in such a way that the mind can make sense of them. That is why humans sleep — to allow the mind to sift through the clutter of a day's experiences. God had improved upon many aspects of Earth on the Island, but the brain had been, by far, His crowning achievement and even He could not devise a more efficient machine to store the memories the souls brought to the Island.

I was not surprised to see that Edward was having the hardest time adapting because he was never one to simply live with confusion. He would need to read, to question and to start building up a structure that he could live with. He had, over the course of many years cordoned off his homosexuality with reason which had been, for the most part, effective.

So, a peaceful night of sleep would not come to Edward until he could find a way to allay his bitterness and doubt when it came to this new reality of God in the flesh and an Island that betrayed his understanding of the Christian universe. He must find the reason, even if he did not understand or agree with it, because then he could feel safe again. There would be a plan, there would be a resolution and Edward could again feel secure putting his fate into God's hands.

Edward closed the Bible, rubbed his eyes and then gazed out the cabin's window, studying the long, wispy clouds crawling through the sky. God was showing off.

Edward did not recognize them as God's vanity, so his mind flipped through various explanations for the clouds since there was no rain. He settled on two likely explanations:

1. They were an illusion created by God, much like the Island's rising and setting sun. God was just trying to make the Island seem more like a natural world, but the clouds had no real use. This seemed unlike God, but I had said the Island was a test run.

2. There was a new set of physical laws in place that, if studied thoroughly, would make sense just as the physical laws back on Earth were all tied neatly together. Perhaps moisture's natural cycle on the Island skipped the rain step.

Both explanations seemed equally viable, yet troubled Edward. He didn't like the idea of a new life without the pattering of rain on a roof, the thrill of lightning storms and the smell of a morning shower. He also missed the sound of birds and insects rising after the rain. He used to walk out after rainstorms and look for earthworms trapped on the concrete. He'd cup them in his hands and walk them back to the grass. They wiggled and startled him every time. No matter how many times he touched a worm, he never got used to how moist and firm they were, how alive and vulnerable they felt.

The Island had no worms, roly-polies, ants, spiders or any other small things to protect. That would be something else he would miss.

He began thinking of the cardinal again when he noticed a shadow passing across the cabin floor. Edward sat up and looked out the window. His bed creaked, and he could hear Tommy yawn above him. A face emerged in the window, sending another shadow into the room.

Edward got out of bed. He stretched his legs and walked to the window. Boys from another cabin were walking to the lake. Across the camp, three girls were also approaching the shore.

"What's going on?" Tommy whispered, then yawned.

"I think they are going for a swim," Edward replied, watching the kids kick off their shoes and walk to the bank's edge.

"Who's swimming?" Simon piped up.

"Some kids," Edward answered.

"Where'd they get swimsuits?"

"Doesn't look like they have any," Edward said. "They're just swimming in their clothes."

"I wanna swim!" Ossie exclaimed, pushing himself off his bed and walking to the door.

Tommy rolled off the edge of his bed and slowly lowered himself down, stepping on Edward's mattress and then dropping to the floor.

"Are you going?" Simon asked as Tommy tugged his shoes onto his bare feet.

"Yup, I'm a beach bum, so I've got to get my fix. You coming, Eddie?"

Edward didn't want to; he had too much reading to do, but he reached for his shoes anyway. Tommy walked to the door, jerked it open and took a long, overly exaggerated breath. He slapped his chest, exhaled and strode outside. The others in the cabin were tilting their heads up and looking out the door. Petrov rolled away from the warm sunlight, scooting close to the wall.

"Hold on," Edward grunted, tying his shoes in loose knots and pushing up off the ground. "Are you coming, Simon?"

"I'll be there in a little bit," Simon smirked.

"Well, I'm going," Ossie said.

"I thought black people can't swim," Simon smirked. Edward froze with his hand on the door, and the rest of cabin fell silent.

"Yeah," Ossie sighed. "We're like cats that way, but I promise I'll stay in the shallow end."

Billy chuckled and Edward grimaced just as he turned to catch up with Tommy.

"Just joking," Simon sighed, throwing up his hands innocently as Ossie shook his head and followed Edward out the door.

Edward had to jog to catch up to Tommy, who was in full stride approaching the lake. Shrieks and laughter drifted through the campground. The morning air was crisp. Tommy hurried to a jog, and Edward trotted behind him, feeling the morning dew collecting on his ankles.

"This is going to be really cold," Edward said.

"If you're too delicate, you can go back to the cabin," Tommy grinned, looking back at Edward.

Edward pushed Tommy in the back and then reached down to tug off his shoe, hopping on one foot towards the lake. He tossed one shoe towards the shore, then the other and they both sprinted towards the waves. As Edward ran into the water, his foot slipped on a rock and he fell. The frigid water sent a jolt through his body and his heart sped straight into a hummingbird rhythm. He found his footing and jerked his head above the surface.

The others laughed as Edward gasped for air and rubbed the water out of his face. His heart stammered but then continued beating fast and hard as it tried to adjust. He was soon laughing too as he trudged his way deeper to where the other kids were. The boys were splashing; the girls were screeching. A few others were diving off the pier.

Tommy lunged on top of Edward. Before Edward could react, he was underwater with a mouthful of lake. He rose and spit the water at Tommy who was swimming away.

I was watching from the shore, writing down notes while Jay leaned against a building, sulking.

"Wanna go swimming?" I asked, looking up from my organizer.

Jay shot me a bitter sneer and then walked back into the campground. I chuckled and returned my attention to my notes.

I don't confess to being an expert on the origins of man, but I believe water played a greater role in evolution than most realize.

It's hard to get a soul to stop thinking about the Heaven it left behind, or even the life that preceded paradise. But the children changed once they hit the water. I don't fully understand why, but the effect is the same on the Island as it was on Earth. Maybe they were supposed to stay in the water, develop gills, flippers and shed their hair in favor of streamlined bodies. One theory that I'd heard on Earth that I particularly liked was that God's Garden of Eden was deep in the ocean among endless stretches of vibrant coral, abundant food supplies and the simplicity of aquatic life, but after

Eve's apple, God expelled them to the shore where only torment, greed and hunger awaited.

Tommy swam far enough away from shore that his feet no longer touched the bottom. Edward followed him wearily.

"Hey," Edward struggled to say as he kicked to keep his head above the water. Treading water, Tommy lazily stroked his arms back and forth.

"You okay?" Tommy smirked, watching Edward lurch his arms up and down to stay afloat.

"Yeah," Edward gasped. "I haven't ... swam in a ... long time."

"Okay, well, don't drown," Tommy replied, turning in the water to look out toward the far shore. "I swam every day, out in the ocean."

"Really?" Edward grunted, then fell below the water. Tommy didn't notice, and once Edward resurfaced, he was visibly annoyed at Tommy's apathy.

A thought crossed his mind as he watched Tommy tread water and raise his face to the sun. He wondered if Tommy was placed on the Island and paired with Edward as some sort of test, that God had put the boy on the Island as a temptation for Edward to overcome.

"Couldn't be," Edward mumbled. "Not here."

"I was a great swimmer," Tommy continued, laying back in the water and floating on his back. "I bet I could make it all the way across the lake."

"I don't know," Edward puffed. "That's a ... long way."

"Wanna bet me?"

"No ... not really. I'd rather you stuck around for a while."

Tommy smirked, turned to Edward and grabbed his arm to begin pulling him back to shallow water.

"Eww!" a group of girls on the shore shrieked. The wooden boards of the pier thudded as Simon ran toward the edge. He was completely naked. Girls standing in his path jumped down into the water, screaming until they submerged beneath the waves. Simon leaped off the edge of the pier, tucked into a ball and flipped wildly down into the water. His chest and stomach smacked against the water and I grimaced.

The kids laughed and clapped. Once Simon rose to the surface, he howled in pain. A group of girls near him were laughing, so Simon began swimming toward them. They shrieked and scattered in different directions as if he were a shark attacking a school of fish. He growled like a monster and had soon cleared out a large, empty circle of water around him.

A large, shimmering object plunged into the lake behind Simon, sending water high into the air. Simon turned and saw a mass of light under the water, like a giant, glowing jellyfish skimming toward him. The water crested into waves ahead of the object and Simon frantically tried to swim away.

The light overtook Simon and he was pulled underwater. The light, an angel, emerged from the water with Simon in its grasp. Simon floated within the light as it approached the shore where his clothes were piled up.

Even though most of the angel's body was lit up around Simon, the creature still only looked like luminous, sparkling fog. The clothes floated up into the light as the angel swept Simon into the campground.

The cabin door opened ahead of the light and Simon and his clothes disappeared inside.

The lake was silent. The swimmers glanced around at each other and then at me.

"Don't give it a second thought," I called to them. "Though it might be best if you come out — we'll be eating soon."

The children started trudging through the water towards the shore. They were already shivering, a few of them a pale shade of blue.

Edward swam closer to the shore, but stopped when he noticed Tommy still staring toward the other end of the lake.

"You coming?" Edward called.

Tommy didn't respond at first but eventually leaned his head into the water and began a casual backstroke. Despite Tommy not putting much effort into the stroke, he still beat Edward's awkward doggy paddle back to the shore.

"You'll find fresh clothes in your footlockers," I called as they passed.

Edward grabbed his shoes but didn't put them on as he walked over to me.

"Is Simon going to be okay?" he asked.

"What can they do to him?" I replied, patting him on his wet shoulder. "Send him back to Heaven?"

Edward smiled and nodded.

"You going to write down that he got in trouble?"

"Of course," I answered. "Streaking deserves at least a footnote, don't you think?"

"You have a point," Edward grunted with a chuckle.

He turned and jogged gingerly on his bare feet to catch up with Tommy.

******

"There's your powdered eggs, Ossie," Tommy grimaced as they watched the steam rise from the unnaturally smooth scrambled eggs piled on his tray.

"Mmm!" Ossie replied, jabbing his fork at the rubbery beige globs.

Tommy looked at the female camper serving behind the sneeze guard. She was a chubby cheeked girl with short, brown curls named Martha.

"How are you doing this morning, you fine young thing?" Tommy winked.

"What else do you want?" Martha sighed.

"Just a smile."

Martha scowled instead.

Tommy beamed. "And some bacon would be nice."

She used tongs to pick up a piece of bacon that was as flat and round as a coin. Tommy watched it drop on the tray and rock around like a quarter.

"You know," Ossie offered, "you could hold onto that bacon and we can play shuffleboard with it later."

"Or use it for currency if we ever go to a pre-Hispanic South American nation," Edward added.

Ossie and Tommy laughed, which made Edward smile.

"Who cooked this?" Tommy asked.

"Doesn't matter, just eat it," Martha answered, then motioned with her tongs for him to move down the aisle.

"Thank ya, ma'am."

Martha nodded and looked to the next in line.

Tommy grabbed a biscuit and made his way through the tables, following the others. Chattering voices filled the mess hall. Some campers ate ravenously; some couldn't stomach the smell of the food and just nibbled on biscuits. None of the food tasted quite like the food they remembered, but it wasn't far off from what they'd eaten on Earth. It had all the nutrients it was supposed to but just didn't come from the same sources. God chose not to let any of the children know the true source of their meals, which I suppose was for the best.

Tommy slid down next to Edward, who kept the Bible in his lap. Across the table, Billy was chomping away at an egg, bacon and gravy sandwich.

"How can you eat that?" Tommy asked.

"You spend any time in the Marines," Billy mumbled through a mouthful of slimy eggs, "and you can eat damn near anything. Just put it between two pieces of bread and you're good to go."

Tommy chuckled, picked up his fork and began cutting the eggs into pieces. The front entrance of the mess hall swung open and Simon leaped in like a superhero. The mess hall settled into silence as the campers watched Simon stand proudly. He glanced back out the door, kicked it closed and raised a hand in triumph.

Some of the children, mostly boys, cheered and Simon soaked in the adulation. He took a grand bow, which inspired laughter.

"I guess Bali was right?" Ossie whispered. "What are they going to do to us?"

"I wouldn't test them too much," Billy said, then downed his glass of milk in one gulp. He wiped his mouth and grabbed his empty tray. "We're meant to be stupid kids, so as long as we only do stupid kid crap, they probably won't do anything."

"Makes sense," Tommy nodded, still stabbing his fork into his eggs.

He watched Billy stand and walk away. He then leaned toward Edward.

"Now it's just a matter of figuring out what exactly we can get away with," Tommy whispered.

Edward inhaled sharply and he felt his face glow. Biscuit crumbles tumbled down his windpipe and he began coughing and hacking violently. He took a drink and choked it all down.

"Not going to throw up are you?" Tommy smirked.

Edward shook his head, then swallowing hard as Simon approached the table. Simon paused as he saw the only available seat next to Ossie.

"Hey," Simon said. "Sorry about the whole swimming remark earlier."

"Don't apologize," Ossie replied, not looking at him. "Makes it hard for me to feel superior to you."

Ossie grinned and then motioned for Simon to sit down.

"What'd they do to you?" Tommy asked through a mouthful of eggs.

Simon glanced around the mess hall and then leaned over to Tommy.

"Not much, just got lectured by the Big Man," Simon sighed. "That little punk Jay was there too, I think he liked watching me get bitched out."

"So, God lectured you?" Edward asked. "Was it weird?"

62

"Yeah, but oh, well," Simon shrugged, leaning back from them and picking up his circular bacon. He dipped it into a pool of syrup and crunched into it.

"Is that good?" Edward asked.

"Who the hell cares?" Simon grunted as he chewed.

Edward and Tommy glanced at each other and shrugged. They dipped their bacon into Simon's pool of syrup and chomped into the dry and sugary concoction.

"Hmm," Edward grunted with mild surprise. "Not bad."

"So, what's on the schedule for today?" Simon asked.

"Arts and crafts, I think," Edward replied, then drank the rest of his milk to force the last of the bacon down.

Simon chuckled and shook his head.

"I hope it's not something gay like making macaroni pictures or beading necklaces."

******

God was scribbling on a clipboard as the children sat outside at long picnic tables wedged between the mess hall and the volleyball courts. God wore orange flip-flops over calf-high black dress socks. His pale blue polo shirt stretched over His gut and hung halfway over His bright pink swim trunks. His eyes were hidden behind silver reflective glasses.

The children had gathered in the center of the campground next to the volleyball pits while some campers passed out the arts and crafts supplies. The children had sat down with their cabinmates, and

Edward's group glared at the thin, sickly boy who placed a bowl of dry macaroni in front of them.

"Unbelievable," Simon sighed.

Ossie's high-pitched, ridiculing laugh sailed through the camp, and Edward elbowed him to stay quiet. Ossie calmed down but kept his mocking smile.

"Sorry, Dad," Ossie mumbled to Edward.

Edward smiled a little.

Petrov took a handful of macaroni and piled them beside his piece of brown construction paper and a bottle of glue. He scratched his face as he stared down at the paper. The others dipped their hands in the bowl and grabbed handfuls of pasta.

"Okay, I'm going to say it and I don't care what any of you think," Ossie said, scooping up his own macaroni and glue. "I love macaroni art. It's just so deliciously awful."

"This is so gay," Simon whispered, but Edward kicked him under the table.

God stood up and handed his clipboard to Jay.

"Art is the human skill that is most like my own," God said. "I want you to do something to celebrate Me and the world I created for you."

God leaned toward me.

"Write that down," He whispered, and I nodded. I opened my organizer and pretended to write but instead just drew wavy lines.

God motioned for the children to start on their projects, then he pulled out a cloth handkerchief. He held it over His nose and honked loudly. The children's eyes widened as they held their heads down and tried not to laugh. Even Ossie managed to swallow his reaction. God honked two more times, sucked the remaining snot down His throat and put the handkerchief back into His pocket. From the same pocket, He pulled out a whistle and hung it around His neck.

"Let's set up the volleyball nets," God told Jay.

"Oh ... my ... God!" Tommy mouthed to Ossie, who exclaimed "I KNOW!"

Edward hushed them both.

"Sorry, Dad," Ossie mumbled again.

They all glanced back as God walked to the volleyball net. God grabbed the net off the ground, not noticing His foot was on it. It snagged around His ankle. He then began hopping on one foot while Jay tried to pull it off Him. God fell over on Jay. Ossie's eyes were red and watery; his face was purple brown and he hiccupped another laugh. The other campers burst out, and soon their whole table was laughing.

I turned my back to God so I could write in my organizer.

"Need any help there, Champ?" Tommy called.

"No!" Jay shouted, freeing God from the net. "Get to work!"

The kids calmed and ducked their heads, trying to stifle their snickering. Edward noticed that Petrov wasn't smiling. He was staring down at the paper, his face stern and confused.

"Hey," Edward whispered. "Are you all right?"

Petrov didn't answer.

"Billy," Simon said. "Check it out."

Simon lifted his paper, showing a naked woman made out of macaroni with circles of white glue for the breasts. Billy chuckled but cut his laugh short as a light emerged behind Simon.

Simon turned to look just as the angel lifted him into the air.

"Oh, come on!" Simon growled as he floated up above the table. "It's Eve in the Garden of Eden! It's biblical!"

God walked over to the table and picked up Simon's picture. He shook His head and tore it up.

"Do you think this is why I brought you here?" He snapped at Simon.

"No, sir."

"This is the second time today that I have had to deal with you," God growled.

Jay dropped the volleyball net and ran over to God and Simon.

"Sir," Jay called, keeping his eyes lowered to the ground.

"Not now!" God snapped, His eyes still fixed on Simon. God floated off the ground, raising three feet into the air as he glided closer to Simon.

"What do I need to do to get through to you, child?"

"I'm sorry, sir," Simon gasped, trying to jerk free.

Simon rose higher until he was ten feet above the children's heads. God followed him, moving close enough that they were face to face.

God stopped only an inch from Simon's nose. His eyes narrowed into a sneer. Simon's eyes widened and he struggled with the angel to free himself.

"Sir!" Jay called again, but God kept his focus on Simon.

"Are you mocking Me?"

"No, I just …" Simon grunted.

Simon felt the temperature drop and noticed his breath form into white puffs. None of the other children could feel the air freezing, but they saw Simon's breath and noticed his skin paling. Simon's lips turned blue as he shivered.

"I'm ... sorry," Simon struggled.

"Sir!" Jay shouted.

God looked down to Jay, frowned and then floated away from Simon and lowered back to the ground. Simon's skin warmed, he stopped shivering and he glared at God.

"Take him to his cabin," God grunted, looking at Jay, and then to me. "He will sit out the rest of arts and crafts."

"Hrrmmph!" the angel bellowed and then swept Simon away towards the cabin.

"Make sure you spell my name right, Bali!" Simon yelled.

God turned to Simon, then looked over at me. I lowered my eyes and closed my organizer. The others hunched down over their papers. Ossie held his hands over his and glanced over to Edward with a grimace. Ossie raised his hand just enough to reveal he had made a naked man with his macaroni. Ossie slid the paper under the table.

God's scowl lifted to a smile, as if the event had never happened. He walked to Petrov and leaned over the boy's shoulder. Petrov shrunk away slightly as his fingers were sliding nervously through the pile of macaroni. His construction paper was still blank.

"Nothing yet?" God asked warmly while patting the boy on the shoulder. "I expect great things from you. You were always one of my favorite artists, Petrov."

Petrov nodded without raising his head from his paper. God couldn't see that Petrov was crying.

"Well, I'll let you get back to it," God called to us all. "Remember, do your best. It took me six of the hardest days of my existence to create your world for you. Here is your chance to repay me."

God looked over at me, and motioned for me to write down what He had just said. I nodded and opened my notebook. God turned to return to the volleyball net and I closed my organizer without writing.

Ossie crinkled up his picture and threw it under the table. He raised his hand.

"Can I get another piece of paper?"

****

Simon returned just in time for volleyball. The teams were divided up by cabins, except with male and female cabins combined. God sat on a raised umpire chair, his face hidden behind the reflective glasses and the whistle hanging loosely from his lips.

He was officiating all three courts simultaneously, but wasn't particularly effective.

There were seven players on each side, with the others rotating in. Edward's cabin was down two players—Simon, who wasn't allowed to play the first game as punishment, and Petrov, who was still sitting at the arts and crafts table. His paper was still blank.

Edward wished he could switch places with Petrov so he could read instead. Athletics were never one of Edward's strengths.

Tommy and Billy were the only players on the team with athletic ability. The first time that Tommy dove head first to save the ball and emerging with a face full of sand, Billy began to reconsider his opinion of the

pretty boy. Ossie was normally a passably decent
volleyball player, but couldn't stop staring at God's
black socks long enough to hit the ball.

Edward heard the thump without seeing the ball. He
turned towards the net just as a white blur consumed his
vision.

"Whap!" Then a fountain of stars.

Edward heard the laughter before he saw anything
again. Finally, a white pool of light grew as he blinked
to clear his watering eyes. Tommy and Billy were
looking down at him. He felt the sand around him, and
he heard the laughter. His nose was aching and he
tasted salty blood in his mouth.

"You're not supposed to hit it with your face, son,"
Billy smirked, holding his hand out to Edward. Edward
took it and was yanked up onto his feet. The kids
clapped and Edward raised his hand.

"Leave the court until the bleeding stops," Jay
sighed.

God didn't look down from the umpire chair. With
His reflective glasses, it wasn't clear where His
attention was. It was very possible he was actually
asleep.

Edward stumbled off the court and continued
toward the arts and crafts table. As he approached, he
saw that Petrov was still crying. He turned toward the
others, seeing that they had restarted the game with
Simon in his place.

"Are you okay?" Edward asked Petrov as he sat
down. Petrov didn't look up at him.

"Why don't you take a break and play volleyball,"
Edward whispered.

"I don't know how to play," Petrov grumbled.

"Well, you couldn't do any worse than me."

Petrov glanced up at Edward, whose face was splattered with blood and sand.

"Does it hurt?" Petrov asked.

"Not as much as I thought it would. Not like it would on Earth."

Petrov nodded and lowered his eyes back to his paper.

"You can't worry too much about that," Edward said. "If you can't think of anything, it's not the end of the world."

"No!" Petrov snapped. "You heard Him, this is why I am here. He only asks one thing from me, to create."

"You can't create with macaroni shells," Edward whispered. "No one can … well, aside from Ossie. Be patient and He'll let you work with paint or something."

"Do you know this for a fact?" Petrov asked. "How do I know I will ever see a paintbrush again, or clay, or a canvas? This could be it for me, these macaroni shells."

Edward shrugged and then looked back at the volleyball court. His team was cheering for something; Simon was dancing around with his elbows cocked behind him like a rooster. God whistled repeatedly until Simon stopped. The entire court grew quiet until God blew the whistle and motioned for the teams to continue the game.

"What if I can't think of anything to create?" Petrov asked. "That is all I am—an artist. If I can't do that, then there is nothing else for me."

"You're in a new place," Edward whispered. "You're not used to it, but once you normalize, it'll get better. I knew this guy who was a musician and went into seminary. The first few months, he couldn't get interested in music because he was so consumed with trying to get used to his new life and being away from home. After a while, he got used to it and began playing again."

"What did he play?" Petrov asked.

"Guitar."

Petrov grunted and slid all the macaroni onto the construction paper. He took the glue and squeezed a long stream down onto the pile.

"There," Petrov sighed. "I'll call it *Creation of the Universe*. I hope He likes it."

chapter v

Heads poked up across the camp at the sound of the clanging bell. Along the clear surface of the lake, children's eyes popped out of the water like hippopotamuses. Others stalked out of the forest and tossed away branches doubling as swords or walking sticks. Several clusters of kids were whispering and giggling in various cabins across the campground, sending lookouts to scan through the window to ensure the wrong person didn't overhear. They adjourned their clandestine meetings and emerged into the open with veiled smiles.

Their secrets were silly and simple, but private. It was the harmless gossiping of bored children and it didn't bother God. That was for the best since there really was no stopping it anyway.

As the children shuffled across the campground, I stepped up the stairs of the gazebo and then waved them towards me. God and Jay strode out from the mess hall with towels over their shoulders, chatting to themselves as their flip-flops popped and smacked with each step. God glanced up at the approaching crowd.

"Are you going to be okay?" God asked me.

"Go ahead, sir, I'll keep the rabble under control."

God nodded and returned his attention to continue whatever it was those two talked about while they were alone during their mountain retreats.

"Where are they going?" Simon asked. "Lake's the other way."

"Jay doesn't find the lake as inviting as you. He and the Almighty One," I said with an ever so slight hint of sarcasm, "have their own place somewhere near the mountain peak."

"Oh, really," Simon whispered, the gears grinding in his head as he looked back to the trail they'd taken towards the mountain.

I regretted divulging Jay and God's oasis, but they'd never invited me up, so I wasn't terribly overwrought with guilt.

I motioned all the other campers to sit in a half circle around me on the outside of the gazebo.

The crowd shuffled around as cliques settled into their own turf. The girls and boys were largely segregated, aside from a pale-faced boy named Barry and a mousy brunette named Mary, who'd already become inseparable. It made the other girls giggle and the boys roll their eyes. With those sickeningly precious rhyming names, it was perhaps inevitable.

They certainly wouldn't be the only children to pair up in the coming weeks. It would be more unnatural if they didn't.

As Edward approached, nose still buried in the Bible, I called to him. He glanced up and I motioned for the Bible. He reluctantly closed it, handed it over to me and found a place to sit amidst the crowd.

"So, what do you think of this place?" I asked over the murmur of children's voices. They steadily grew quiet, a few shrugging, a few grumbling, and the rest murmuring "it's fun" or some other bits of unenthusiastic praise.

"Well, if you have any problems, you can come to me. I'll see if there's anything we can do to help you adjust."

I sat on the handrail of the gazebo, my feet dangling off the ledge. The children were semi-attentive, but I knew I would lose them entirely before long. I scanned the faces and realized there was one missing.

"Edward, where's Tommy?"

Edward stood, a little too formally, and looked around the camp.

"Well," Edward began. "In the bathroom, I think."

"You think?" I asked, and a few children giggled. I shushed them and looked back at Edward.

"He was swimming and I was reading when we heard the bell," Edward said. "He told me to go on and said he had to go to the bathroom. I'm sorry, I should have gone with him."

"That's okay, Edward; I'm certain he can figure out how to flush a toilet on his own."

More children giggled. I waved them quiet and flipped open the Bible. While flipping through the pages, a faint shimmering light distracted me. I glanced up into the sky to watch it descend and grunt.

I sighed, closed my eyes and concentrated until I could see Tommy in my mind.

"He's swimming; he's far out — I think he's trying to cross the lake."

The light backed away and then soared out over the lake. The children were quiet and nervous. A few whispered to each other and Edward stood, stepped out of the pack of children and jogged to the lake to watch.

Before long, there was a splash followed by yelling. The light appeared above the mess hall holding Tommy. Tommy yelled, squirmed and tried to flail at the light.

"Take him to his cabin so he can change," I called to the angel. "Tommy, come straight here after you're done; no distractions."

"Go to hell, Bali!" Tommy growled.

"Charming," I murmured, then motioned for the angel to take him away. Tommy was whipped across the campground and he disappeared into Cabin Five. I rested back on the gazebo and looked over the children as Edward returned to his spot on the ground. Some giggled and whispered. Edward tucked his head down, guilt tugging his eyes to the ground.

"Here it is," I said, holding up the Bible. "The only book in our possession, and apparently the only book you will ever need. We will be dividing you into groups for daily readings here in the gazebo. It will be taught by Jay or myself at first, then perhaps we'll let you guide your own Bible studies in the future."

"What about God?" Edward asked, looking up at me. His face was weighed down by frustration, his spirit was brittle and the insomnia seemed to be catching up with him. "Will He ever guide any?"

"Doubtful," I answered. "Believe it or not, being Creator of a universe comes with quite a large number of pressing concerns. He spares what little time He can, but not enough for Bible study."

"Where did God and Jay just go?" a girl's voice asked, but I couldn't find the source.

"To take a bath," Simon grinned. "Together!"

"Eww," kids groaned.

"Children, please," I called over the chatter, throwing Simon a severe glare. "They've chosen an alternate place to bathe, a place where they can discuss matters that are none of our concern."

"Is the bath in an enclosure, perhaps some sort of gathering place with walls and a roof?" Ossie asked with a grin. "What would you call that?"

"Your Divine Creator does not go to a bath house, if that is what you are suggesting," I growled, doing my best to stifle a smile.

"What do they talk about?" Edward asked, still solemn.

I shrugged.

Whispers followed, then more snickering.

"Okay, okay!" I called over the voices. "Let's get this over with so we can get on with our lives ... afterlives, whatever."

The kids quieted down and watched me with only a few occasional whispers sifting through the crowd.

"Does anyone have any questions about the Bible?" I asked. "Any perplexing issues that have dug at you?"

All their eyes darted up, wide and curious. They glanced around at each other, watching for the first hand to raise. As I expected, it was Edward.

"Where in the Bible does it talk about this place? I've been searching for something that might refer to it, but..."

"It doesn't," I interrupted. "The universe is quite expansive, and this book — though there are many, many, many words — isn't nearly vast enough to go into it all ... thank the Lord."

"Amen to that," Ossie chimed in.

"That, and God's universe is constantly shifting, tweaking and evolving," I continued. "And yes, humans did evolve, dinosaurs existed and the Earth didn't just poof into being at the dawn of mankind — just to get those out of the way early."

"Are we the only ones?" a toothy, bean sprout of a boy named Timothy asked. "Are there are other souls out there?"

"Humans are unique, to be certain, but the only living things with souls? No. Earth wasn't the only source of intelligent life in the universe. How many of you took a good look at Heaven while you were being flown into this place?"

They all raised their hands.

"Looks a lot different from above, doesn't it?"

Children chuckled and nodded.

"Well, less than 5 percent of those souls originated on Earth," I said, and all their faces twisted in disbelief, shock and fascination. "You must realize, God has always been and will always be around. Infinity is a dreadfully long time, and a human life, a civilization, a planet or even a universe only exists for a short time, in comparison."

The kids mumbled and whispered to each other. Edward's hand raised again.

"So how many universes have there been so far?"

I shrugged; no one knew that but God. Maybe He didn't even remember. God refused to make lists, which drove me to wit's end on a daily basis. I chose not to imply, in front of the kids, that God was capable of forgetting anything, let alone the number of universes He'd created.

But God forgets more than even I like to admit.

Billy was the next to brave a question.

"How much of the Bible is literally true?" Billy asked. "Not like some story or parable, but an actual hard fact?"

I chuckled and looked at the Bible. I opened it and flipped through it.

"Well," I sighed, glancing through the pages, "Anytime you have so much information that was either passed along by oral tradition or written down many years after the fact, there are going to be divides between what really happened and what was said to have happened. The spirit is there though."

"But if I had to put a number on it," I continued. "I'd say about 75 percent is more or less true. Exodus should be viewed an extended morality tale rather than a history lesson. As I said, this book looks big, but it's not nearly big enough. It wasn't really ever meant to be viewed as strict historical text."

"What about Revelation?" Edward asked. "How much of that is true?"

"To answer that," I replied, "we happen to have someone here who lived through at least part of the apocalypse."

"Who?" Billy asked as he and the rest of the children scanned each other.

Petrov kept hunched over, perhaps wishing that the others would fail to notice. I considered letting it go, but the children were already beginning to look in his direction.

"Would you like to enlighten us, Petrov?"

Petrov glanced around and then back at the ground.

"It wasn't what I expected," he mumbled.

The crowd was silent. Most of them probably hadn't even considered the possibility that their world no longer existed, but thought that it continued to spin somewhere out in the ether.

Ossie raised his hand.

"What's God's true stance on sexuality?"

It was the first time I'd heard him sound vulnerable. I took a deep breath.

"You mean back on Earth or here?" I asked, but Ossie just shrugged. "Well, your bodies aren't mature enough for sex to be an issue, so it is not a big concern, presently. On Earth … it was more handled on a case-to-case basis, like most sins."

"I didn't really expect to be here," Ossie said, trying to ignore the other kids' stares.

"Would you like to discuss this later?" I asked softly.

"No," Ossie declared. "No, I really want to know now, and I don't really care if they know."

I looked over the group's curious faces.

"Fair enough," I shrugged. "Ossie is a prime example of how complicated sexuality is when it came time for judging souls. Upon puberty, Ossie realized that he was gay."

The group went rigid, as if stricken with a spell. After the first moments of shock, some hid their looks of disgust. Some stared at Ossie in wonder.

"He repented many of his sins, went to church, but never halted his homosexual lifestyle," I continued. "In fact, he had a monogamous relationship for … what, forty years or so?"

"Forty-four," Ossie corrected, his face stern and unaffected by the others'.

"There are many of you who have had indiscretions, sexually and otherwise," I said. "All I can say is if you made it to Heaven, then clearly you did more right than you did wrong. You were all judged on your faith using the same measuring stick, so I don't want any of you to treat Ossie any differently because of this, okay?"

Mumbles and nodded heads.

"I am serious. I know most of your secrets. I've seen the Book of Life, or at least your entries. I don't mind divulging the details."

More mumbles and nodded heads.

"But I thought you got into Heaven because you accepted the Lord Jesus Christ in your heart," Martha snapped.

I chuckled and nodded.

"Correct," I grunted. "So, Ossie is here because he is meant to be here. He deserved it just as much as the rest of you."

Unsatisfied, Martha stood and continued.

"That doesn't make sense. The apostle Paul said in First Corinthians 'Flee from sexual immorality. All other sins a man commits are outside his body, but he who sins sexually sins against his own body'."

"Paul said a lot of things," I sighed.

"He also said 'you must not associate with anyone who calls himself a brother but is sexually immoral or greedy, an idolater or a slanderer, a drunkard or a swindler. With such a man do not even eat'."

"Paul also said that it was best not to have sex at all, but also said that not all men could live as he did," I countered. "If it could not be helped, then it was better to marry, and Ossie, was, if not legally, then at least spiritually, married."

"But…" Martha began.

"Are you God, Martha?" I growled. She ducked her head. "Answer me, are you God, Martha?"

"No," she whispered.

"Do you have faith in God, Martha?"

"Yes."

"Then why are you questioning His judgment now?"

Martha sat down slowly and hid her face. She was not crying, she was furious. The other children were still stiff and skeptical.

Ossie would be a pariah to many of the children. I wasn't sure why he chose reveal his secret so readily, but I wasn't terribly surprised.

"Any other questions?"

There were more questions, there had to be, but it is hard to follow a bombshell. Instead, the children remained quiet and their questions would wait for another day.

"Okay, go enjoy the rest of your afternoon," I called, waving them away. "Return at the dinner bell."

When Ossie stood, many of the kids walked away, as if he had a virus they could catch. Billy stared directly at Ossie.

"Really?"

"Yeah," Ossie replied with a nod. "I don't like hiding."

"Well good for you," Billy said, his voice thick with bitter sarcasm.

Billy walked away, as did most of the group. Tommy was jogging back from the cabin and met the group.

"What did I miss?"

"Ossie's a fudgepacker," Billy grunted as he walked by.

Tommy smirked and glanced over at Ossie curiously.

"Really?" Tommy asked.

Ossie nodded. Tommy walked to Ossie and patted him on the shoulder.

"Thanks for telling us."

Edward watched them retreat to the cabin, and then glanced at me. I held up the Bible for him as he approached. He looked at the Bible but didn't take it.

"Would it be possible for us to talk more about the Bible?" Edward asked me, the worry cutting lines around his cheeks and at the corner of his eyes. He seemed old again.

"Of course," I replied, still holding the Bible up. He finally grabbed it. "Not today, but maybe after you've settled in."

Edward nodded, and then retreated from the gazebo. He stopped and turned toward me again.

"Is God tempting us?" Edward asked.

"Tempting you?"

"Yes, is He—is this a test?"

The question sent my mind spinning with possible responses. I stifled what I wanted to say and instead settled on "no."

"It feels like we are," he countered.

"You are not being tested, just don't do anything spectacularly stupid and you should be fine."

Edward nodded with a troubled smile. He glanced over and found Petrov walking alone back to the cabin. He jogged to catch up with Petrov and they talked quietly as other kids watched and whispered.

Edward's cabinmates were certainly living up to expectations.

******

"Petrov, would you like to talk about it?" Edward whispered as he kneeled beside Petrov's bed. Petrov was curled up in a fetal position, pressed up against the wall. He didn't appear to be crying.

"No," Petrov murmured. "Thank you."

Edward glanced back at Tommy, who stood beside the window. Tommy shrugged with a thin smile. Ossie leaned against his bunk and nodded to encourage Edward to try again. Edward placed his hand on Petrov's shoulder.

"If you ever feel like you need to talk," Edward whispered, "you can tell me anything. It won't change the way I look at you, I promise. I was a pastor and I talked to a lot of military personnel who'd gone through wars. There's not much you could tell me that I haven't heard before."

"Thank you, Edward," Petrov whispered, still not turning around. "But right now, no."

"Okay, can I at least get you something? Are you hungry?"

Petrov shook his head, so Edward squeezed his shoulder and stood up. Tommy smiled approvingly. The door opened and the rest of the Cabin Five residents shuffled in. Billy noticed Petrov curled up on his bed.

"Is he going to be okay?" Billy asked Edward, and Edward nodded.

"What happened to you?" Billy asked Tommy.

"Went for a swim."

"Right on," Simon grinned. "You guys want to go into the forest with us? I know where God and Jay went. There's another place to swim, I think it's in the mountain. Maybe like a hot spring or something."

Edward glanced back at Tommy.

"Sounds interesting," Tommy smirked.

"You've already been in trouble twice today. Sure you want to incur His wrath again?" Edward asked.

"What's the worst that could happen?" Simon replied with a shrug.

"I guess we'll find out," Billy said, opening his footlocker and digging through the clothes. He lifted out a pair of socks and took off his shoes. He put the socks over the ones he was already wearing and then put his shoes back on. The others stared at him.

"I get bad blisters," Billy answered without waiting for anyone to ask. He glanced up at Ossie who was standing against the far wall, away from everyone.

"Really gay, huh?"

Ossie nodded.

"I'll be damned," Billy grumbled as he stood up. "Why'd you just decide to tell everyone in one grand gesture like that?"

"I was gay all my life," Ossie said. "I didn't come out until I was in my early 20s and decided I wasn't going to hide anymore."

"Huh …. well, I guess I can accept that," Billy grunted, grabbing his shoe to slip it on.

"I don't need your acceptance," Ossie replied.

Billy threw his shoe to the ground and swiveled to face Ossie, his eyes wide and his nostrils flaring. Simon took a timid step in-between them.

"Boy, I ain't never been around gay people," Billy growled. Edward and Tommy stood and prepared to separate them. "I certainly never slept just above a faggot. I'm trying to be cordial about this, so you're gonna have to cut me some goddamn slack, all right?"

Ossie straightened his back while looking Billy in the eyes. He was making his stand.

"Billy," Ossie started. "I understand that this is hard for you and probably a lot of other people here. I didn't ask to be here, though. But, as long as you don't ask me to apologize for being gay, I'll do what I can to not make you uncomfortable."

Billy grunted, looking away from Ossie.

"So, I changed in front of you after we swam …" Billy began.

"Jesus Christ, Billy," Ossie exclaimed. "I'm gay; I'm not a pedophile!"

Billy gave him a long, hard look, and finally bent down and grabbed his shoe.

"I guess I can deal with that then."

Billy walked over to Petrov, sat on his bunk and pulled the shoe on. He craned his head to look at the timid boy.

"You comin'?"

Petrov didn't answer so Billy shrugged, finished tying his shoe and headed toward the door. He nodded for Ossie to come along. Ossie smiled and followed.

"Can we talk to Bali first?" Edward asked as he jogged behind them

"You're not going to tell him where we're going are you?" Billy asked, subtly threatening.

"No," Edward answered.

"We can't tell him anything," Simon said. "I don't trust anyone who writes everything down. He says he doesn't show it to God, but I don't buy it."

"Well, theoretically God should already know, right?" Edward asked. "God knows everything."

"Yeah, I don't know about that, son," Billy grunted. "From what I've seen, I'm not buying into that omnipotence thing. The man looks like he's having a hard enough time just dressing himself everyday."

"True," Edward chuckled. "I'm still going to go see Bali. I just want to see if he could get something for me."

"Is it a nudie magazine?" Billy winked, making Edward blush.

chapter vi

Simon's hands cramped and a splinter dug and twisted against the tendon in his knee. The branch under his foot crackled and bowed under his weight. A breeze passed through the forest on its way to his perch, so he tightened his grip. The wind brushed through the limbs and rustled the pine needles. The tree swayed gently and then settled.

"What the hell am I doing up here?" Simon grumbled.

"Can you see anything?" Edward called from fifteen feet below.

"Keep your panties on!" Simon growled back. "If you're bored just make out with Ossie a while."

"Oh, ha ha!" Ossie replied. "I'm going to laugh when you come tumbling down out of the tree!"

"Thanks for the encouragement, brotherman!" Simon yelled.

Simon took a deep breath and then reached for the next highest branch that appeared strong enough to hold him. It was about as thick as his arm and the highest limb that he could comfortably reach. If he couldn't see through the canopy of branches from there, he wouldn't be able to.

The small group of children had jumped off the trail about fifteen minutes prior so they wouldn't run into God and Jay. Now, predictably, they were lost.

Simon stood up on his toes, clung onto a thin branch and then leaned his right knee onto the upper branch. He hugged the tree and slowly stood up. It creaked and wobbled, but held. He straightened up and could see a small opening between trees. He leaned away from the trunk, shifted his weight and then:

CRACK!

The limb gave way; Simon lunged for a lower branch. The splintered limb cut against his ribs as he fell. He twisted and jerked his hands over to another limb. It held for a few moments, but it started to bow. His fingers slipped and he fell, grasping at smaller limbs that were too thin to cling on to. He crashed into a branch, clung onto needles and twigs momentarily until his feet found a larger limb. The needles ripped off in his hand, leaving him wobbling on the thin limb. He waved his arms around, desperately trying to keep his balance. He couldn't and fell through a web of smaller branches. They held his body for a moment, but began crackling.

"Shit," Simon grunted, grasping desperately for anything that could support his weight. His body started slipping through the bed of thin limbs. "Shit, shit, shit, shit, shit, shit, shit!"

He slipped through and plummeted the final five feet until his body hit the ground with a thud.

"Language, Simon," Ossie smirked.

The other children stared warily and grimaced as Simon groaned.

"You okay?" Tommy whispered.

"I just fell out of a fucking tree!" Simon growled as he rolled and clung to his ribs.

"Boy, don't make me take a bar of soap to that mouth," Billy smirked, kneeling down beside him and lifting his shirt. There were long red scratches along Simon's hip where the bark had cut into him and a welt where he'd hit the ground. "That was about the slowest fall I've ever seen."

"Thanks, ass!"

"Settle down," Billy said. "I'm going to check your ribs."

Billy ran his hand along Simon's side, pressing against his rib cage which made Simon grimace.

"Where else does it hurt?" Billy asked. "Can you breathe okay?"

"I guess," Simon groaned.

"Do you know where you are?" Billy asked.

"On the bottom of a fucking tree!"

"Laaan-guage," Tommy sang, while Billy held Simon's face steady as he stared at his pupils.

"You're all right, wuss," Billy grunted, patting Simon's cheek and then pulling him up to his feet.

"Did you see it?" Edward asked.

Simon took a deep breath, then glared up at Edward.

"Your concern is touching," Simon sneered.

"Yes, we're all sorry that you fell and thank you for going up there in the first place," Tommy rattled off with a roll of the eyes. "Did you see anything?"

Simon straightened, twisted his waist and grimaced.

"We're going the right direction," Simon said. "It's not far."

"Well, let's get going," Billy grunted as he turned uphill. "We don't have much time until dinner."

"Can I get a second?" Simon snarled. "I just fell out of a tree. I know you have to get back to your girlfriend ..."

"She's not my girlfriend," Billy corrected, not looking back. "I just don't want to miss dinner."

"Yeah, whatever," Simon sighed.

"I can piggyback you if you can't walk," Ossie ventured.

"No, that's all right, stud," Simon chuckled as he stretched his back. "Okay, let's go."

Billy led the group deeper into the forest. The farther they traveled from the camp, the more tangled the brush grew.

After thirty minutes of trailblazing and the occasional grumble and moan from Simon, the group's visibility was cut off in all directions. Edward regretted not asked Bali for a compass. He then wondered if a compass would work here, if there was an actual magnetic north pole.

"Where's your Bible?" Tommy asked Edward.

"I left it back at the cabin," Edward shrugged. "I was tired of carrying it."

"Hmm," Tommy smiled

Edward couldn't hide a grin and quickly turned away.

"So," Tommy called to the rest of the group. "Why do you think we were all alive at the same time?"

"What do you mean?" Ossie asked.

"Well, humanity was around for several millennia," Tommy continued. "I've talked to a few other people in the camp and everyone, I guess except Petrov, was all alive at about the same time."

"I'd thought about that," Edward grunted as Billy helped him up onto a boulder. "I think it's because we can all relate to each other better."

"Maybe it was a golden era," Ossie ventured, then taking Edward's hand to climb up the boulder. "Maybe everything got worse after us and God's trying to go back to that era to figure out what went wrong."

"Could be," Tommy said. "What do you think happened to all the others?"

"What others?" Billy asked.

"The kids that came before us," Tommy said.

"Whoa," Simon gasped, waving his hands. "Let's take a second, okay?"

Simon sat down on the ground and lifted his shirt to look at his ribs. Billy cocked his head to look at the scratches, which had already faded to the point they were almost completely gone.

"What makes you think that there were kids before us?" Edward asked.

"I think Tommy's right," Billy said shaking his head. "I'd thought it was weird that there were paths already beaten into the forest."

"Right," Tommy said. "Plus, our cabins aren't exactly new; they look like they've been here for a while."

"Maybe God made it that way," Simon ventured.

"God doesn't really work that way," Edward answered. "Outside of creation stories in Genesis, which I believe are clearly just metaphors, and then the odd miracle here and there, God is much more likely to work within the normal flow of reality. If there is dust in the cabins and trails in the forest, that is because the cabins hadn't been cleaned in a while and people walked the same route over and over again."

"But if we're not the first ones here, where are the ones who came before us?" Tommy asked.

The group fell silent. Edward looked around them, then motioned everyone in close. They huddled around him.

"I've been thinking about that cardinal a lot," Edward whispered. "I think there might be something else across the lake, something we're not supposed to see."

"Like what?" Ossie asked.

"I don't know," Edward answered in a whisper. "But, I was hoping that if we got to the top of the mountain, we might be able to see."

"Okay, but why are we whispering?" Tommy asked.

"Because I don't know where God is," Edward answered.

"Isn't God all-knowing and all-seeing?" Billy countered.

Edward frowned.

"Have you ever seen one adult watching over a room full of little children? The ones that get away with the most are the ones who never draw attention to themselves."

The kids looked back up the hill, which was still veiled by branches, bushes and tall grass.

Tommy shook his head and glanced back at Edward.

"I don't think we'll find any answers on this mountain. Why would God put something we're not supposed to see in a place where we could find it? Of course we're going to climb the mountain; of course we're going to try to get to the other side of the lake. Why would he put something there that we're not supposed to see?"

"To see if we'd look for it," Ossie answered.

The children looked up and around the trees again.

"Should we still go up there?" Simon whispered. "I mean, what happens if we see something bad? What can they do to us?"

"Bali said nothing can happen to us," Ossie answered.

"I trust that guy about as far as I can throw him," Billy said. "I'm not opposed to heading up there, but I think we might also keep on our toes. Ossie might be right—this might be some kind of trap and from what went down between God and Simon, we know the Big Man has a dark side."

"I agree, but this is going to drive us crazy," Edward said. "If we don't go up there now, all we're going to do is think about it the rest of the time we're here. That might be a long time. So let's just get this over with."

"Wow, look at you," Ossie smirked. "Guess your balls finally dropped."

"Gross, Ossie," Edward grunted, straightening up out of the huddle. "Let's go."

"No, wait," Simon said, pulling them back down. "I've got something I think we should consider."

"What?" Billy asked.

Simon looked up and down the hill, then looked in the sky.

"Okay, this is really important, okay?" Simon said.

"Are you gay, too?" Billy asked.

"No, no," Simon said, standing and turning. He reached into his pocket. "Hold on. Stay hunched over, I don't want the angels to see."

He bent over and unleashed a loud, rumbling fart into the huddle. The huddle broke and Billy slugged Simon in the shoulder, who then let loose a squealing laugh and he danced up the hill.

The rest groaned and followed.

"Jesus, they don't smell any better in Heaven," Billy grunted.

Simon laughed harder and continued to skip towards the mountain.

As they ascended, the hill progressively grew steeper and the trees began to thin out until the boys finally reached a clearing. From their vantage point, the mountain seemed several times taller than they'd remembered. The face was rocky and there was a winding path that zigzagged up and disappeared into the clouds.

"How long do you think that'll take?" Tommy asked.

"Awhile," Billy answered. "We might not make it back for dinner. Is anyone tired?"

"I'm fine," Edward said, with the rest grunting in agreement.

Edward began walking towards the path, with the others trailing behind him.

"Hey!" a voice shouted from behind them.

Edward turned down the hill. Jay and God stood just inside a grouping of trees. They wore towels and flip-flops, Jay seemed to be completely dry, but his hair was messy like he'd recently taken a bath.

God's hair was still wet and He wasn't wearing His glasses.

His eyes were a milky white, as if he had cataracts. Edward was transfixed momentarily, and then self-consciously looked away.

"What are you doing here?" Jay growled, stepping out from the trees and walking toward them.

"Just exploring," Billy shrugged. "What are you doing out here?"

"None of your business!" Jay shouted. "Get back to the camp!"

God stayed within the grouping of trees. He didn't seem angry, instead he seemed intrigued. He stared at Edward, and Edward lowered his eyes from God and glanced back at Tommy.

"Go!" Jay continued, pointing down towards a trail leading down the hill. "You have no business here!"

"Okay, we're going!" Billy growled back.

The group began walking towards the path. Edward stole one more look back at God, who had stepped out from the trees to watch them retreat.

As they lumbered down to the base of the mountain, they muttered and grumbled.

Edward jogged to catch up with Billy.

"We're coming back again, right?" Edward whispered.

Billy glanced over at him, amused.

"Damn right, we are."

chapter vii

Slivers of moonlight pranced along the waves. The breeze cooled as it wafted across the lake and a silvery glow was cast on Sophia's face. She stood just at the shoreline, stealing glances back at the campground. When she saw Billy approaching, her lips lifted into a demure smile.

Billy shoved his hands in his pockets and kept a casual pace as he approached, but he wanted to run.

"Play it cool," he thought.

Billy wouldn't admit that he had worried throughout the day that she wouldn't show tonight. He never felt comfortable counting on someone else, but in Sophia, he saw safety. Maybe not passion, but safety.

"It's a beautiful night," Billy called, and Sophia nodded without looking directly at him.

He eased down on the sand, and began mentally rifling through stories, jokes and other small talk, searching for a way to break the silence that seemed always to encase her.

But instead of speaking, they both sat on the shore without a word and looked out across the waves. Billy shifted his weight just enough that the thin peach fuzz on his arm brushed across her forearm. They both pretended they hadn't touched.

Giggling voices drew Billy's attention away. Further down the shore near the pier, two figures emerged, holding hands and walking out towards the water. They kicked off their shoes and waded into the water, stopping once the water reached their knees.

"Who's that?" Billy asked.

"The girl's named Mary," Sophia said, watching the figures walk through the water. "I think the boy's name is Barry."

"Barry and Mary?" Billy smirked. "Jesus."

"Don't use the Lord's name in vain," Sophia whispered.

"Sorry."

Sophia looked back out across the lake. Billy watched the couple and briefly entertained the idea of sliding his hand around Sophia's. He decided against it, but did glance over at her face. Her eyes shifted over towards him. She smiled, and a goofy grin stumbled off his face.

"How was your day?" Sophia asked.

"Good," Billy replied. "Well, we got yelled at by Jay."

"Tsk, tsk, tsk. What did you do this time?"

"Well," Billy grunted, jutting out his chest and smirking at Sophia. "We went up to the mountain just to see what was there. We ran into Jay and … Him, and I guess we weren't supposed to be there."

"Did you get into a lot of trouble?"

"Not really," Billy said. "Jay told us to go back to the camp. I think we just surprised them."

"Really?" Sophia asked. Their eyes tripped across each other and Sophia quickly looked back to the water. "What do you think they were doing?"

"Swimming," Billy answered. "I think there might be springs or something in the mountain."

"How odd," she whispered, more to herself.

Down along the shore, Tommy appeared. He walked barefoot out to the water and trudged into the waves until they reached his waist.

"He seems to spend a lot of time in the water," Sophia mumbled.

"Yeah, I guess he does."

Edward emerged, sat down on the shore and opened the Bible. He kept one eye on the Bible and the other on Tommy, and after a few minutes, he began to untie his shoes. He met Billy's eyes. He looked away and subtly tied his shoes and started reading again.

A bell rang in the distance, calling them to bed.

******

Edward poked at a rubbery hard-boiled egg with his fork. The egg squirted off his tray, bounced across the table and fell onto the floor. It skipped beneath kids' legs and settled to rest a few tables down.

Edward glanced around to make sure no one had seen. A camper noticed the egg by his foot and then looked around to see where it came from. Edward ducked his head.

"Hey Tommy," a pair of girls echoed as they carried their trays to a table across from them.

Tommy nodded with a clever smile and Edward stewed.

"Hey girls!" Simon chirped but the girls ignored him.

Once the girls passed, Billy resumed muttering and whispering about the mountain. There was not one mention of Ossie's coming-out statement. Ossie had envisioned a spectacular coming to terms moment with his bunk mates, but instead the issue had been outshined by the mystery at the top of the mountain.

Ossie grabbed his toast and took a large, bitter bite.

"What do you think, Ossie?" Simon asked, just as Ossie started munching.

Ossie rolled his eyes, and motioned for them to wait while he chewed. He finally swallowed hard.

"About what?" Ossie asked.

"Going up again today?"

"I don't know," Ossie said, glancing back to the corner of the cafeteria where Jay and I sat at a small table. "We might want to wait a day or two, see if we can figure out when they are likely to not be there."

"That's not a bad idea," Billy said. "Though, I think if we see an opportunity, we go."

Tommy lifted a piece of bacon to his mouth, but stopped. He wiggled the bacon as he said "You know," as if to emphasize the point. He took a small bite and continued, "I wouldn't mind going to that cliff where we flew in, take another look at the infinite beyond."

Billy nodded, shoving the last of his toast in his mouth and then washing it down with the last of his milk.

"Sounds good," he said. "We'll see what ridiculousness they have us doing today, and when we have time, we'll go. You going with us this time, Petrov?"

Petrov hadn't been listening and was surprised to hear his name. He glanced up, but didn't say anything.

"We're going to the place where they flew us in," Edward said patiently to Petrov. "You want to go with us?"

Petrov shook his head and lowered his focus back to his food.

Billy shrugged, stood up and walked to the counter where dishwashers were working. A rotation of names determined who would clean each day and who would serve. The girls always served; the boys always cleaned. Ossie had spent twenty-seven years as a chef in his earlier life and was annoyed he couldn't get into the kitchen. He wasn't surprised that Heaven was just as misogynistic as churches had been.

The others finished and caught up with Billy as he waited outside. Petrov trailed behind them and stopped when Jay called his name. He walked over to our table.

"How are you, Petrov?" I asked. He only shrugged and kept his eyes lowered.

"We've got a job for you today," Jay said as he forked hashbrowns into his mouth. "Dooh nyow moo …"

"Jay," I snapped. "Swallow, then talk."

Jay rolled his eyes and chewed laboriously while holding up his finger to prevent Petrov from escaping. Jay swallowed and continued:

"Do you know how to use a screen press?"

Petrov shook his head.

"Really?" Jay asked as he forked up another mess of hashbrowns and studied Petrov. "Well, you're the artist, so you need to find someone who does and then go to the equipment building. Know where that is?"

Petrov shook his head again.

"It's the big building between the cabins and God's house," Jay said, then shooed Petrov away.

Petrov shuffled out of the mess hall with his eyes on the ground. He caught up with his cabinmates at the tetherball pole. Billy was hanging onto the ball and swaying back and forth on the heels of his feet as they talked about the cliff.

"Does anyone know how to work a screen press?" Petrov asked.

"I do," Edward answered. "Why?"

"I need someone to show me how."

"Are they making you do shirt designs or something?" Simon asked.

Petrov shrugged.

"Christ," Simon laughed. "This place is so lame."

"Hhrmmph!" a voice grunted behind Simon.

Light shimmered and Simon was lifted off the ground.

"All right, catch you guys later!" Simon yelled as he was whisked off towards Cabin Five.

The others chuckled as Simon disappeared into his cabin.

"Okay, Petrov," Edward said. "Where is the screen press?"

******

The long, fabricated building stored a stockpile of equipment that we used at the camp rarely, or not at all. God was a bit of a pack rat, and there were two storage areas in the building even I wasn't allowed to look in.

The building reminded Edward of World War II-era barracks, the kind he had spent time in as a young chaplain. The doors were all rusted, so Edward had to throw his shoulder against one repeatedly until it squealed open. Dust swirled up into the light and hovered in the room. The large screen press was tucked in the middle of boxes and shelves. It was the same kind Edward had used at the camps his church had run. It wasn't terribly effective, but worked well enough to make free shirts for campers who didn't want them.

The next room was separated by fencing and a wooden door. There was just enough room around the screen press for two people to work at once.

"This is pretty easy," Edward said as he dropped the Bible on a table and dug out a box full of paints from underneath it. "Basically, you have these screens with designs on them; you put the print on the T-shirt, pour paint over it, smooth it out, and when you lift it up, there should be the design all crisp and sharp."

"Oh," Petrov mumbled.

A knock at the door startled the pair. They turned to see God standing in the doorway. He wore a Hawaiian shirt unbuttoned down to the middle of His chest. Patchy chest hair sprouted out in tight curls. His glasses were slowly shifting from a brown tint to the color of watered-down tea. He was holding cardboard designs in his hands.

"I've brought these," God said, holding up the designs. "These are just ideas. Somewhere in the back room there are some x-acto knives and supplies. If you have a better idea, then you can try it out."

Edward nodded and walked over to take the designs from God. Edward realized as he looked up at God's glasses, seeing the colorless eyes behind them, that he'd lost all sense of awe of His Creator.

"So, uh," God yawned as he walked out the door. He turned back to them. "Get about seventy shirts done, then you can have the rest of the morning to yourselves."

"I'm not sure if we can do seventy in one morning," Edward said. "Petrov's never done this before, and I'm going to have to relearn it."

"Oh, well if you need to work through lunch, that's fine. Just make sure if you do something different than the designs, you show me first."

"Okay," Edward sighed.

God glanced down at the Bible on the table.

"Getting a lot of reading done?" God asked.

Edward nodded.

"I'd love to talk to you about…"

"Hmm, good," God interrupted and then disappeared out the door.

Edward chuckled mockingly and shook his head.

"Oh, and," God said, reappearing in the doorway. "Um, I know I said to come up with ideas, but maybe you should just stick to the designs for now. I'm going to be a little busy today and we really need those shirts done."

"Why?" Petrov asked. God glanced at Petrov, cocking His head slightly. He seemed surprised to hear Petrov question Him.

"Because they need to be done," God grumbled, then disappeared again.

Edward tossed the designs onto the screen press and patted Petrov on the shoulder.

"Well," Edward grunted. "I guess there are shirts around here somewhere. You look over on that side; I'll look over here."

The pair dug through the boxes, finding poorly crafted pinch pots, ash trays and beaded necklaces.

"Who made these?" Petrov asked.

"Not sure, but clearly we weren't the first ones through here," Edward said.

Edward tossed a box of necklaces behind him and then stared down at the next box.

"Petrov," Edward whispered. "Come over here."

Petrov shuffled over and looked over Edward's shoulder. A mop of thin strands glowed in the sunlight as they hung between a box and the wall.

"A cobweb?" Petrov asked.

"It's the first one I've seen in the campground," Edward whispered. "They're not supposed to be here, remember?"

They both squatted to look around the box to find the spider.

"Gentlemen!" a voice called from behind them.

They both spun and faced the door, trying to stand in front of the cobweb. I stood at the door, knowing what they were doing but deciding to not let on.

"Sorry to startle you," I said, walking in. "Do you have any questions about the screen press?"

"Where are the shirts?" Edward asked.

"Oh," I said, walking to the wooden door leading to the back room. I tried to turn the knob, but it just spun loosely. "Figures."

I leaned against the door, then jerked back to force it open. It cracked and wobbled, then swung wide.

"There you go," I said, holding the door to ensure it didn't fall over on me. "They should be in boxes in there. There are different colors; unless God said differently, the choice of hue is up to you."

I winced at the unintentional rhyme.

"Thanks," Edward smiled, walking past me into the next room.

"Oh, Edward," I said, walking back to the outside door. I reached around the door to pick up a wooden case that I'd left outside. "I got what you asked for."

I sat it inside and Edward jogged over to it. He took it to the screen press table and sat it down. He opened the latch and found a large sketch pad and an easel set of pencils, pastels, brushes, pens and erasers.

"Thanks, Bali!"

"My pleasure."

Edward pushed the case to Petrov.

"Here you go," Edward said. "See if you can do something with this. I know it's not macaroni and T-shirts, but …"

Petrov watched Edward for a few moments, and then looked down at the case. He timidly moved his hand towards it and ran his fingers over the brushes.

"Thank you," Petrov grinned as he stared into the case. "Thank you."

"So, unless you have any other questions, I'll leave you to it," I said with a wave, which they didn't return. I began to move toward the door, but paused.

"Oh, Edward, how are you doing with the good book?" I asked. "I know you said you wanted to talk about it."

"Um, no, not right now anyway," he said, reaching for the book and then tossing it to me.

I caught it, then studied him as his attention was diverted over Petrov's shoulder.

"Are you done with it?" I asked.

"I'm just tired of carrying it around."

I nodded my head and left them alone.

"Hey," Edward said, nudging Petrov in the shoulder. "I'll take care of the press, why don't you sketch up some ideas."

"Okay," Petrov said, taking the case and walking over to a box below a window. He sat down, took out a pencil and began sketching furiously, as if trying to catch up in a race that had started without him.

* * * * * *

Edward rubbed at the blue paint on his fingers, rolling the paint into little balls that he would then flick off his fingertips, like throwing little blue lawn darts and trying to form the tightest cluster possible a few feet away from him.

He sighed and glanced down at the white shirt. It was supposed to be a blue image of a cabin with a grassy path out front and "Island of the Blessed" written on the bottom. There were seven of the shirts hanging up around the room drying; some were splotchy, some looked faded.

The one on the press had the image painted on twice in slightly different places. The result was similar to what would happen if Edward stared at the shirt and crossed his eyes.

"I think I'm losing my stride, Petrov," Edward mumbled.

Petrov glanced up from his sketch pad, rubbed his eyes and then stood up. He blew on the paper, swiped off shards of eraser, then set it down beside the box he'd been sitting on.

"I think it looks interesting," Petrov smirked as he walked over to the shirt. "Kind of a pop art ... thing."

"Thanks," Edward sighed.

A knock drew their attention to the door.

"Excuse us!" a voice called. "But we have some reading material about the Church of the Latter Day Saints that we would like to share with you!"

"Come in, Simon," Edward called.

Simon emerged with a chuckle as the rest of Cabin Five filed in behind him. Tommy and Billy carried trays of food.

"Soup's on, boys," Tommy said as he handed a tray to Edward. Centered on the tray was a mushy ball of white paste with brown chunks underneath.

"What is that?" Edward cringed.

"Not sure, but some girl refused to eat it because she was a vegetarian," Billy chuckled. "Jay said it wasn't meat because they don't have animals on the Island, so she asked what it was and Jay just said 'it's better if you don't know.'"

"Yummy," Edward mumbled as he paled.

"How far off from finishing are you?" Billy asked.

"A long way," Edward sighed. "Couple hours at least."

"So, are we supposed to be wearing these?" Ossie asked as he surveyed the shirts.

Edward shrugged. He sat down on a crate to eat. Petrov sat on the floor in front of the chair with his sketch pad behind him.

Ossie walked over to the press.

"Can you make one with the image upside down or reversed?" Ossie asked. "Might be worth more, kind of like a rare stamp."

"I'll see what I can do," Edward replied as he chewed.

"Is that a sketch pad?" Ossie asked.

"It's Petrov's," Edward said. "He's been working all morning."

Ossie reached for the pad while asking "Can I see?"

Petrov stood and blocked Ossie's way.

"No, please, there's nothing ready to look at," Petrov answered apologetically.

"Come on," Ossie pleaded, clasping his hands tightly together.

"Not yet. Sorry."

"We're planning on heading to the cliff this afternoon," Billy announced. "Do you want us to wait on you?"

"The cliff?" Edward asked. "Where the landing strip is?"

"Yeah," Simon answered. "Did you hear the plane take off? We think the big man is taking it for a spin so we figured we'd investigate all Scooby Doo-style."

Edward took a bite of the muck and glanced over the shirts as he swallowed.

"Sounds like fun, but we might not be out of here until dinner," Edward said.

"You go," Petrov said. "You've done all the work so far, I'll finish up."

"No," Edward replied. "I can't do that to you."

"I insist."

Edward smiled, then took a bite of the white concoction and winced. He swallowed hard and put the tray on the ground.

"Do we have a lesson or something we're supposed to do this afternoon?" Edward asked.

"Not sure," Billy answered.

"God was supposed to do some lecture or something but never showed," Simon said. "Guess he had better places to be."

"Really?"

"Where would God go?" Petrov asked.

chapter viii

Simon and Ossie danced like wood sprites ahead of their cabinmates while singing with a volume and pomp that only increased every time Billy growled "you sound like castrated mules" or "my farts have better pitch than you two."

Inspired by a newly realized mutual affection for the 80s pop band INXS, Simon and Ossie were attempting to best each other in annoying Billy, and to a lesser degree, the rest of the explorers weaving through the forest on their way to the cliff.

Edward guessed INXS probably sounded better in its original form, but he had never really followed music outside of the dull chamber music played in his church. He'd gone to a few jazz clubs when he was young, but there was just too much temptation.

Ossie and Simon rarely hit the same pitch, and only through pure chance. Their singing was not so much a celebration of the music, but more a gleeful and purposeful mutilation.

They neared the cliff as Ossie and Simon blurted out lyrics about the devil. Edward wasn't sure of what the substance of the song was since the duo would hum the words they didn't know (which were most of them) but Edward understood enough to make him uncomfortable.

When the clearing came into view, Billy grunted "about goddamn time," then "shut that shit up."

"Language!" Simon exclaimed in a piercing falsetto.

The worn airstrip was just a flat, red-tinged dirt road that ran parallel to the lip of the Island. The sky above was blue, but along the horizon the boys could see the vast expanse of souls weaving into the fabric of Heaven.

"I really wish we would have come when the plane was still here," Simon whined.

"Were you planning on stealing it?" Tommy asked.

"Thought had crossed my mind."

They edged toward the cliff and looked down. Tommy nudged Edward on the shoulder and motioned toward the trees.

"What?" Edward asked.

"You don't see them?"

Edward looked again and saw a small cloud of gnats in-between the group and the trees. They swarmed and zoomed around in an airy ball.

Edward was always awed by the unity of gnats, how they all seemed to be buzzing in their own senseless patterns, and yet when they moved, the swarm moved together. Hundreds of independent minds all finely tuned to sweep collectively at a moment's notice. The cloud was impressive and beautiful to watch, yet when he saw that same herd mentality in humans, he attributed it to naivety and weakness.

This explained a great deal why Edward had so few friends among his parishioners. He found it hard to fully embrace any individual who so willingly forfeited his or her own personality.

"Why would God even need the Cessna?" Billy asked. "He could just poof wherever He wanted to go."

"Yeah, I guess even for the all-powerful, it's still the safest way to travel," Simon said.

Ossie chuckled and then sat down at the edge of the cliff, throwing his feet over and looking down. Simon picked up a pebble and tossed it over the lip.

"Hey, don't do that!" Billy growled. "There are people down there."

"Oh, like a pebble is going to hurt them," Simon groaned while rolling his eyes.

"Just don't."

"Sorry, Dad."

The others sat down along the edge and stared at Heaven. The cliff dove straight down. The jagged rocky face bore subtle bands of differing colors just as Edward had seen in canyons back on Earth. The bands of color sometimes resulted from changes in the area's environment, showing that at one point the land was underwater, at other times not. Edward wondered why the Island would have those same bands.

Near the base of Heaven was a thin halo of mist, and beyond that, Heaven. The longer Edward stared, the more he could make out individual souls. Each seemed to be a ball of energy at the front with a tail like a comet.

Simon giggled and leaned over to Edward.

"They look like sperm," Simon whispered. "It's like God shot his load all …"

"Simon!" Edward gasped, scooting away from him. Simon laughed and mumbled something about a "money shot."

Edward shook off the crass comment and looked back down to Heaven. The ball of each soul would emerge and then plunge back into the quilt, with the tail following for a few moments and then fading. He wished he'd asked for a telescope, too.

He tried to think of the souls as a universe of comets winding around each other, but now he could only think of sperm.

"What was it like for you guys down there?" Tommy asked.

"You were there, too," Billy answered.

"I know, but maybe it feels different for everyone."

No one responded, instead they all gazed back down at Heaven. Ossie began humming another song. Simon joined in.

"Stow it," Billy grumbled.

"Sorry, Dad," they replied in unison.

Edward glanced from Heaven back to the swarm of gnats. They were still there. The mass would drift all together, then shift over quickly for no apparent reason. Edward felt Tommy's finger brush up against his. Edward looked over at him. Tommy slid his eyes up, barely meeting Edward's. Tommy quickly looked back down at Heaven as he moved his hand.

Edward's heart beat heavily and his armpits started to sweat. Edward couldn't help but smile, and began to think of Heaven again.

"It was warm," Edward said. "Down there, I just remember it being very warm and very safe. And simple."

"Yeah," Tommy whispered.

"It was like I was just a small part of everything else," Ossie said. "I still felt like an individual, but I was also being supported, if that makes any sense."

Billy grunted with a nod.

Edward let his eyes trail back up to Tommy, hoping he would glance over again. He didn't.

"Where do you think God went?" Ossie asked.

"Maybe he's running around with some other hussy Heaven," Simon replied. "Some younger Heaven that'll do things for him that we won't."

"You know, there's probably an angel watching us," Billy said. "He's going to toss your ass off this cliff."

"Whatever," Simon sighed, then discreetly looked behind and around him.

Tommy chuckled and laid back against the dirt. Edward leaned back too and tried, and failed, to appear relaxed. He had a light glaze of sweat on his forehead.

"Everything was just so much simpler down there," Tommy whispered.

"It was," Edward replied.

"Just floating," Tommy murmured. "Floating."

Their eyes met briefly. Tommy smiled and then returned his gaze to the blue sky above them.

"I bet I could climb down," Simon said. "If I had the right equipment, I could make it all the way to the bottom."

"You'd just fall and I would laugh," Billy smirked.

"No, I wouldn't, I'd be like Spiderman, all 'Thwipt, Thwipt!'"

"Thwipt?" Edward asked.

"That's the sound Spiderman makes when he shoots out a web," Ossie informed him.

"I see."

Leaves rustled and branches creaked. Edward sat up and looked at the tree line behind them. In the distance, he could hear a stiff wind pass through trees.

Tommy stood and studied the trees.

"The wind is picking up," Tommy said. "You don't think there'll be a storm, do you?"

"Bali said it didn't rain here," Billy replied as he stood and brushed red dust off his shorts.

The trees rustled again, the branches bending and weaving. The breeze swept past Edward, nudging him.

"Maybe we should head back," Edward said.

"You're such a pansy," Simon jeered, still staring at Heaven.

"They might be looking for us," Edward said. "Plus, if it does rain, I don't want to get caught in it."

"Okay, Mom," Simon sighed, rolling back from the cliff and standing up.

The wind rushed through the trees again, closer. A loud crack startled Edward.

"What was that?" he asked.

The tree line jerked as air pounded against it. Leaves and branches came hurtling toward them. The wind punched against them like a wave. Edward fell back to the ground. Tommy tried to stay on his feet, but he staggered backwards and rolled toward the edge of the cliff. Billy caught his arm and Edward scrambled over to grab Tommy's other arm.

The wind roared around them as Ossie and Simon scurried to the edge to help. Tommy was shouting, but his voice was washed out by the raging wind. His feet struggled to find a foothold on the rocks jutting out below, but just slid off. Edward held Tommy's forearm with one hand and braced against the edge of the cliff with the other.

The wind died and Tommy, panicked, cried "Don't let go!"

"We won't!" Billy answered. "We'll get you up. Ossie, Simon, grab onto us! We'll pull up together!"

Ossie grabbed Edward's legs and watched Billy. The temperature had dropped dramatically, and Tommy's gasping breaths were forming into white puffs.

Tommy looked below, watching Heaven as his feet still slid against the rocky wall. He turned to look back up at Edward. Tommy's face was suddenly calm.

"We'll get you up," Billy said, whipping his other arm down to grab onto Tommy's shoulder.

Tommy craned his head to look back down at Heaven.

"No!" Tommy said. "Wait!"

"What?" Edward asked.

"Let me go!"

"What?" Billy shouted.

Tommy stared up at Billy, then Edward.

"Let me go," Tommy said. "I want to go back."

Billy and Edward glanced at each other.

"No, we're pulling you back up," Edward said.

"Please, Edward. Let me go."

Edward held his eyes steady on Tommy. Tommy mouthed "please" again.

"You don't know what will happen," Edward said.

Tommy struggled to smile.

"What's the worst they can do?"

Edward's grip loosened.

"Dammit!" Billy growled, adjusting his grip. "Are you sure?"

"Positive," Tommy called.

"Okay," Billy said. "Keep hanging on back there!"

"We got you," Simon replied.

"We let go on three, okay?" Billy asked Edward. Edward nodded. "One … are you sure?"

"Do it!" Tommy yelled.

"Two … Three!"

Edward released and watched Tommy drop. Their eyes were locked as Tommy plummeted backward down the cliff.

Another breeze brushed passed him, whooshing down the cliff. As it soared down to Tommy, it began glittering with sparkles of light.

"An angel," Billy said.

Tommy turned and faced Heaven. His body jerked and slowed. The angel glowed as it seemed to wrap completely around Tommy. They came to a stop, and then began ascending back up the cliff. Tommy's body hung limp, still facing Heaven. He was lifted above Edward and then sat back down near the landing strip. Edward stood and ran toward Tommy as the light around him lifted and evaporated.

Tommy's body remained still as he laid facedown on the ground. Edward could see Tommy's chest heaving; he was crying. His breath formed small clouds that tumbled along the ground. Edward knelt down beside Tommy. He ran his hand over Tommy's shoulder.

"I'm sorry," Edward whispered.

Tommy didn't answer. He kept his face hidden in the dirt.

******

Goose bumps formed on Edward's bare legs and his breath formed long white plumes as they walked back through the cold forest toward the camp.

Billy stopped suddenly, turned to Simon and slugged him in the chest.

"Oomph," Simon winced as he fell backward onto the ground. He held his chest, grimaced and looked back up at Billy. "What was that for?"

"You were the dumbass who threw the rock!"

chapter ix

Why would God need to leave the Island?

The question is beyond even my knowledge of God's ways and means. The very thought that God would ever or could ever abandon His creation is staggering, if not devastating. Even the mere thought that God could not control the entirety of His creation from any place in the universe is troubling.

Humans often believe God is all-knowing and all-seeing because they then feel watched over and protected. How can God be the divine and supreme judge of men's hearts and characters if His entire focus is not on us?

Is the question a legitimate concern or just another example of humanity's warped pride and jealousy?

I must confess that this riddle has haunted me ever since I first thought of it many, many years ago.

Light shimmered off the face of an angel as the wind picked up. With the sparkles erupting at such frequency, a vague outline of the angel could be discerned—the noble chin and strong jaws, the inhumanly beaked nose, the swept-back forehead and the massive wings tucked behind his thick frame. He seemed to shiver from the cold, or perhaps impatience, as he waited for my directions.

I tried to keep the pages of my organizer from flapping in the wind as I read over my notes and frowned. Children passing on their way into the mess hall stared at the angel in awe and intimidation, swerving away from us as they neared the door.

I'd sent the angel into the water earlier to ensure all the children had made it out of the lake when the winds hit. There were more children to account for off in the woods, along the shoreline and scattered throughout the campground.

Above the Island, vast expanses of dark gray clouds were racing from horizon to horizon. On Earth, the clouds would indicate a front, but on the Island there was no telling what the clouds meant. I would have assumed God was up to something, had some experiment under way or was simply in a vile mood, but God wasn't on the Island.

I watched as Edward and his cohorts slunk into the campground, cautiously scanning for angels. The boys' faces were flushed from the sharp, frigid winds. Tommy was trying not to cry, but whimpered abruptly from time to time as Edward walked alongside and whispered encouragements. Billy kept an eye on me while he led the group back to the screen printing room.

I turned to the angel. His face sparkled as the wind kicked up and, for a brief moment, I could look into his small, severe eyes and sharp, inhuman smile.

"We need one of you to go find God, immediately," I told the angel, then turned my organizer toward him so he could see a small map of Heaven I'd devised. It was drawn more out of assumption and educated guesses than real knowledge.

"I think he might be in the lower outskirts. Find Him; tell Him what's happening. Go ring the bell, have the others collect the children. I want them all to stay in the mess hall. We'll ride it out there, have dinner early and wait for God to get back."

The possibility arose that God might not be in Heaven at all. He'd been known to disappear altogether, but if that were the case, there was nothing I could have done about it any way.

The angel grunted and began to back away.

"Hey, hold on," I said, closing my eyes.

It was hard to picture the Island with the cold wind biting at my skin. I took a deep breath and scanned the outer perimeter, up to the mountain, along the shoreline and into the forest.

"There is a group on the northern side of the campground—four of them, about a hundred yards into the forest," I said. "Another group near the mountain, just east of the base. Just two there. The rest are near enough that they won't have any problem hearing the bell despite the wind."

The angel grunted. I opened my eyes to see his massive, sparkling wings beating as he lurched into the air.

The door to the screen printing room edged open and a pair of eyes looked out at me.

"Bali!" Jay shouted as he emerged from God's house. He waved and began running toward me. Jay looked out at the lake while he approached.

"What are we going to do?" he asked, stopping next to me and watching the choppy waves.

"Round up the children and get them into the mess hall," I said. "An angel is going to get God; the rest will collect all the kids. We'll just ride it out."

Jay turned to me and nodded.

"What do you need me to do?" he asked.

"Let's go see if we have any long-sleeved shirts or extra blankets to keep the kids warm," I said as I looked through my organizer. "There should be enough for all the children."

I tucked my organizer into my armpit and led Jay toward the screen printing shop.

"Edward and Petrov have been printing shirts, so we might take those over, too."

We jogged to the door. I knocked before opening, hearing hushed voices arguing inside. As the door opened, the boys all stood and faced us.

"Hey," I called as Jay and I entered and closed the door behind us. I rubbed the goosebumps on my arms and studied the guilty parties. "How are those shirts coming?"

"We're done," Petrov said. The sketch pad and the case were tucked behind him, hidden on the other side of a box.

"Good, grab all those shirts," Jay barked. "Have you seen any long-sleeve shirts?"

Petrov and Edward shook their heads.

"What's going on out there, Bali?" Billy asked.

"There's been a disruption," Jay answered.

I turned to Jay and leaned close.

"Don't," I whispered.

"No," Jay sneered, pushing me aside and walking toward the group. "If they make a mistake, they should be held accountable."

Jay approached Simon, his fear of the weather outside shifting into anger as he glared down at the smaller camper. Simon avoided Jay's eyes but frowned bitterly.

"Sorry," Simon mumbled.

The bell began ringing and Jay glanced away. He smirked at me and then walked toward the door.

"What's going to happen?" Billy asked.

"We're not sure," I answered. "It might get colder. We're having everyone gather in the mess hall until God returns and bringing everything we can find to stay warm."

"Where did He go?" Edward asked.

"That is none of your business," Jay growled.

Edward narrowed his eyes, stood straight up and took a step toward Jay.

"Why not?" Edward asked.

Jay looked to me, and I shrugged.

"You don't know, do you?" Edward furthered. "Do you even know if He's coming back?"

"He'll be back," Jay replied, his voice weaker. "How do you know?"

"Because I have faith," Jay grumbled. "Something you seemed to have lost, Preacher."

Edward's face flushed and he took a step toward Jay, his fists clinched. Billy lunged in front of Edward and held him back. He met Edward's eyes, Edward nodded and retreated back to the others.

"What if He doesn't come back?" Billy asked, turning back to me.

"He'll be back!" Jay yelled, opening the door and storming out. He froze just on the other side of the door, his mumbled "oh no" barely audible over the roaring winds.

I motioned for the kids to wait inside and I walked out to Jay. Gray clouds were overtaking the sky. Two waterspouts twisted up from the other side of the lake, reaching high into the clouds. They weaved and wound around each other erratically. Waves were crashing farther up onto the shore and sweeping over the pier.

"I can't get wet," Jay mumbled, his face pale and his vibrant green eyes locked on the water.

"I know; get to the mess hall," I said.

Jay sprinted across the campground and waved children to follow him. He opened the mess hall door and ushered other children in before following them. I stepped back inside the screen printing room and closed the door behind me.

"Okay, real quick," I said. "Don't worry about the rock, Simon; it had nothing to do with what's going on. Sometimes this happens when God leaves. He'll be back soon, though; you have my word."

"Why would Jay say that this is my fault if it isn't?" Simon asked.

"I don't know. He just does that, but this is happening because God's not here to regulate the weather. It will be okay—the angels will protect us until He gets back. Now, grab all the shirts and go to the mess hall. I'm going to see if we have any blankets. Keep all the kids calm until I get there, okay?"

They nodded, then started grabbing boxes of shirts. I opened the door for them and watched the waterspouts. The funnels had hit the far shore. A third spout had sprouted from the clouds and jutted down

into the middle of the lake. Ossie ran out of the room
but stopped to stare at the spouts.

"Don't look!" I shouted. "Just go! Hurry!"

******

The campers huddled in the center of the mess hall
as Jay stood up in the middle of the group and read
passages of the Bible aloud.

The temperature continued to drop outside and there
was no heater, the Island wasn't supposed to get cold
enough for one to be needed. The legs of the tables had
been folded in and then the tables were stacked along
the walls. Piles of shirts and blankets surrounded the
children; many of them had wrapped themselves in
several shirts and then clutched blankets tightly over
their cold bodies.

Even amid the pandemonium, I could acknowledge
the delightful irony of the serene image on the front of
the T-shirts contrasting with the chaos outside. Though
I thought it was funny, it just fed many of the children's
burgeoning resentment.

Tommy separated himself from the group and
Edward followed. They sat against the inside wall of
the building, Edward whispering, Tommy staring at the
floor emotionless.

They startled at the first lightning flash. As far as I
knew, it was the first lightening bolt to strike the Island.
The thunderclap rattled the windows as the winds
picked up again. Jay watched the windows warily, and
when the gusts subsided, he returned to reading the
Bible. He was skimming through various selections
from the letters of Paul, finding anything to give the

children, and himself, solace. The children weren't listening.

I'd stuffed my organizer into a plastic bag and then wedged it into my waistband. I went looking for the hot chocolate machine in dry storage and found Barry and Mary huddled in a corner whispering to each other. I didn't say anything, just grabbed the small machine and a large can of chocolate sauce and left them there.

Sophia had volunteered to help set it up and was working on hooking up the water line.

"Okay, we need to let it warm up," I said as I finished pouring in the chocolate sauce. I ran my finger inside the can and licked the chocolate off. "Go wait with the others."

"One of the funnels is getting closer!" Billy called from a window, sending a wave of nervous chatter through the group.

"Shut up and get back over here!" Jay shouted. "If that window explodes, it'll cut your face to shreds."

A few whimpering cries followed.

Jay slammed the Bible shut and stood.

"That is enough!" Jay growled. "God will not abandon us! I am ashamed that some of His most strident followers are breaking down because of a little foul weather!"

"This isn't supposed to be happening in Heaven!" one of the girls called.

"This isn't Heaven!" Jay replied.

The children looked up at him. Jay grimaced and shook his head.

"I mean, it is and it isn't," Jay struggled. "God will come back; just have faith."

Martha stood and tossed down the shirt she was using as a blanket.

"Blessed is the man who perseveres under trial!" Martha growled. "Because when he has stood the test, he will receive the crown of life that God has promised to those who love him!"

Jay patted her on the shoulder and then sneered at the others.

"See, not all of you are cowering like mice," Jay shouted.

"What happens if those waterspouts get to us?" Edward asked. "If it sucks us up and kills us, what happens then?"

"It won't," I called, walking over to the group. "There are angels all around the mess hall; they'll protect us."

"There are more than sixty of us here," Simon said. "Can they save all of us? Are there enough of them?"

"Yes," I answered, knowing that it wasn't the truth. "As long as you're in the campground, they will keep you safe, okay?"

Another lie.

"What if I leave the campground and go to the waterspouts?" Tommy asked, standing.

The children turned to the boy, who hadn't spoken since returning from the cliff. I glanced at Jay, who grimaced and shook his head.

"Please stay," Edward whispered to Tommy.

"Why?"

"For me."

Tommy sighed and then sat back against the wall.

"Everyone stays in the mess hall, okay?" Jay called. "We will be fine!"

"Is there not one storm cellar in this whole place?" Ossie asked.

"No," I answered. "We'll just have to wait in here and stay away from the windows."

"Can I at least get some hot chocolate?" Ossie asked.

I grinned, but another stiff wind shook the windows.

The children watched the glass and huddled even tighter in the center of the hall. The roof and the walls creaked, a piece of sheet metal jarred loose in a supply shed outside and began banging as the wind beat against it.

I heard light tapping begin slowly on the windowpanes and roof.

"Is that rain?" Ossie asked as the tapping grew to a patter all across the roof.

"No," I answered. "It's from the lake—the funnels are picking up water from the lake and it's falling all around us."

A heavy thud shook the roof. Girls screamed. Whatever had hit the roof slid off to the side of the building facing away from the shore.

"Stay here," I said, walking to the window. I saw what it was and then turned away to make sure none of the children could see.

"What was it?" Billy asked.

"Nothing."

Jay separated from the group and jogged to me. He looked out the window.

"We need to make sure the angels get that before we let the kids outside," Jay whispered, and I nodded.

Water began streaming down along the windowpane and Jay backed away. He looked across the mess hall to the children.

"It'll be okay," I whispered to Jay. He turned back to me and smiled. "Go read to the children."

I patted Jay on the shoulder and walked over to the other side of the mess hall to watch the lake. It was now as dark as night. The waves were high enough to pour over the pier. Two of the waterspouts had spun into tornadoes and had ventured deep into the woods on the other side of the lake. I could make out trees and debris swirling in the funnels.

The third spout appeared—it was approaching the shore near the mountain. I walked to the northernmost window to get a better view. The funnel dipped from the clouds near the middle of the lake but the neck of the funnel bent and stretched out toward the shoreline.

The funnel suddenly veered toward the campground and I stumbled back from the window. The roar consumed the building, as if a train were rumbling through it. Children were screaming, but their voices were drowned out. Jay closed his eyes and his lips trembled out prayers.

I eased back to the window. Branches and water were blowing across the lake. The windowpanes were rattling; a square of sheet metal tumbled across the shore into the lake. Glittering angels were almost completely visible as they soared around the building. They looked like bears with wings, but with longer necks. They were as impressive as eagles and as clumsily assembled as platypuses.

I retreated back to the group. The children huddled tightly; many of them were crying hysterically. Jay was still praying.

Edward pulled Tommy up and led him to the rest of the group. Edward was yelling at me, but I couldn't hear him.

The building groaned. I looked up to the ceiling just as the structure crackled and broke. A swath of the roof and ceiling ripped away. Windows broke all around us. Glass and water swirled around the building. Tables tipped over. I ran to the children and put my body over a group of them huddled together.

Then, silence.

The wind deflated. Water dripped from the open ceiling for a few moments, then stopped. I scanned the damage— the broken glass, the broken beams from the roof, the tables scattered across the mess hall, puddles of water on the floor. No blood, no hurt children.

As I watched, the glass swept up off the ground and reformed into the windows. The puddles of water turned to mist, lifted off the floors and billowed out of the open ceiling. The gray clouds were clearing, giving way to blue sky. I heard the hum of engines and then saw God's airplane pass above the hole overhead. Wood and tiles then flew to the hole and reformed the damaged ceiling.

I stood up and looked over the group. They were drenched with water and shaking in fear, their breaths puffing out in thin clouds. The sun was out, but it was still bitterly cold.

Ossie stood staggered across the mess hall. He picked up the hot chocolate machine, which had leaked chocolate sauce. He tipped it upright and grabbed a nearby mug.

"Who's thirsty?"

Jay stumbled away from the group, pushing kids out of the way and holding his head. He struggled to stay on his feet, leaving a trail of blood in his wake.

"Stay here!" I told the children and followed Jay into the kitchen. I grabbed a pile of T-shirts and ran over to him, catching him just as he stumbled to the ground.

I didn't realize until I left the mess hall that my organizer had fallen to the ground. I'd worried that the children would take it out of the plastic bag and look through it. They didn't. Instead, they just stared at it as they shivered.

In the kitchen, Jay tried to stand by bracing himself against a stove, but he slipped and fell to his knees. Blood was pouring down from his scalp.

"I'm wet, Bali!" Jay moaned as his hands shook. "I'm wet!"

I knelt down and pressed the shirts against him, trying to dry his skin.

"It's okay," I said. "We'll get you dry; no one will see."

"Is everything okay?" a voice called.

I turned to see Barry and Mary watching us from the dry storage area.

"Get in the other room!" I growled.

They shuffled out of the kitchen and disappeared into the mess hall.

"Do you know where the other cups are?" Ossie called as his head poked in.

"Other room!" I yelled.

"It hurts so bad," Jay murmured as he laid down on the tile floor.

"I know, I know. We'll get you dry."

chapter x

Edward thought of fireflies as he watched the sparks from the bonfire dance and swirl up into the sky. The crackling logs and the smell of the rich, enveloping smoke relaxed him. He wanted to sleep, they all wanted to sleep—but the storm had left them without cabins or beds. They used the shards of lumber that were once the cabins to make the campfire.

In the distance, Edward could hear Martha reading the Bible aloud to a small group of girls, mostly passages about temptation, judgment and penitence.

As with most other things, God would tend to the campers lost homes in His own time.

The children were wrapped in blankets as they gazed, tired and withdrawn, at the fire. No beds to sleep in, not enough energy left to talk, all that was left was to dwell on the lives they had left behind: Billy on foreign wars, Sophia on missions in small African villages, Simon on detox centers and Petrov on his entire life after age twelve.

Tommy, alone, smiled as he gaped at the flames. Once the storm had passed, so had his sorrow. He joked about Jay in ways that made even the boldest children uncomfortable, he started a semi-successful round of

"Row, Row Your Boat" and then he initiated a rendition of Milli Vanilli's "Blame it on the Rain" with Simon and Ossie.

Edward was pleased to see Tommy's mood lifted, but he was troubled by how severely it had shifted. Edward had seen this kind of erratic behavior in troubled youth before, yet it didn't diminish his fascination with Tommy. If anything, it heightened Tommy's allure.

The glint of an angel's shimmer appeared from above and another log dropped into the fire, sending a blossom of sparks up into the sky. The wind shifted and blew smoke over Tommy. It was warm and enveloping. It reminded Tommy of his father and made him hungry for marshmallows—the roasted kind with molten sugar concealed beneath the crispy surface that coated the tongue in scalding heat.

There would also be overcooked hot dogs that were black and flaky on the outside, but still tender and juicy on the inside. Then, in the morning, there'd be his first taste of coffee, which he'd hate but drink because his father would grin at him like his son had just shed a layer of his childhood. They'd blow steam off the surface of the coffee and talk about God, football, his father staying straight and, of course, his father's ambitious plans. His father always had exciting schemes and they were always different every time Tommy saw him. It made Tommy believe his father was capable of anything, until later in life when Tommy realized his father's life had amounted to nothing.

His father was supposed to move in with Tommy's mother and sisters to be a family again, but ended up in jail again a month later.

And, as quick as that, Tommy's face sank, his smile
faded and he was distant again.

"Hey," Simon whispered to Tommy and Edward.

Simon was hunched over, the blanket covering his
entire body like a burka. Simon's hands were shifting
around inside the blanket as he searched for angels in
the sky.

"Check it out," Simon said, sliding his hands
outside the blanket. He opened his right hand to show a
rock to them. Simon tossed it into the air, caught it,
tossed it again, caught it. He tossed it a third time and
the rock hung in the air. It seemed to freeze as Simon
did small circles with his hand underneath, wriggling
his fingers slightly. The rock finally dropped back to his
hand.

"Whoa," Tommy smirked. "Cool trick; how'd you
do it?"

"I don't know," Simon said, pulling the rock back
into his blanket.

"Oh, okay," Edward said, rolling his eyes as he and
Tommy turned back to the fire.

"No, no, seriously," Simon whispered. "I was trying
to do another trick I used to do back when I was a
magician, and it just sort of happened. I can't make it
hang up there long, but I feel a connection to it."

"Good for you," Edward sighed.

"I'm not kidding," Simon urged. "I'll do it again."

Edward turned back to Simon as his hands appeared
back out of the blanket.

"What are you doing?" Billy asked from behind
them.

Simon startled and dropped the rock. Simon
shushed Billy and grabbed the rock. He looked around

and then motioned Billy over. The four then formed a tight circle with Simon's hand hidden in the middle.

"Now, watch closely," Simon said.

"You're not going to fart or something stupid like that are you?" Billy grunted.

"No," Simon gasped, offended. "Now, this isn't a trick. Don't tell anyone, though. I don't want to get in trouble again."

"Okay," Billy conceded. "You fart or whip out your Johnson, and I'll throw you in the bonfire."

Simon's hand reappeared, pinching the rock between his finger and thumb theatrically. He then tossed it in the air. He caught it, tossed it, caught it, tossed it and it hung in the air.

"Jesu …," Billy mumbled, then stopping and glancing around for angels. None came, so he looked back at the hovering rock. They watched it closely for five seconds until it dropped to Simon's palm. "Do it again!"

Simon scanned around them.

"Okay, last time."

Simon repeated the process, this time fighting back a smile. The rock hung in the air again. Billy moved his hand around the rock and then underneath it. It continued to hang in the air, undisturbed.

"Close your eyes," Billy said.

Simon did and Billy grabbed the rock and tried to pull it away, but couldn't. After the fifth second, Billy's hand jerked away with the rock inside. Billy opened his hand and looked over the rock.

"How do you do it?" Billy asked, looking up at Simon whose smile was wide and beaming. "It's a trick, isn't it?"

"No," Simon shrugged. "I promise."

"Then why are you smiling like that?" Billy asked, tossing the rock back to him.

Simon caught in and slipped it back under the blanket.

"'Cause it's magic, man," Simon said. "I've always wanted to be able to do something like that."

"What else can you do that with?" Tommy asked.

"I don't know, just figured it out with the rock."

"Teach me how to do it?" Billy asked.

"Can't—it's magic and I can't divulge my secrets," Simon winked, then turned back to the fire.

"Bastard," Billy whispered as he moved around to sit next to Simon. They chatted softly, then laughed.

"That's weird," Tommy said to Edward, and Edward nodded. Tommy smiled wide and nudged Edward on the shoulder. "It's been quite a night, huh?"

"It has," Edward replied.

"Are you okay?"

Edward took a deep breath, then leaned in toward Tommy.

"I'm really worried," Edward said.

"About?"

"About this whole place," Edward whispered, glancing around them for angels. "Doesn't it seem to be unraveling to you? Tonight we almost died in a tornado, bugs and animals are popping up when they're not supposed to, now Simon is a magician."

Tommy nodded as he watched the fire. His smile faded to a distant smirk.

"At least they're keeping it interesting."

"Yeah," Edward conceded with a weary sigh. "I just don't like not knowing what the rules are, you know? I could accept bad things happening on Earth because even if they were unjust, at least there was a consistency to the way the world worked. Here? I just don't see the same structure, and it bothers me."

"You need to learn to relax and enjoy the ride."

"That's never been my strong suit," Edward mumbled.

"Well," Tommy said as he wrapped the blanket tighter around himself. "No matter what happens, I'll protect you."

Edward's face flushed and his stomach fluttered. He felt weak, nauseous and overcome with nerves. He ducked his head away as a smile broke through to the surface. Tommy bumped his shoulder again, sending a wave of sparkling energy through his body.

"Hey, everyone!" Jay called.

Edward and the others had to stand and walk around the bonfire to see Jay. He was holding a clipboard with a pencil tucked behind his ear. There were no signs of blood left on his clothes, but Edward thought he still looked pale.

"Listen up," Jay continued, glancing at the clipboard. "The angels should have the cabins repaired soon, then we'll send you guys to bed. Is anyone hungry or thirsty?"

"Got any s'mores?" Ossie asked.

"No," Jay replied with an exasperated sigh. "Just stuff we have in the cafeteria."

No one said anything, so Jay looked back down at the clipboard.

"God will be coming by in a second to talk to you—just hang out and stay warm," Jay said. "Let Bali know if you have any problems or issues, or need to use the bathroom."

Edward raised his hand. Jay glanced at him, but didn't acknowledge him any further. He turned and began walking toward God's house, where God's silhouette could be seen through a window, pacing and looking back out at them.

"Jay!" Edward called, but Jay kept walking.

"What is it Edward?" I asked.

Edward turned to me.

"Why doesn't God just poof the cabins back, like he fixed the mess hall roof?"

"Because there is no imminent danger," I answered. "God only intervenes when there is danger that the angels can't handle."

"Well," Simon said. "I'm in imminent danger of freezing my nuts off, what's God going to do about that?"

"I suppose God could just remove them," I replied. "Would you like me to make an inquiry?"

******

"Where'd He get a fur coat from?" Billy whispered to Edward, who just shook his head.

God was approaching in a spotted tan-and-white fur coat with a hood pulled over his head. His hands were jammed into the coat pockets; he wore black dress pants underneath.

"It's a parka—looks like American lynx to me," Ossie answered, then leaned in close to them. "It's actually a woman's coat."

The group chuckled as they huddled close.

When God reached them, he motioned to Jay to bring the clipboard. He wore matching mittens and awkwardly attempted to flip the pages on the clipboard. Finally, unable to grab the sheets through the mittens and aware the children were trying to stifle laughter, He just handed the clipboard to Jay with a disgusted look, as if the clipboard and/or Jay had failed Him.

Jay flipped the page for God and held the clipboard up so God could read it.

"What do you call snails on a boat?" God read aloud.

The group deflated slightly and shot narrow looks back and forth to each other.

"What?" Ossie finally called to God.

"Snailors."

None of the children, even Ossie, dignified the joke with even a polite chuckle.

"Snailors," God mumbled to Himself, then motioned for Jay to make a note on the clipboard.

He pulled off the hood of the parka, revealing a pair of earmuffs underneath that matched his mittens. Chuckling erupted from the group, which grew into laughter. God smiled, motioned for Jay to scratch out the previous note.

"Snailors," He grinned.

"Okay, calm down!" Jay called to the group.

"Thank you, Jay," God said, then cleared phlegm from his throat and spat. The children backed away as the loogy hit the ground in front of them.

"Oh, sorry," God mumbled to the children, then looked out to the whole group. "I know it's been a rough day for you, and I understand that it is cold. I will warm it up tomorrow, but for the time being you will have to tough it out."

"Can we get coats or more clothes?" Edward asked.

"No."

"Can I have your coat?" Billy asked as he stood up from the group.

"No!" Jay growled. "Sit down and show respect!"

God frowned as he looked over the group. He motioned for Jay to make a note.

"What about the earmuffs?" Simon called as he stood up.

"I could just freeze you out tonight!" God shouted as He swiveled and strode around the campfire to Simon. "Or I could just warm you up right now, is that what you want?"

Simon ducked his head and sat down. The children were silent until Tommy stood with his blanket still wrapped around him.

"You can warm me up," he said.

"It's not a pleasant experience, boy," God growled, not even turning toward Tommy.

"Nothing on this rock is pleasant," Tommy snapped back.

God turned toward him with a bitter smile, then muttered, "Okay."

God walked toward Tommy, jerking off his mittens. He raised his hand and placed it on Tommy's shoulder. Jay jogged toward God.

"Sir," Jay said.

"He asked me to warm him up, and that is what I'm doing," God responded flatly.

Tommy began to wince, sweat started forming on his face. He began gritting his teeth, but he looked directly into God's eyes defiantly.

Edward began to smell fabric burning as smoke wafted up through God's fingers.

"Sir," Jay said. "Please."

Tears started welling in Tommy's eyes. The smoke continued drifting from his shoulder and his fists were clinched tightly. Tommy grunted and flinched away, but God kept His grip on Tommy's shoulder.

"Sir!" Jay shouted.

God lifted his hand. The imprint of His palm was burned through the shirt where Tommy's skin showed through, dark red.

"Thank you," Tommy grumbled, tears rolling down his face. He remained standing, staring at God.

"You are not my only responsibilities!" He sneered, turning to the rest of the children. "I have an entire universe to look after—I'm not going to babysit you and let the rest of My creation languish! I created this island for you, and I have not heard one 'thank you' from any one of you."

"Thank you, Sir!" Ossie called. "Now can we go back to heaven?"

God glared down at Ossie, who responded with a casual smile.

"Please," Ossie added.

God looked over to me and motioned for me to write. I did. I quoted them both word for word.

God turned away again and stormed up the hill, pulling on his mittens and jamming His hands back into His pockets. Edward urged Tommy to sit down, which he finally did, wincing from the pain in his shoulder. Blisters were bubbling on his skin.

Jay watched God storm off, then looked over the group, his eyes resting on Tommy. He broke his gaze and began pacing in front of the children, mumbling to himself and shaking his head. He stopped, threw the clipboard into the group and strode away.

I let Jay go, then motioned for one of the children to hand me the clipboard. I knelt down amidst the children.

"Your cabins are going to be ready soon," I said. "Try to get some sleep and let's just pretend this night never happened, agreed?"

They did.

"Tommy, your shoulder should be fine in an hour or so. If it isn't, let me know."

Tommy nodded.

"Ossie," I said, turning to him. "Please don't ask that again."

"Only if I can get another cup of hot chocolate," Ossie nodded.

"Deal."

Tommy raised his hand weakly and I pointed to him.

"Do you have any coffee?"

chapter xi

Edward was amazed that even freshly built cabins still smelled musty and old. It was, at first, an annoyance which was only heightened by the fact that the Island hadn't warmed since God reappeared.

But as Edward watched his breaths form white plumes that drifted up above the beds, curled and dissipated as they reached the cabin ceiling, Edward also begin thinking about the meaning of the dust.

"Perhaps God really did design the Island to look lived in," he wandered, then wiping his wet, cold nose with his blanket.

Perhaps, he thought, there really wasn't anyone else on the Island, they really were the first and only ones there. The trails, the pinch pots in the supply room, all part of a deception by God to get the children wandering about what was on the other side of the lake.

"To tempt us," Edward whispered.

All the children's minds raced and wandered that night since the cold brought phlem-laden coughs that chased away sleep. They all rolled in their beds, pulled the covers tight and looked like shivering burritos.

The sun flicked on, suddenly. It didn't rise gradually but burst into a warm blossom above the horizon. Edward was the only one who seemed to notice. He'd become accustomed to watching the sun rays creep across the campground. That morning, it was as if God had just flipped on the sunlight after losing track of time.

Before long, the tightly curled children unwound and relaxed into a comfortable sleep. Just as Edward felt dreams seep into his mind, the breakfast bell sounded.

"Man," Billy groaned. "Is everyone else's pillow completely crusted with snot?"

"Eww," Ossie grimaced. "Billy, that is gross."

"Just wondering," Billy yawned.

"My face actually stuck to my pillowcase last night," Simon said. "I tried to roll over and my pillow rolled with me."

Edward chuckled and proceeded to flip his pillow over.

"I'll dare someone to lick my pillow," Simon said. "I'll give you my breakfast dessert to do it."

"No, thank you," Ossie laughed, then kicking up at the springs of Billy's bed. "By the way, those must have been some dreams you were having last night."

"Who, me?" Billy asked.

"Yeah you," Simon chuckled. "Sounded like you were being eaten by a bear, kind of freaked me out."

"Me?"

"Yeah," Edward sighed. "It's kind of a nightly thing with you, but I guess no one else is ever up. I thought about waking you up, but was worried you'd wake up swinging."

"Huh," Billy grunted, then unconvincingly added, "Don't remember that at all."

Edward chuckled, but it staggered into a series of violent coughs. He rolled over off the bed and continued coughing until he'd gotten the phlegm out of his lungs.

"Ugh," Edward gasped. "I hate sleeping in the cold."

Edward slipped on his shoes and walked to the window, hoping the sunlight had warmed it. God was standing near the pier talking as He kept His hands tucked in a bulky pullover. Edward wasn't sure if He was talking to Himself or an angel—he hoped it was an angel.

The glimmering light of an angel emerged from a storage shed. It was carrying a large, long object wrapped in a white blanket. Edward studied the object for a few moments before convincing himself that it couldn't possibly be what it looked like.

Jokingly, he announced:

"I think God is stashing a dead body. Somebody must have complained about the food."

Tommy dropped from the bunk bed, then pranced across the cold floor. He hopped over to the window.

"Kinda does look like a body." Billy grinned, then hopped back to his footlocker to get his shoes. "I'm jealous of the dead guy."

The angel carried the object to the pier and then sat it down in a rowboat. God carefully lowered himself down into the rowboat and began paddling away from the pier.

"Where's He going?" Edward muttered.

"Who?" Billy asked.

"God— He's taking the boat."

Billy slipped on his shoes and shuffled back over.

146

"Do you think He's going to just drop that in the lake?" Edward asked.

Billy shrugged, then answered, "Better stuff some rocks into the intestinal cavity or it'll just float to the surface."

God continued paddling across the lake until He was just a black dot on the water.

"He's going to the other side," Billy said.

"Why?"

"I don't know. But after we see what's on top of that mountain, I say we find a way across the lake to see what there is to see."

chapter xii

"Mmmmmm, brains!" Simon groaned as he gazed blankly ahead. His arms were stretched out in front of him, his mouth gaped open and he walked stiffly toward a group of girls who shrieked and ran away.

"Brains!" Tommy echoed, closing in from the other side of the girls.

The girls huddled and turned toward the boys. Sophia stood out in front, protecting the girls from the two zombies. She lifted up a sock with other balled-up socks shoved inside to give it weight. The other girls lifted their sock weapons.

"Now!" Sophia yelled. The girls screeched and charged Simon, pelting him repeatedly over the head until he went limp and fell to the ground.

Other children, wearing headbands and groaning for brains, emerged from behind Cabin Four and tried to encircle the girls.

"Charge!" Billy shouted from behind the mess hall. He led a small group of boys toward the zombies as they tossed balled-up socks like rocks. The zombies dispersed; the ones that were hit fell like sacks of potatoes to the ground. Billy reached down and picked up Sophia, carrying her off on his shoulder as the others followed.

One girl collapsed to the ground in front of Tommy and cooed "Oh no Mr. Zombie, don't eat me!"

She fainted back and waited for Tommy to grab her. Instead, he stepped over her and continued staggering onward.

"Hey!" the girl shouted. "Get back here!"

"Braainns," Simon growled as he crawled to the girl.

"Not you," the girl snapped, sitting up and kicking him away. "Your dead anyway."

She jumped to her feet and tried to run away, but Simon grabbed her shoe and attempted to bite her ankle. She finally jerked away and ran off.

"You're such a psycho!" she called over her shoulder as she ran to join the last of the surviving humans.

"Help!" Edward yelled.

Billy lowered Sophia to the ground and looked back toward Edward who had been surrounded by the zombies. Twelve undead children were overwhelming Edward as he swung his sock back and forth, trying to fend them off.

"Back, you monsters!" Edward growled.

"Brains!" Tommy howled.

Edward swung the sock at him, just narrowly missing.

"We have to save him!" Sophia gasped, starting to run toward Edward.

Billy chased her down, wrapped his arm around her, holding her tight against him.

"It's too late," Billy grunted. "He knew the risks going into this."

Edward continued swinging his sock frantically as the zombies closed. He whapped Ossie in the forehead, and Ossie fell to the ground, but Tommy bear-hugged Edward and the two fell to the ground.

"Brains!" the group cheered.

"That poor bastard," Billy grumbled, then pulled Sophia away.

"You all should be ashamed of yourselves," a female voice called.

Billy looked over to a small group of girls watching the game of zombies versus humans from the porch of Cabin Six. The group had started out as an insular clique with Martha as its leader, but Billy was beginning to think they were becoming a full-blown cult.

Martha stepped out from the group and approached Billy. Billy ignored them and walked back to his band of survivors.

"This game is an abomination," Martha sneered. She seemed to be constantly glazed with sweat and the fat in her neck wobbled when she moved. "God will punish you for this."

"Ignore Martha," Billy grunted. "She's just mad that they won't serve her doughnuts by the pound."

The girl grimaced at the comment, but followed them undeterred.

"Sophia, you used to serve God; how can you participate in this affront?"

"It's just a game," Sophia sighed.

"Do not love the world or anything in the world," Martha proclaimed. "If anyone loves the world, the love of the Father is not in him. For everything in the world…"

"Shut the hell up!" Billy growled.

Martha stepped back as the group of girls enveloped her. Bolstered by their numbers, she smiled and continued:

"The world and its desires pass away, but the man who does the will of God lives forever," Martha finished with a sanctimonious smile.

"Back off!" he growled and Martha ducked her face as the group flinched backward. "Get lost, you miserable harpies!"

Martha kept her eyes averted from Billy but didn't retreat.

"God will punish you."

"Let him," Billy snapped, then turned and motioned the others to walk back to the mess hall.

"Brains?" Simon called as he wandered alone through the campground like a child looking for a lost dog. "Brrai-aiiinns?"

Simon turned and saw Billy and the other survivors scampering to the mess hall.

"Brains! Brains! Brains! Brains!" Simon shrieked as he hopped up and down and pointed. The other zombies emerged from behind the cabins, Edward now one of them.

"Cooome baaack, braiiins!" Simon pleaded

The zombies formed a swarm and began shuffling toward the mess hall.

"Dammit," Billy grumbled, turning toward the children who were huddled behind the other side of the mess hall. "How much time do we have left?"

Raul, a swarthy kid from Cabin Four, checked a stopwatch that hung from his neck.

"Twenty minutes."

Billy sighed, looking back at the herd of zombies.

"Okay, let's flank them. If we can stun them all, they'll be down for fifteen minutes. Whoever survives should be able to scramble for the last five minutes to win."

Billy looked across the group of survivors. They nodded unenthusiastically.

"Look, I know we've been at this a while," he said, pacing out of ahead of them, methodically whapping the sock against his hand. "We've watched a lot of our brothers fall, but the human race must survive, and it will survive! I want each of you to pair off boy/girl, so that when those bastards starve, and they will, then whoever is left can repopulate the planet."

"Ewww," one of the girls groaned, and the children giggled.

"And!" Billy growled, regaining their attention. "If the worst should happen, and those monsters overtake us, then we will have gone out on our terms! We will have never surrendered, but fought until the end! Now, are you with me?"

"Ehh," Sophia shrugged, inspiring a few chuckles.

"Are you with me?" Billy hollered.

"Sure!" the children shouted, and then "whatever!"

Billy held out his hand to Sophia, and as she grasped it he pulled her up into his arms. He raised his sock with his other hand and, in his best John Wayne impression, barked out "Let's show these bastards how the cow ate the cabbage!"

152

Sophia giggled, but then nodded solemnly. The other children paired off and Billy looked over at the zombies.

"Okay—they are in one pack, so if we flank them on the left and right side, we might be able to get them to trip over each other, get really congested and then we can annihilate them. How many grenades do we have?"

"Only five," a girl said, holding up an armful of knotted socks.

"Okay, spread them out," Billy said. "Do not throw them until we are at point-blank range. We cannot waste a shot."

The girl handed out the grenades, Billy barked a few more orders and then shouted "charge!"

The children scrambled out from behind the mess hall and sprinted at the zombies, who in turn quickened their awkward, stiff-legged hobble. The survivors hollered a war cry, the zombies moaned for brains and as the two small armies came within twenty feet of each other, a voice boomed:

"STOP!"

The children slowed to a standstill and looked over at God. He stood next to Jay, His arms folded and a sneer fixed on His face. Behind the pair were Martha and her cabinmates, snickering.

"What is this?" God growled, walking to the children.

"A game, sir," Billy answered. "We were told that we had the afternoon to ourselves."

"So you play a game about pagan monsters?" God asked. "About humans coming back from the dead. Where do you get these disgusting ideas?"

"Well, in the Bible ..." Ossie began, but he was swatted by Edward.

God glared at Ossie, who just beamed back a smile. The other children kept their eyes averted from God as He walked between the two armies. He approached Billy, who stood straight up and lifted his eyes defiantly.

Behind God, Simon lifted his arms up ahead of him. His eyes glazed over, his mouth went agape and he began staggering toward God.

"Brains," he whispered until I jogged to him and held him still. God didn't notice.

"Brains?" Simon whimpered. I shook my head and he pouted.

God continued staring down at Billy.

"Where is Petrov?" God asked.

Billy shrugged.

I closed my eyes to search for Petrov.

"He's at the pier, sir," I finally answered.

"Go get him for me," God grumbled, turning His back on the children and walking toward Cabin One.

"Billy," I said. "Could you go tell Petrov he is needed?"

"Sure," Billy replied. "Can we finish our game?"

"I'd advise against it."

******

Ossie could feel Edward's stare and tried to ignore it as he talked to a group of girls about pop stars of the 1970's. Finally, Edward stood and approached. He tapped Ossie on the shoulder and then motioned him to follow.

The two walked toward the lake while Edward glanced around for Tommy. He was talking with Billy, Raul and one of Raul's cabinmates named Todd as they stood in a suspiciously tight group near the mess hall.

Edward had been curious about what they were talking about, but right now he just wanted to be sure no one could overhear the conversation.

Edward led Ossie toward the water, stopping a few feet away from the waves. Edward took a deep breath while Ossie waited impatiently.

"I wanted your advice," Edward finally whispered.

"Oh, um, okay," Ossie answered. "I wondered when this would come up."

"What do you mean?"

"Well, you start," Ossie said.

Edward studied Ossie carefully. Dropped his eyes and took a few moments.

"You don't seem afraid of God."

"Yeah?"

"I'm just," Edward began. "Everyone seems to have trouble here but you and Simon. I understand it with Simon, he's just a few rungs down from a nihilistic sociopath so I'm not sure anything scares him."

"I like Simon," Ossie smirked.

"Oh, I do too, but you see my point?"

"I do."

"So, how do you do it?" Edward asked. "I mean, after everything you went through back on Earth and then going to heaven, how are you okay being here on the Island?"

Ossie chuckled and then sat down on the sand. He glanced up at Edward before patting the sand next to him.

"Edward, Edward, Edward," Ossie sighed. Edward sat down stiffly. "You can't take this stuff too seriously, Eddy."

Edward smiled at 'Eddy.'

"Why do I care about anything here?" Ossie said. "Honestly, I thought it was likely I'd end up in the other place, but I knew that the God I believed in would reward me for a good, if unconventional, life. He did, and I'll one day end up back in heaven. This place? I don't know what it is, I don't know why we are here, but I don't really care."

"How can you not care?" Edward asked. "How can you not be bitter? I mean, how do you not feel…"

Edward looks around them, then leans in close.

"Betrayed?"

Ossie laughed, loud enough that it embarrassed Edward. Ossie shook his head and playfully measured Edward out of the side of his eye.

"How did He betray us, Eddy?"

Edward sighed and began to stand up, but Ossie grabbed his shoulder and eased him back down.

"I know how tough all of this is on you," Ossie began. Edward could sense a hidden meaning behind the statement, and then began to grow nervous that Ossie knew.

"But I don't remember any contracts back on Earth or at the gateway to heaven," Ossie continued softly, glancing back out across the Island. "God isn't legally obligated to me and fighting against all of this silliness isn't going to change anything."

"But the Bible is a contract, it's His contract with us."

Ossie nodded and thought for a few moments.

"Where in the Bible does it say that a place like this can't exist?" Ossie asked.

"But aren't you disappointed?"

"In what? Heaven? No, not really, it's been fine."

"No," Edward whispered, leaning in even closer. "Aren't you disappointed in God?"

Ossie grunted and leaned away. He craned his head up to look over the campground and noticed God leading Petrov and Jay to Cabin One.

"You mean that guy?" Ossie asked.

Edward turned and looked over at God.

"Yeah."

"I don't know that guy," Ossie shrugged. "He's not the God I prayed to, he's not the God that rewarded me with heaven. He's just a guy that doesn't know the first thing about human fashion. If I believed he was really God, then yeah, I guess maybe I'd feel let down, but I don't believe for one second that is the person I spent decades praying to."

"Then who is He if he's not God?" Edward asked.

"Who cares?" Ossie asked.

"I do," Edward answered, his eyes glazing with tears. "How does it not drive you crazy not knowing why we are here?"

Ossie took a deep breath and rocked up to his feet to stand.

"Because, Eddy, I'm above it. If that sad, little man is really God and He derives pleasure playing these games with our lives, then I'm better than Him and am not going to waste any of my time worrying about what He thinks of me and why He put me here."

Ossie held out his hand to Edward and helped him onto his feet.

"I wish I could switch it off too," Edward said. "All these questions, they are just weighing me down, but there has to be sense to it all."

"Why?"

Edward didn't answer, just ducked his head and shrugged.

"Edward?" Ossie whispered and Edward raised his head. "Is that it? Is that all you wanted to talk about?"

"Yeah," Edward replied weakly. "Thanks."

"Okay," Ossie said. "But if there is anything else you…"

"No," Edward answered. "That's it."

Ossie paused, studying Edward. He shrugged, patted Edward on the shoulder and walked back to the mess hall.

Edward's eyes shifted to Tommy who was huddled with the whispering children. Edward wanted to walk over to find out what they were planning, but instead veered off to the volleyball court and leaned against God's umpire chair as the wheels worked in his mind.

Edward glanced back to God's cabin where he could see Petrov's head through the window. He wasn't sure what was going on between God, Jay and Petrov and that worried him. Edward knew there wasn't anything that could be done about it, though.

After the zombie game had been disrupted by God, Martha and her friends quickly retreated into their cabin. Billy and Tommy talked quietly for a few minutes and then seemed to start recruiting other campers into some new scheme. They've been huddled together ever since.

Edward wondered if Billy was planning retaliation.

As it turned out, Billy wasn't—or at least not against Martha. In fact, in the huddle, Martha's name had not been mentioned once.

The vicious cold snap was still concerning Billy and many of the other children. Humans are the most efficient and resourceful scavengers in all of God's creation, or at least in what of it I have seen so far. When presented with a problem, humans immediately look to their environment for a solution.

Raul and Todd had actually been the ones who had hatched an idea, figuring Billy and Tommy were already planning something, recruited them as co-conspirators.

The plan would provide for the possibility of another frigid night but would also let the children vent their frustration with God.

Todd was a cunning child and former lawyer (yes, a handful of them did make it to Heaven after all—on a technicality) who had been the most successful at staying under God's radar. Despite Billy's bluster and Simon's defiance, Todd had actually gotten away with more violations of campground rules, including:

1. taking food into his cabin.
2. taking supplies without permission such as shirts, blankets and toilet paper.
3. taking the boat for a brief trip across the shoreline (but never far from the campground.)
4. listening to private conversations between God and Jay.

He had even seen what was in the fog on the western side of the lake, but had told no one. I am the only one who knew he disappeared from his cabin that night.

Well—perhaps God knew, but it was impossible to tell.

"How many coats can he really have?" Billy asked Todd.

"Even if He just has three," Todd said, "then that is three more than we had before. I just have no interest in spending another cold night in this place."

"It's pretty ridiculous," Raul grunted in agreement.

"So, we need a really good distraction," Billy said. "From someone who is willing to take the fall in a spectacular way."

"Sign me up, I'm ready for whatever," Tommy said. "Should we get Simon in on this? We know he's not afraid of God."

The group chuckled.

"No, we actually want to be able to get away with it," Todd said. "We need someone who isn't quite as obvious, someone who isn't constantly being tailed by angels."

Tommy glanced over at Edward and Edward perked up. Edward had no idea what they were talking about, but he knew Tommy was at least thinking about him. Tommy leaned back into the group and they mumbled back and forth. Tommy then looked back at Edward and waved him over.

Edward jogged over with an eager smile. Simon pretended to listen to Ossie talk television with a flock of chattering girls, but kept the huddle in his periphery. Simon could tell something was up, and he was annoyed that he was being excluded. He hated missing out on mischief.

Edward reached the small group and Tommy draped his arm over his shoulder and leaned over to whisper, "Hey Eddy, ever row a boat?"

chapter xiii

It seemed that Edward had arrived at a precipice, a moment where events could begin unfolding beyond his own control. His decision would force him either down a path of blind devotion at the expense of his individuality, or along a path of self-assertion at the expense of his relationship with his Creator.

But, to me, the decision had seemed inevitable even before the poor pastor set foot on the Island.

Then comes the question of whether choice exists in a reality where God is all-knowing, all-seeing, and has created a world to exact specifications. Can the human mind overcome the nature instilled in it by God? Can humans actually play a sizeable role in the outcome of their own lives?

We can say that Edward's choice to follow a path toward God or away from God was not pre-determined, but then we assume that He did not create this Island specifically to induce Edward one way or another.

If He did, then is free choice only an illusion? If not, how can humans prove it is not?

Perhaps this is too dangerous a line of thought and I should just continue with the story.

"Are we really doing this?" Edward gasped as he floated in the water, ducked beneath the pier with Tommy.

They stared at the rowboat gently rocking in the water as Edward's heart fluttered in his chest.

"Holy shit," Edward mumbled, feeling sick.

"Edward!" Tommy gasped. "Language! From you of all people! I really am a bad influence on you."

Edward chuckled and their eyes met. It was a long second as Edward felt like he was falling into Tommy's smile. There was a connection — Edward was sure of it — but he had no idea what to do about it.

Somewhere in the recesses of his mind, the urge to confess tugged at him, to divulge to Tommy that day back on Earth when they'd met. He could then spill the larger and much more urgent confession.

But, what was the confession, really? What was it that consumed Edward's thoughts, love or just naïve infatuation?

Impossible for Edward to tell and irrelevant since whatever it was that took hold of his heart was so wondrous and over-whelming that Edward was prepared to follow Tommy across the Island, off the far edge and down into hell, if need be.

"Let's go," Tommy whispered, tugging on Edward's sleeve and then wading further into the water.

Edward followed as he scanned the shoreline. There was nothing they could do about angels, they would be caught eventually. In fact, that was the plan.

Tommy swam up to the rowboat and clung onto the side; he lifted his body out of the water and then rolled into the boat. Edward followed and crawled to the oars.

Tommy untied the boat from the pier and sat next to Edward. They both began rowing gently, trying to make as little noise as possible.

Edward assumed they'd be caught immediately, but as the bow began skimming away from the pier, nothing happened. The only person who seemed to see was Simon, who ran out onto the shoreline and jumped and pumped his fist in frustration that he'd been left behind. Tommy waved Simon away and then pointed at the sky. Understanding that Tommy was motioning at angels, Simon threw up his arms and stormed away.

Edward chuckled nervously and continued to row. Tommy grinned and whispered, "Thanks for doing this with me."

Edward nodded.

The progress was slow and the pair had trouble coordinating their efforts. The boat would veer to the left and to the right, but after the first few minutes of rowing, they had managed a more or less straight line toward the center of the lake.

Edward hadn't rowed since he was very young on Earth, and it seemed easier than he remembered. His arms were burning after only five minutes, but he was growing more confident that, if given enough time, he and Tommy would be able to make it to the other side of the lake.

"What if we actually make it to the other side?" Edward asked softly. "What then?"

"We run into the woods and find a place to hide so God can never pull us back to that campground again," Tommy replied.

Edward looked over at Tommy, anticipating the clever grin, but Tommy just gazed back at the campground solemnly.

Edward imagined a new life in the woods where it would be flush with wildlife, bird calls would wake them up in the morning, they would cut out an acreage to grow vegetables, they would fashion spears and fish along the shore.

Edward imagined peace on the far shore, the kind of peace he'd only felt in his dreams while floating in Heaven.

"How are you holding up?" Tommy asked.

"Wonderfully."

The boat began veering to the left again, but not because one child was out-rowing the other, but because a current was tugging the boat. It seemed to be flowing toward the fog. Tommy watched the fog curiously as he rowed harder to keep the boat from gliding toward it.

"Come back," a voice whispered.

The children startled and looked around them. The voice had sounded as if it came from someone in the boat with them. Tommy let go of his oar and carefully stood in the boat to look around them.

The campground shore was far enough away that he couldn't tell if anyone was watching them. They could make out figures walking around the cabins and the mess hall, but they didn't know if God or Jay was among them.

"Keep rowing," Tommy said, continuing to stand to watch the shore.

Edward scooted over and took hold of both oars. He began rowing, slowly at first, but building into a steady and urgent rhythm.

"Come back," the voice repeated, louder.

The children scanned all around them, but couldn't see anyone. Tommy looked down into the water and jerked back and fell against Edward.

"He's in the water!" Tommy gasped.

Water exploded all around them, soaring up above the boat and climbing into the air. The boat jerked and rocked as it lowered with the lake. Water continued soaring out of the lake as if falling into the sky, forming a wall all around them.

The boat cracked as it hit the lake bottom, all just mud and flopping fish. The water soared up all around the boat, leaving a small patch of sky visible high overhead. Within the surging wall of water, fish rolled and struggled against the immense current. Mist swirled around the children and thunder crackled. Electricity sparkled and snapped as it jumped from one side of the funnel to another.

Tommy pushed himself up and stood on the stern of the boat.

"Come on!" Tommy shouted over the roar of water. "Come get us!"

Edward leaned up to grab Tommy's hand. Tommy jerked away.

"We are here!" Tommy screamed. "You don't scare me, not anymore! Just come get us and send me to Heaven or Hell! Just get me out of this place!"

"Tommy!" Edward called, standing up to try to calm him.

The wall of water opened up like curtains and God walked along the lake floor toward them. With each footstep, God's foot would sink into the mud, and He would then have to jerk it back out for the next step. The roar silenced, but the water continued rushing around as the fish struggled to swim out of its current.

Despite the chaos, the lightning flashes and the racing currents, the only sound was the mud sucking at God's yellow rubber boots.

He wore a slicker and held a black umbrella over His head. The flopping fish in front of Him evaporated as He approached. He stopped just in front of the boat, closed the umbrella and shook out the water.

"You stole from Me," God sighed, tapping the boat with the end of his umbrella.

"So, what are You going to do to us?" Tommy growled.

"Please," Edward said, standing up and getting between Tommy and God. "We'll go back."

"Do you want to go to the other side of the Island?" God asked, calmly looking past Edward to Tommy. "Is that what this is all about? You want to leave the campground?"

"We want to go back to Heaven," Tommy replied, stepping past Edward and bending over to climb out of the boat.

"Stay in there, please," God said, and Tommy lifted his leg back and stood in the boat.

"Is that what you want as well, Edward?" God asked.

"I ..." Edward began, but lowered his head.

"Oh, no, please, don't hold back, Edward," God sneered. "Let me know how displeased you are with everything that I've given you."

"We didn't ask for this!" Tommy growled.

"No, I suppose you didn't," God replied, then motioning to the boat. "You might sit down."

Tommy didn't initially, but God smiled and motioned again. Edward sat down and tugged at Tommy, who finally conceded.

"I can't send you back to Heaven," God replied, looking around at the wall of water, watching the fish struggle. "I will let you go to the other side of the Island, if that is what you really want."

Tommy glanced back at Edward, and Edward nodded.

"Okay," Tommy said. "Let us go then."

God laughed and pulled a fish out of the water. It struggled for a few moments, then stopped and stared at God, its mouth gasping for water to breathe. God wedged the umbrella under His arm and petted the fish.

"I said I would let you go, Tommy, but only you," God chuckled. He placed the fish back into the water and shook the droplets from His hands. "Edward comes back with me."

"No," Edward began, but then grimaced from a sudden pain stabbing at his stomach. His face flushed. Sweat began streaming off his skin. He grunted and fell backwards in the boat. Tommy leaned over Edward and touched his skin. Edward's temperature had soared. He groaned as sweat poured off him, his face and skin a dark red. He began convulsing.

"Edward!" Tommy cried.

Edward became still for a moment. He reached up to Tommy's face and brushed his fingers against Tommy's cheek then passed out.

Tommy jumped up and turned to God.

"Stop it!" Tommy screamed.

"Come back with us, and I will," God smirked.

Edward's body lifted off the boat and floated lifelessly up the wall of water.

"I would sit down and hold on if I were you," God said, soaring off the ground and floating behind Edward's body up and out of the funnel of water.

Tommy sat down and gripped the edges of the boat. The roar of the rushing water returned. The wall started to crash down on him and the boat jerked up as the water rushed around and under it. The boat tipped violently and Tommy fell out as both he and the boat were immersed.

Tommy kept his grip on the boat as it rose quickly to the surface. It emerged and capsized as waves crashed against it. Tommy clung desperately as the water rose and fell with large, quick swells.

"You said you were a good swimmer!" God called as He floated away, Edward's limp body trailing behind Him. "Swim back to shore and bring My boat back with you!"

******

Billy, Ossie and Simon swam out to help Tommy pull the boat ashore. Petrov grabbed Tommy and helped him out of the lake. Exhausted, Tommy crawled on the sand and laid down. Petrov leaned down and pulled him farther up the shore, away from the waves.

"Where is Edward?" Tommy asked.

"Sleeping in the cabin," Petrov said. "He'll be all right."

"I fucking hate it here," Tommy grunted.

"I know."

"Did they get the coats?"

"No," Petrov answered. "We tried, but we were caught. I tried to keep God and Jay distracted as long as I could, but He knew. I think He knew about the plan before we'd even thought of it."

Tommy studied Petrov. He stood and straightened.

"You didn't rat us out did you?" Tommy asked.

"No, I swear, I did the best I could."

"Don't lie to me," Tommy grunted.

"I'm not, I promise you," Petrov pleaded.

Billy stepped between them and pulled Tommy away.

"Listen," Billy growled. "That boy was the one who caught the worst of it. I can guarantee you he didn't snitch on us."

Tommy nodded, sighed and then staggered toward the campground. Petrov followed.

"When you are feeling better," Petrov said, "we are going up the mountain."

Tommy stopped and looked back at Petrov.

"You're going, too?"

Petrov nodded.

"Why?"

Petrov dropped his eyes.

"I am just curious, like the rest of you."

chapter xiv

God and Jay shuffled away from the camp, towels draped over their shoulders and their flip-flops clapping with each step. Bitter whispers traveled across the arts and crafts table as children worked on popsicle-stick houses and talked about the previous day's mini-rebellion. The children had watched from afar as Edward and Tommy challenged God in the lake, but no one really knew what had happened aside from the exploding wall of water.

Edward returned to Cabin Five, and within an hour, felt fully recovered from the intense fever. Tommy stayed by his side the rest of the day. Just as on Earth, pain and mortality bonds human relationships tighter.

Billy and Raul had only seen God pull Petrov into Cabin One after the failed robbery. They couldn't tell what was happening inside, but heard Petrov's screams.

The chill was spreading throughout the campground and the day's art projects were produced with barely a whisper.

Edward began to feel a sense of inevitable doom on the Island as he feared the worst was still ahead of them. He saw Tommy and God as two forces that could not co-exist. There would come a time where one force would have to be taken out of the equation, and Edward knew that God was there to stay.

That left an urgency to his affection for Tommy. He was shaken by God's viciousness, awed by the omnipotence demonstrated in the lake, but he felt even more distanced from his Creator than ever before.

Nothing more was discussed about the failed attempt to sneak into God's cabin and Edward guessed it was because of the group's collective guilt over leaving Petrov behind.

For his part, Billy was unnerved by how quickly the group was discovered, almost as if they had been lured into a trap. The moment Billy had slipped into the window, he heard Petrov's voice approaching from outside, trying to warn him just before the front door burst open.

Billy had just enough time to run. No one knew what happened after that aside from God screaming at Petrov and then pulling him by the arm into the cabin.

When Petrov finally returned to Cabin Five, he had changed. He was still quiet, but no longer meek.

Now they were set on going up the mountain, which Billy was starting to believe was a bad idea. Petrov insisted they go as soon as possible, and Billy felt obligated to lead them there.

Billy, Simon and Ossie muttered back and forth, discussing the mountain. Tommy, Edward and Petrov had nothing to offer, but listened intently.

The question of including Raul, Todd or any other members of other cabins was floated by Simon, but quickly discarded. To get away with it, Billy insisted the group stay as small as possible to attract the least amount of attention.

Billy developed the plan fast. The mission to the top of the mountain took on an importance as if the mystery perched on the summit would unravel the complexities knotting up their lives. God's show of force might terrify some children into obedience, but Billy and his cabinmates were rallying.

Only the bitterness of being denied something fundamental, in this case freedom, could unite the children in a bond so feral at its core. Spurning the comfort and authority of the campground for such an ill-defined and distant ideal as freedom was a quality that many millennia of humanity could not civilize out of the species, nor could the perfect haze of heaven.

It was always thrilling to watch, like a tight-rope walker defying gravity and mortality for no better reason than to demonstrate his fate was of his, and only his, choosing.

Could I have prevented this equally fool-hardy ascent up the mountain? Could I have reasoned with the children and brought them back into God's flock?

Yes.

But then, why would I?

The conversations were closed off from the rest of the campers and Billy felt the invigoration of usefulness again. He was needed; he had a purpose.

He was better equipped to deal with the Island than his fellow cabinmates, it wasn't too far removed from Scouts and the Marine Corps. But on the Island, he didn't feel he was there to learn anything or to accomplish anything. Instead, it was more like a prison.

Edward wasn't sure what they'd find on the mountain, but he was desperate for any kind of answer, even just a hint that helped explain this place and why God was putting them all through this. He also needed a purpose, one that involved more than ridiculous crafts, T-shirts and inane Bible lectures. He needed something to focus on other than the confusions of the flesh that were only amplified by idleness.

Edward finished his popsicle-cabin first, holding the unstable house that leaned to the left so severely it teetered at the point of a catastrophic failure. He held it up for me to see, and I nodded despite my reservations about the structure's stability.

He sat it on the table and began working on Petrov's pile of sticks, which Petrov was just staring at with a frown. Billy finished and then helped Edward complete Petrov's house. Simon and Ossie just shrugged off their unfinished cabins and retreated with the others to plan.

The dinner bell rang as God and Jay emerged from the hill. God looked over the table full of popsicle cabins and He was pleased. He didn't seem to notice that the majority of the contraptions would crumble back into their components if a stiff breeze hit them. It was enough that the children had tried and, more importantly, followed directions.

For once, Billy's cabinmates managed to keep up with Billy's ravenous appetite as they consumed dinner as quickly and as haphazardly as they'd built the popsicle-stick cabins. Hurrying out of the mess hall, they ducked their heads to avoid raising suspicion and cautiously disappeared into the woods.

"Look at the sun," Edward said to Tommy as they found the trail.

Tommy glanced up to the sun. It sat at the center of the sky, straight above them as if it were the middle of the day.

"That's weird," Tommy said.

"Yeah, it hasn't moved all day, not since noon."

The others looked up with them, holding their hands just in front of the sun.

"Do you think it'll go down tonight?" Billy asked.

"Why," Simon smirked. "Can't miss your starlight date with what's-her-name?"

"Shut up," Billy grunted, slugging Simon in the arm. "And her name is Sophia."

"Billy and Sophia sittin' in a tree," Ossie sang. Billy turned and slugged Ossie harder, making Ossie wince and then laugh.

"I can do this all day!" Billy growled.

"I'm just concerned, seeing how we never got inoculated against cooties," Simon shrugged. "Just sayin'."

Billy swung at Simon, but he dodged away, laughing.

"Do you think He's just trying to keep the Island warm after that one night?" Tommy whispered to Edward.

"Maybe," Edward shrugged.

"Let's get moving," Billy sighed, leading them along the trail.

Simon jogged up to Billy and put his arm around Billy.

"Billy," Simon began solemnly. "Cooties strike one in three sexually active adults."

Billy pushed Simon away, but Ossie appeared on his other side.

"Even with continued use of preventative treatments, it's still possible to spread cooties to your partner," Ossie said.

Billy raised his fist, but then shook his head and continued walking up the trail. Undeterred, Ossie continued:

"Sexual activity should be avoided during cootie flare-ups, and side effects can include vaginal discharge, testicular elephantitis and anal malaise."

******

The clearing at the base of the mountain came into view and Billy paused to search the tree line. They'd hurried along the path to the mountain in hopes of getting to the top and back before anyone noticed they were gone. Once Billy finally stopped to look across the landscape, the others sank to the ground and gasped for breath.

"Hey there, champ," Tommy wheezed. "Let's pace ourselves a little, okay?"

"Do you want to see the top or not?" Billy grumbled, scanning the clearing. Satisfied they weren't being followed, he strode out toward a trail winding up the side of the mountain.

The others sighed, but struggled to their feet and followed.

Billy was annoyed with himself that he'd forgotten to bring any extra water or look around the campground for sunblock. He thought about slowing down so as not to push the others to exhaustion, but was also thinking that if he pushed Simon and Ossie hard enough, they would be too tired to start singing again.

They reached a path leading up the face of the mountain which was paved in long shards of obsidian that reflected the heat of the sun back up at the children.

If the children would have had their eyes on the path rather than the top of the mountain, they would have seen one of God's little hints. The placement of the shards, the size, the groupings, it was all methodically arranged. These same hints could be seen amidst the trees, the placement of the cabins and all across the Island. It all had something to do with the mathematic relationships of the Island.

God explained the path to me once, brimming with pride over His cleverness. He worried that it might be too obvious, but after hearing Him explain it, I still had no idea how the designs, dimensions and spacing communicated anything. Unsure of what to say in response, I responded with a smile and a shrug.

He must have known I was humoring Him because he never explained the trees or cabins to me, which is fine.

I can't say for certain why he chose to infuse so many symbols in the landscape. Perhaps he'd been annoyed with humans' inability to see the patterns hidden on Earth, and he'd decided to make them more obvious on the Island. Mathematics, as it turns out, was meant to be the definitive proof of God's existence, and He couldn't fathom why mankind never figured it out.

Billy's furious ascent up the mountain slowed when he realized the others had given up trying to keep pace. He stopped and looked out across the forest and down into the campground. The children in the campground looked like ants scurrying between the buildings.

The others finally caught up, sweat soaking through their shirts, leaving large, dark saddle bags under their armpits.

Relieved that Billy had finally stopped for a rest, Edward leaned against the wall and used his shirt to clear sweat off his face. He glanced out across the Island and wondered if angels were tracking them.

Surely, he thought, they would have stopped them by now.

Of course, they nearly made it halfway across the lake yesterday, so either the angels were not as ubiquitous as the children were led to believe or they are letting them go to the top of the mountain.

At this elevation, Edward could make out more of the far side of the lake, seeing that the forest on the other side stretched out farther than he had thought. He'd assumed they were on the larger side of the Island, but now it looked like there was far more space across the lake.

On the far shore of the lake, he saw the gap again, where the trees and water seemed to fade into fog. On the other side of the fog was another vast expanse of trees.

"When we got close to that fog," Tommy gasped, pointing to the edge of the lake. "There was a current pulling us toward it."

"Any idea why?" Billy asked.

Tommy shook his head.

"Well, we'll put it on our to-do list," Billy grunted. "How's everyone doing? Ok?"

Edward nodded with the others, then looked back out toward the gap.

"Come on," Billy called to Edward. He took one last look at it, and then followed the others up.

Their mouths were dry, their feet were sore but they were finally approaching the end of the path where it disappeared into the clouds above them.

Edward glanced at his forearms. They were turning pink. He looked back up at the sun, still affixed straight above them. It wasn't moving at all.

"How the hell do they take this path in flip-flops?" Billy grunted.

"Language," Ossie replied, deflated by exhaustion.

They continued on, their pace slowing. They were taking more breaks and as they reached the cloud cover, Edward paused.

"Guys," he called to the others.

They slowed and turned to look down at him.

"Is this a bad idea?"

"It's an absolutely horrible idea," Simon replied. "So let's hurry up and get it over with."

Edward grinned weakly, then followed the others into the fog.

The mist swept over them with a cool, moist relief. Their pace quickened again. Whatever was waiting for them at the top, felt close.

"How much farther do you think it is?" Simon gasped.

"No idea," Billy said. "Let's go on for about another thirty minutes, if we don't find anything, we'll head back."

"Pussy," Ossie smirked.

"Kiss my ass," Billy replied. "Actually, forget I said that."

"You sure?" Ossie asked sweetly.

"Positive."

Edward noticed a light above them through the thick mist.

"Does anyone else see that?" he asked.

"Yeah," Billy answered. "That might be what we're looking for."

Billy began striding up the hill and the others struggled to keep up. The path leveled out as it wound up toward the light. The water vapor warmed as they neared, beading on their faces and soaking their shirts. The bluish-white light moved and flickered above. Billy was almost jogging, pulling away from the others and disappearing into the fog.

"Oh, my God," he gasped from the front of the group.

"What?" Tommy asked.

"Just get up here!"

They ran to catch up, emerging out of the fog and into the light. Thousands of fireflies fluttered just above a pool of water. The fireflies cast a light-blue shimmer on the water and on the children. Steam rose from the water, drifting up and joining the clouds above the fireflies.

"This is much better than the lake," Ossie whispered.

The others chuckled. Billy walked up to the pool, kneeled down and dipped his fingers into the water.

"It's warm," he said.

"How warm?" Tommy asked as he followed Billy.

"Bathtub warm."

"Well," Simon said, kicking off his shoes and pulling off his socks. "We came this far, let's take a dip."

He jumped, splashing water up into the air. The fireflies fluttered up and away, but settled back into their halo above the pool. Simon emerged from the water with a grin. He spit water out at the others.

"I wouldn't drink it, might give you the shits," Billy smirked.

The children quickly shed their shoes and socks and eased into the pool.

Edward settled into the water and dipped his hair back. He then swallowed a mouthful of water, despite Billy's warning. It tasted clean and smooth, as if it'd been filtered. Petrov stood on the shore, his shoes and socks still on.

"You coming?" Ossie asked.

Petrov shook his head and then sat down to watch them.

Ossie shrugged and then dipped his head below the water. His head jerked back out of the water.

"Shit!" he gasped.

"What?" Edward asked, then looked down into the water.

A thick, red fluid was rising from the bottom of the pool.

"Jesus, Jesus, Jesus," Simon gasped as they watched the red fluid overtake the pool.

"What's going on?" Billy panted as he backed away from the liquid. It flowed around him and he lifted his hand from the water.

"It's blood," Billy said.

The fireflies above them flickered and then disappeared. The fog overtook them. Edward looked back across the pool, but could only see shadows.

"Shit," Simon growled. "What do we do now?"

Light burst from the water. They all swam quickly to the edge of the pool and climbed out. They turned back to the light and saw an image shining on the surface of the water. It was a grown man with closely cropped hair, wearing a suit with the tie undone and walking with a limp. He was shouting and the sound was distant and thin, like an old, tin can recording from the advent of the record player. He strode through a house looking from room to room with frantic urgency.

"That's me," Billy said, then mumbled, "Fuck."

The man kicked open a door, limped in and then pulled open a closet. Curled inside was a woman crying and protecting her head with her hands. The man reached in, grabbed her by the hair and dragged her out of the closet. He picked her up and threw her against the bed. She backed against the wall as the man shouted at her. He lunged, raised his fist to hit her, but stopped. He punched the wall instead, leaving a mark of blood. He leaned off the bed and limped out of the room, his bleeding knuckles leaving a trail behind him. He opened a hall closet, pulled a pistol off a shelf, checked the chamber, and lunged back to where the weeping woman still cowered. He grabbed her by the hair and jerked her head up, shouting indistinctly at her. Everyone watched in silent horror as he put the barrel of the gun against her forehead and held it there for a long moment.

He released her, put the muzzle in his mouth and pulled the trigger. The blast sent the image to all white and the fireflies glittered for a few moments, but faded away again.

A dim light glowed across the water. The other children glanced at Billy, who had his face hidden in his hands.

"I guess that explains why you can't sleep at night," Ossie whispered.

Billy grunted and wiped his eyes.

"You don't know the half of it."

Light flickered on the pool; another image appeared—a different man, this one a strikingly handsome but dirty and underfed man with long, ratty blond hair, wearing a loose-fitting and stained sweatshirt. He sat in the front seat of a car, his hands twitching as he rocked back and forth behind the wheel. The car was parked along the side of a neighborhood street at night. The man was watching a house. Another person came walking along the street toward the car.

"That's me," Tommy said. "The one in the car."

The figure waved to Tommy's image. Tommy got out of the car and walked over to the house. They crept to the side, jumped the fence and hurried to the back door. The other figure had a crowbar and forced it into the doorjamb. He broke the door open and they ran in, closing the door behind him. The figure went to the living room, Tommy ran upstairs. When he got to the second floor, he saw a shadow move behind a bedroom door. Tommy pulled a knife out of his back pocket and walked toward the room.

A man emerged with a bat. Tommy jumped at him, jamming the knife into the man's chest. Tommy left the knife in the man and ran downstairs and out the front door. The image faded.

"He was a teenager," Tommy muttered flatly. "His parents came home to find him a few days later. They'd gone on vacation; I thought he'd gone with them."

Another image surfaced. It was a casino.

"My turn," Simon mumbled.

A man in a glittery white suit walked across the casino floor. He stopped at a blackjack table, pulled out a deck of cards, spread them out and held them out to an elderly woman. She pulled out a card, looked at it and then replaced it. The man in the glittery suit made a card appear behind her ear. The people at the table clapped and the woman gave the man a chip.

"I don't get it," Billy said. "You're doing magic?"

"We're also stealing," Simon sighed. "You can't see it, but my girlfriend is stealing chips as I'm distracting tables. We did it for years."

Simon in the glittery suit walked to another table. He held out the chip, threw it up in the air, caught it and then opened his hand. It had disappeared. He waved his hand around, but the chip fell out of his sleeve. The table laughed.

Simon shrugged to the table bashfully. He then walked up to a security guard and pointed at a brunette woman walking away from the blackjack tables. She looked back over her shoulder to see Simon talking to the guard. She hurried her pace.

"We'd stolen over $90,000 from casinos," Simon said. "We'd had a good year, and I got greedy. The casino offered a reward for information leading to an arrest, and that's me turning her in."

The image disappeared.

"These are our sins," Billy said. "I guess the lowest points in our life."

"What is this place?" Edward asked.

Another image appeared. There were men in tuxedos, women in dresses. A black man stood next to a preacher.

"Bullshit," Ossie growled.

"So that's you?" Edward asked.

"That's the day I got married. Why is that showing? Is that really the worst thing I did on Earth? God, I hate this fucking place!"

Ossie threw a lava rock into the water, and the image fluttered from the waves. He grabbed another rock and flung it into the fog.

"Why?" Ossie yelled at the pool, then turned back to the fog. "Damn you!"

The other children held their heads down until Ossie finally sat down in a heap, crying silently.

"You got married to a guy, huh?" Tommy asked, and Ossie nodded.

The image faded. The next image was of Tommy as a young adult.

"What?" Tommy growled. "Why me again?"

Tommy was sitting in an office, talking. He stood and took off his shirt, then his pants.

"Christ," Billy grunted.

Tommy walked around the desk and a man's hand emerged, running along Tommy's chest.

Edward paled.

"You're gay too?" Billy growled.

Edward began to nod, but realized Billy was talking to Tommy. They didn't know that it was Edward's hand, it was Edward's office, it was Edward's sin.

"I've been a lot of things," Tommy mumbled. "I was 19 or 20, on the streets, starving and strung out. I just — this is all so fucking stupid. Why is this that bad? Why is this as bad as killing someone?"

Tommy stood up, spit into the pool and began walking back down the mountain. The others stood as well to follow.

Petrov stopped, turned around and leaned toward the water. He dipped his finger into the water. The blood swirled around his fingertip and another image appeared. The children stopped and Tommy shuffled back up the mountain to see.

The image showed a man running through the streets of a small town. As the man ran, he would duck behind cars and hide from groups of soldiers being led by priests. The priests led the soldiers house to house, pulling out men and women. Long lines of people would be laid down in the street, then shot in the back of the head.

The man ran through an alleyway and into a house.

"That is me," Petrov said. "Of course."

Petrov closed the door behind him. A woman came up to him, but he waved her away as he ran through the house. He went to the back door, ran out and opened up the door to a storm cellar. He ran down the stairs and shouted. Another man stepped out of the shadows of the cellar. Petrov pulled the man out of the cellar and pushed him outside. He motioned for the man to leave, the man pleaded with him. Petrov pulled out a pistol and pointed it at the man. The man backed away. Petrov shot in the air, and the man ran away.

"I couldn't hide him; they would have killed us, too," Petrov mumbled as the image disappeared. "But, they did, eventually. They killed everyone."

The fireflies lit up again, the blood faded and the water was clear again.

"What was that, Petrov?" Simon asked.

"The rapture."

"No, it couldn't be," Edward whispered.

Petrov didn't answer.

"I thought you lived way off into the future," Simon said. "But that didn't look too futuristic to me. When did you die?"

Petrov sighed, stood up and began walking back down the path.

chapter xv

Billy's fork clinked against his tray as he stared down at the mush of lasagna and green beans. His hands were crusted with dried mud and dirt, as were everyone else's who'd climbed the volcano. They smelled like they looked and had been given a wide berth in the mess hall.

"Hey Tommy, like the new look," a girl called, then giggled. Tommy responded with only a nod.

"Unbelievable, doesn't matter what we do to you," Billy grunted.

"If they only knew," Simon smirked, but Tommy shot him a sharp glare.

The children were supposed to be sleeping, but the sun hadn't set. Instead, I had decided to bring them to the mess hall for a second dinner, hoping the sun would drop into the horizon eventually. I'd written God a note and had it delivered to Him, but still the sun hung above us.

Billy stirred his fork down into the glop, pulling out a limp noodle and then dropping it back in. The other cabinmates shared his faraway stare while they sat at the table watching their food cool.

The rest of the mess hall buzzed about the sun and how it related to the storm just two nights ago, about Jay and God who hadn't been seen in hours, about what had happened in the lake, and about where Billy and his cabinmates might have gone. I was left alone to field questions and assure the children that, though I knew as little as they did, things were really going to be okay; that they weren't being punished; and no, sacrificing something to God wouldn't get the sun to start moving again. I then ushered them outside and told them to play, like a weary older brother who didn't have the energy to further deny their family was falling apart.

Ossie sighed, finished his milk and then stood up with his still-full tray.

"Stick around, Ossie," Billy said. "All of you, hang out for just a little longer."

Ossie nodded and sat back down. They hadn't spoken more than a few words since returning from the volcano hours ago. They'd retreated down the path and hid in Cabin Five until the dinner bell sounded. They'd filed into the mess hall with the other children, still not uttering a word of what they'd seen on the volcano.

They all kept their distance from me, and I was relieved that there were six fewer people that would be asking impossible questions that night.

All their impossible questions would instead be aimed at each other.

Billy watched the last of the other children file out. He pushed away his tray and leaned toward the others. The others pushed their trays out of the way and huddled close to him.

"Okay, first things first," he whispered. "Who else is gay?"

The others glanced around at each other, except for Ossie who avoided all of their eyes. Tommy glanced up briefly at Edward. Edward jerked his eyes away, instead looking at me to see if I was paying attention.

I pretended to be distracted as I scribbled circles in my notebook.

"No one else?" Billy asked. "Just Ossie and Tommy? That's right, Tommy, you're gay, right?"

Tommy sighed. "I've been a lot of things."

"Spectacular," Billy grunted. "Clearly, we can't just pretend what we saw up there didn't happen, so let's just get this shit settled between us right now. Okay?"

They nodded with their eyes fixed on the table.

"Not you, though," Billy said to Edward. "You need to go ahead and leave."

Edward looked up at Billy, and then around to the others.

"You got to see our dirty little secrets, but we didn't see yours," Billy continued. "So I don't think you have the right to be a part of this conversation."

"Unless you are going to add something to it," Tommy added, his eyes steady on Edward.

Edward couldn't tell if Tommy knew about the vision. Edward's legs were shaking and his palms were sweating.

"Well, Eddie?" Simon asked. "Are you going to throw into the pot like the rest of us?"

"You can trust us," Petrov whispered beside Edward.

Edward met Petrov's eyes, considered it, but shook his head. He grabbed his tray and walked away.

Tommy was the only one who watched him go. Edward

quickly retreated from the mess hall, and I waved as he passed by me. He didn't see me.

"Edward!" I called. He turned and walked back to me. "Let your cabinmates know when they are done that they have dish duty at breakfast tomorrow."

"Okay," Edward nodded, his eyes on the floor. "Is there anything else?"

"Guess not," I replied.

Edward walked out of the mess hall and planted himself on the outside wall while he waited for the others. He slid down the wall, sat and hid his head in his hands so he could cry without being bothered.

"Okay," Billy said inside as he watched to see if I was eavesdropping. I had my nose buried in the Bible. "What you guys saw from me is by far not the worst thing I did in my life. I guess it's what God disliked the most, but if I hadn't killed myself, I'd have killed her. She didn't deserve it, she stayed with me and took care of me and took all my crap, and that made me hate her more than anything. I was hurting really bad at that time and killing myself was probably the only decent thing I did in years."

"Yeah, I'm pretty pissed about mine," Ossie said. "You know, I'd honestly thought that marrying Isaac was the right thing to do, God-wise. When I found myself in Heaven, I'd really thought God agreed. I'm just livid right now."

"At least you guys only had to see one of your mistakes," Tommy said as he pulled his tray back in front of him and forked up a lump of pasta. He put it in his mouth and chewed slowly while the others nodded in agreement.

"Well, I think we all know that I was a scumbag for a good deal of my life," Simon laughed. "Billy offed himself, Ossie was gay and Tommy was a druggie gigolo. Petrov was just born in the wrong time. I'm okay with all that."

"Me, too," Ossie said. "I really feel comfortable with all you guys, but I'm really starting not to like God so much."

They chuckled and leaned back. Billy glanced back at me.

"Okay," Billy said. "If any of you have any questions, feel free to ask. I'm not telling you everything, but I'll let you know what I think you need to know. And as far as Edward goes, he can stay on the outside of all this. Agreed?"

"Yeah," Simon nodded. "He's pretty boring and I'm sure he had a fairly uneventful life, but he's hiding something."

"He is," Petrov said. "I don't think it is as bad as he thinks it is."

"You don't think he diddled kids do you?" Simon asked.

"No," Tommy shook his head. "Not Edward."

"He was a preacher, though," Simon countered. "Not unheard of."

"No," Tommy repeated. "I think, whatever it is, he got really good at suppressing it."

"Huh," Billy grunted, then stuffed a forkful of lasagna into his mouth. He grabbed his tray and stood up. "Let's get out of here."

"Yeah, you gotta get cleaned up for your date," Simon chirped, grabbing his tray and skipping behind Billy.

"Go to hell," Billy grumbled.

"Bali!" Simon called to me. "Billy's got a potty mouth!"

******

The campground was restless. By my count, it should have been 4 a.m., but the sun was still fixed in the center of the sky. The temperature had climbed to one hundred degrees. The cabins were ovens, and the children were lounging outside in whatever shade they could find. Some had pulled out their pillows and were sleeping in the woods.

Billy sat just outside of his cabin, waiting for Sophia to emerge from hers. He yawned, he rubbed at his eyes and shook his head. His body was tired, his mind was finally numbing from the experience at the volcano but he refused to sleep until he saw Sophia.

Sophia was inside her cabin, watching Billy and waiting for him to start walking to the lake. She finally got tired of the other girls in Cabin Eight teasing her, and went out. She walked nervously toward the lake and was relieved when Billy walked to meet her.

Barry and Mary had already beaten them to the shore and were cuddled tightly in the shade of the pier with the waves licking their bare feet.

"It feels really nice over here," Mary called, waving the new couple over.

Billy glanced at Sophia, who wrinkled her brow and ever so slightly shook her head.

"No, that's okay," Billy called back. "It looks a little cramped. Maybe in a little while, though."

"Suit yourself," Barry called back.

Billy led Sophia to a tree near the shore and they sat down in the shade. The lake lost a lot of its serenity in the baking daylight. It was hard to watch the water due to the glaring reflection, but Billy was still glad to be with Sophia. He needed time away from the cabin, time to let his mind untangle.

He leaned back against the tree trunk and glanced at Sophia's thin back and long brown hair. Before she could catch him, he looked back out to the restless water.

After a few moments, he yawned.

"Tired?" Sophia asked.

"It's been a long day."

"I'm sorry, wanna talk about it?"

"Eh," Billy shrugged. "Have you heard anything about the sun?"

"Bali said it'll go down soon," she answered. "He's not sure when, though."

"This whole swing from cold to warm is making me a bit nervous," Billy said. "Do you think He's testing us?"

Sophia shrugged, then glanced over at Barry and Mary under the pier.

"What?" Billy asked.

"They're kissing," Sophia grimaced.

Billy leaned forward and looked over at the couple under the pier. They were trading pecking kisses, the kind children attempt when they don't know how to kiss yet.

Billy wanted to ask, "Wanna try?" but instead he looked across the water and the campground and asked, "Where are the angels at?"

"I don't know," Sophia answered, then giggled as she held up her hand between her eyes and the kissing couple.

Billy laughed as he watched her, his body sparkling with nervous energy.

"Do you think they'll get in trouble later?" Billy asked carefully.

Sophia laughed briefly, but her body stiffened. She lowered her hand and looked back at Billy. His breath turned into a lump in his lungs, he fought to keep his face blank.

"I guess I should tell you," Sophia whispered, her face heavy and suddenly older. "I'm not interested in kissing, or anything like that. I had bad experiences."

She said it so matter of fact that the finality of the statement sent Billy's body sinking into a slouch. He felt bad for showing his reaction, so he pushed up a smile.

"That's okay," he whispered. "They'll probably get in trouble anyway."

"Yeah," she mumbled, looking back out to the waves.

Her head dropped and she pulled her knees up to her chest.

"I'm sorry."

"It's okay," he whispered. He wanted to stroke her hair, hold her hand or slug her in the shoulder. Anything to make her okay, but she was so closed off that he had no idea what she needed.

And the insurmountable challenge of that distance only made her more irresistible.

"If you want to leave …" she began.

"No," Billy said. "I like being here. It really is okay. I've kissed tons of girls."

"Oh," Sophia whispered. "Well. Good for you."

Billy grimaced and then chuckled nervously.

"I'm just saying I don't really care about that," Billy said, which wasn't a complete lie. "I like being here with you. It reminds me of when I used to hang out with my mom on the front porch of our house. She was a smoker, but she didn't smoke inside, so she'd sit outside and we'd talk about all kinds of things. It was one of my favorite memories of her."

"Oh," Sophia whispered, looking back at him with a timid smile. She turned back to the waves.

"So," Sophia said, not turning to look at Billy. "You don't care if you ever kiss me because I remind you of your mom?"

Billy leaned back against the tree and gritted his teeth.

"That's not what I meant," he said with a sigh.

Sophia leaned back next to him, wearing a wide smirk. Billy saw it, then slugged her shoulder softly.

"You suck," Billy grunted.

"I know."

196

chapter xvi

Edward had given up on sleep. The sunlight still poured through the window. He tried to ignore the heat while he scanned the springs of the top bunk. The sweat beaded on his forehead and soaked his pillow. He couldn't muster the energy to wipe the sweat away, even as it rolled into his eyes and burned under his eyelids.

The cabin was flooded with the rank, salty smell of armpits. Tommy shifted on the bunk above him and his hand draped over the side.

"Are you awake?" Edward called.

"Yeah," Tommy mumbled.

"What time do you think it is?"

"No idea," Tommy sighed, then he sat up on his bed and dropped to the floor.

"Wanna go swimming?" Tommy asked.

"Um, yeah," Edward said, standing. "Do you think we'll get sunburned?"

"Probably," Tommy grunted, walking out of the cabin.

Edward jogged to catch up with him. He managed to match Tommy's stride and glanced over at his face. Tommy didn't acknowledge him.

Tommy walked to a tree near the shore and sat down under it. Edward sat next to him, and they both stared across the water.

"I'm leaving, Eddie," Tommy mumbled.

"To go where?"

"Across the lake. It has to be better over there."

Edward sighed and shook his head.

"You don't know that," he whispered.

"I don't care, Eddie. I can't stay here."

Edward inched closer to Tommy.

"I know this is hard on you," Edward said. "I really, really feel bad for you. If there is any way I can make it easier ..."

"Go with me."

"What?" Edward asked, his heart palpitating. He began sweating.

"Go with me," Tommy said. "We'll swim out across the water."

"I can't swim that far," Edward said.

"Yeah, you can," Tommy said. "We'll get some wood, a log or something, anything to keep us afloat. We can't drown, right?"

Edward shrugged.

"Trust me, Eddie," Tommy pleaded. "I need to leave, and I can't leave you behind. Not after what God did to you."

Edward stared up at Tommy, his mouth beginning to move, the confession ready to finally surface.

A group of children approached on their way to the water. They waved at Edward, and he returned the wave. Tommy kept his eyes down. When they passed, Edward leaned close to Tommy. He wanted to confess, but instead he said:

"I've never had a friend like you before. If you go, I'll go, but I don't want to leave. Not yet, not until I understand more."

"Understand what?" Tommy asked. "Understand God? You can't, Eddie. You couldn't back on Earth, you can't here."

"I ..." Edward began, but he closed his eyes and ducked his head. "Give me a little more time, please."

"Why?"

"There is meaning here," Edward mumbled. "I know there is. I just need some time to work it all out."

"Edward, you might be right. This island might make sense, but there are no answers here. If there are answers, I bet we'll find them on the other side."

Edward looked up at Tommy. His thoughts went back to the volcano.

"Just give me a little more time," Edward pleaded. "I'm not ready."

Tommy kicked at the ground, then looked over at the water.

"Okay. But only if when the time comes, you leave with me, no questions, no objections. We just leave."

"I will," Edward whispered, venturing his hand over to grasp Tommy's. Tommy let him. "I promise."

A ringing ping drew Edward's attention back to the cabins. A few more pings rang out and he let go of Tommy's hand as he stood to look back into the campground.

Raul was cradling an acoustic guitar while sitting on the porch of the Cabin Four. Raul was tuning it string by string. A small group of children, mostly girls, were sitting on the shaded porch all around him.

He strummed all the strings at once, adjusted the low E string again and then took a deep breath. He closed his eyes and his fingers began dancing. A flurry of notes rolled out from the guitar. It was a furious, flamenco-style song. The children around him smiled while they watched his fingers slide up and down the neck, prancing and darting.

Many of the notes jangled and whined at first, but Raul grew progressively more precise. He paused, beat the rhythm into the body of the guitar and then clapped the beat in a quick, staggered pattern. The children clapped along and then he resumed jabbing at the strings.

His eyes were shut tight, his teeth gritted as the showering notes swept out of the guitar and sent shivers through his face.

He missed a series of notes, laughed and opened his eyes. He wiped the sweat from his face and flexed his hands open and closed. The kids clapped and smiled.

"Ow," he grimaced, looking at his red fingertips. "I'm a bit out of practice."

He repositioned his hands, and began playing a slower, blues-tinged ballad. He bent the notes like the strings were spaghetti noodles, tapped his foot softly and grimaced each time he dove down to the base of the neck. The song hit a soaring note, and faded. He smiled and shook his hands and rubbed his fingertips.

"That was amazing," a girl swooned.

"How did you get a guitar?" a boy asked, eyeing the attentive girls.

"Bali," Raul said with a grin.

"It's so hot out, I'm surprised you even have the energy," Ossie gasped, swooning alongside the girls.

"This is my favorite time to play," Raul said. "It's so hot, the strings are very loose— I can make them do anything."

A couple girls blushed; a few boys huffed and walked off to find something else to occupy their time.

Raul began playing again, varying every song's style, from machine-gun surf songs to gypsy swing. Everyone was amazed with his talent, but only a few girls remained after the first half-hour. That was enough attention for Raul to continue playing, even after blood started dripping from his fingertips, staining the strings and neck of the guitar. The girls admired his dedication, and he basked in their sympathy which is why he didn't notice God walking through the campground toward him.

The Alpha and Omega wore pink volleyball shorts and a light blue muscle shirt. He had a line of white suntan lotion running along the bridge of His nose. His head was covered with a large Panama hat.

"Where did you get that?" God growled.

Raul's eyes shot open and the girls scattered. Raul didn't stand as he held the guitar tightly. The blood continued to drip down from his left hand. God stopped just in front of the cabin, glaring at Raul. Jay came running through the campground with a clipboard. He stopped beside God.

"Where did you get that?" Jay asked, his face twisted in revulsion as if Raul were holding a dead animal.

Raul's hands moved around the guitar, gripping the body tightly. He watched God carefully, but didn't answer.

"Tell me!" Jay growled.

"I gave it to him," I answered, jogging from the mess hall over to Raul.

"I don't remember giving you permission to introduce music to the campground," God said, turning to me.

He grabbed my arm and pulled me away from the cabin. Jay remained beside Raul but watched us. Jay had the same worried look he always got when he was afraid God was about to lose His temper.

God stopped near the volleyball court and looked around to make sure no kids were close enough to hear.

"You will not do this to this group, Bali," God grumbled.

"Do what, Sir?" I replied weakly, keeping my eyes down and away from His. I opened my organizer and flipped over the pages until I found the entry I was looking for. "Two days ago, just after lunch, approximately 12:30, You instructed me to keep the children's time occupied and to do what I needed to in order for them to remain focused on the campground."

I closed the organizer and looked up to God.

"So, I decided to give a few of the children things that would help them direct their energies at positive projects rather than in other unhealthy distractions," I said. Then added, "Sir."

God didn't respond, but he looked back up at Raul. He motioned for Raul to bring the guitar over. Raul hesitated, but then stood and approached.

"This is your fault," God whispered to me.

God snatched the guitar from his hands and waved him away.

"I will not have any distractions here!" He called to the children, then looked back down to me. "I thought we understood each other, Bali."

"Raul is a musician, Sir," I replied. "It is in his nature. You created him that way."

"Don't tell me about what I created, Bali!" God sneered.

"We cannot deny them their natures," I said, wincing in anticipation of His response, but none came. I looked up slightly and noticing God looking out across the lake, I decided to proceed. "I've looked over my notes, and they seem to indicate a pattern of behavior that is initiated by boredom and frustration. We've tried to keep them from what they are meant to be, but if we can embrace their true nature, perhaps that will be the best way to funnel their energy into more productive activities."

God frowned, glanced down at the guitar then handed it to me.

"Have him learn some decent songs," God grumbled. "None of that vulgarity I heard before. Something pleasant, but not showy."

"But I don't think it was meant to be vulgar, Sir."

God swiveled toward me and moved close. He lowered his sunglasses, showing me His milky, blank eyes. I tried not to stare, but I couldn't stop myself.

God realized what I was looking at, so he backed away from me and raised the sunglasses back over his eyes.

"Sorry, Sir," I said, cowering slightly and holding the guitar behind my back.

Tommy leaned toward Edward to whisper "that is the Man you want to understand?"

God's eyes remained on me. I felt He wanted something else from me, but I couldn't tell what. Fortunately, His attention diverted back to the water. A speck appeared on the lake approaching our shore. The children noticed and began moving toward the water to see what it was.

God walked to the pier to watch a canoe with two people paddling it toward our shore.

"Who is that?" Edward asked me. I knew the answer, but I didn't know how to give it, so instead I followed God to the pier.

The children all moved toward the water but stayed far enough back that they could retreat to their cabins in case God became angry again. Jay walked as far as the mess hall, but he wouldn't get any closer to the water. I noticed Tommy wandering to the pier and motioned him over.

"Give this back to Raul," I told him, handing him the guitar. "Tell him to not play it until he talks to me."

Tommy nodded, grabbed the guitar and ran back into the campground. He slowed as he neared Jay and looked back at me. I motioned Tommy to keep going, even as Jay frowned at him. Raul was still on his cabin's porch. He grabbed the guitar and quickly retreated inside.

God didn't seem to notice the guitar returning to Raul, He was too busy watching the water. He shook his head as the canoe approached the pier. Inside were two women, in their early twenties, wearing brightly colored bikinis tops and khaki shorts. I smirked, then glanced back at the children. The boys and girls gazed, their mouths agape, but for entirely different reasons.

Once the women reached the pier, they edged the canoe next to the rowboat. The girl in the front of the canoe, a tall brunette with olive skin and perky breasts, tossed the rope to God. He caught it, but then dropped it into the water. He turned and walked away. I ran to the pier and reached down into the water, grabbed the rope and then tied it to the pier. I helped the brunette out of the canoe, trying to catch the glint in her fierce blue eyes, but they were directed at God. I then reached for the shorter, thinner blonde still sitting in the boat. I gave her a warm smile as I helped her out of the canoe. She winked and pulled me into a tight hug.

"Good to see you again, Bali," she whispered.

"Always a pleasure."

The brunette jogged after God as the boys' eyes were fixed helplessly on her body. The girls had turned their attention to the pathetic boys, and they murmured among themselves as girls always do.

I quickly scribbled in my organizer, and then jogged to catch up with the group.

"Turn around, dammit!" the brunette yelled at God.

He did, and Jay quickly ran to His side.

"Why are you here?" Jay growled.

"Why do you think?" she replied, pointing at the sun that was still in the center of the sky.

"Not here," God said, coldly. "Let's discuss this in Cabin One."

The blonde jogged to meet up with the others, glancing over at the gawking boys and giving them a sultry wink. Billy half waved and blushed. Sophia turned to look out at the water.

God walked in long strides as He led them toward Cabin One. They disappeared inside. Simon stepped out in front of me and nudged me on the shoulder.

"Can we keep em?"

chapter xvii

The sun dropped like a stone. With night coming so quickly, the angels and I had to scramble to find candles and lanterns. We hustled the children into the mess hall to feed them. In reality, it should have been two in the afternoon, but the screaming between God and the two women in His cabin had kick-started the terrestrial cycles without consideration to the children's internal clocks.

They would simply have to adjust, which is a small thing. That is what humans were designed to do, after all.

The children were beginning to grumble amongst themselves. They were tiring of storms, endless days and sudden nights. Even the most truehearted campers were whispering when they thought I couldn't hear. God was losing His flock.

I decided that perhaps it was time to expand the arts and crafts possibilities. God detested distractions in His new experiment, but the children desperately needed something to occupy their thoughts. I secured modeling clay, more drawing pads and painting materials. There were books on Christian philosophy and great works of literature by some of the God-approved authors like C.S. Lewis and Dante.

I also decided to introduce an upright piano that night. I had the angels bring it into the mess hall and tuck it into a corner. Dozens of candles sitting on saucers were placed all along the top of the piano, lighting it up like an eerie Vegas billboard.

The children noticed it at once as they filed into the mess hall, which itself was dimly lit with lanterns sitting on the tables.

I sat back to see who would take the bait. It was not Raul, as I'd anticipated, but a short, mousy brunette named Edna. The girl had fallen in line the day she arrived and was one of the few not to stray from God's intended path—yet she had never been lured into Martha's more fanatical clique.

Edna never lowered her eyes from Him reverently whenever he was near, never spoke out of turn and closed her ears to all the bitter gossip rampant in the camp.

While the piano glowed in the corner of the mess hall, she ate quickly and dropped her tray off with the dishwashers. She timidly approached the piano.

She turned to look at my table where Jay's chair was empty. I motioned for her to go to the piano. She smiled and pulled out the bench. She uncovered the piano keys and ran her fingers along the ivory. She pressed down middle C gently, and the tone vibrated. A few other students gathered around the piano. Raul was still sitting, but he watched intently.

"What can you play?" a girl whispered.

"I'll try to remember something," Edna said as she closed her eyes. She took a deep breath and placed her fingers on the keys.

She hummed and as her head gently rocked, she visualized the key strokes in her mind, trying to dig up the song in her memory. The first chord rang out, and her fingers were off. It was a slow and unsteady version of "All Things Bright and Beautiful."

The mess hall fell quiet as Edna played. Her tempo evened out as the song continued and she sung just above a whisper. Raul grabbed his tray and ran to the dishwashers, dropped it off and then was out the door in a sprint.

Edna played three somber verses, leaning heavily on the final note. As she lifted her hands away from the piano, she received scattered applause from the mess hall. She smirked bashfully and stood up to half bow.

"Bravo!" Simon yelled. "Play something else!"

Edna shook her head as she kept her eyes lowered. Raul burst through the door of the mess hall with his guitar. He strode to the piano and motioned for Edna to sit down.

"Please," he said breathlessly as he pulled over a chair and sat down.

"I'm not that good," Edna said as she shook her head and blushed.

"No, please, let's play a little," Raul pleaded.

Simon jogged over and took Edna by the shoulders and led her back to the piano.

"No, no," she chuckled. "I'm not nearly as good as Raul."

"You can't tease us like that," Simon urged, easing her down to the bench.

"I don't have any sheet music," Edna said, still resisting despite having already placed her fingers on the keys.

"It's okay, play what you know," Raul urged as he tuned his guitar. Other children chirped supportively.

"You can play for thirty minutes!" I called. "Then we have to get to bed."

"Okay!" Raul replied, then turned to Edna. "Play that same song."

"But your fingers are all bruised and cut up," she said.

"My fingers will be okay."

Finally, the first notes emerged, this time precise and confident. Raul's guitar sang out in notes that bent impossibly as they sang over the song. Edna's piano trod ahead steadily as Raul's guitar danced and soared. The cuts on his fingers opened up halfway through the song, but he didn't seem to notice.

Simon pulled a chair up to the piano and rocked back and forth with his eyes closed and a soft smile that twitched along with the music.

Barry and Mary held hands under the table, thinking no one would notice. Billy and Sophia had slipped away and were sitting on the shore close to the mess hall, listening and watching the waves. Petrov finished eating and shuffled out the door.

When the song ended, Raul hugged the guitar and clapped for Edna. The other kids joined in the applause and Edna smiled with tears welling in her eyes.

"Ugh, I don't know why I'm crying," she laughed, looking down at Raul. "I'm sorry, I wish I where a better piano player."

"No, you did wonderful—what else do you know?" Raul asked.

"Without sheet music? Um, some Christmas songs, I guess. I know a little Beethoven."

"Play Beethoven," Raul said, repositioning his hands on the guitar.

"Do you know 'Moonlight Sonota'?"

"You play, I'll follow," Raul urged.

She began in a tender, yet unexpectedly urgent melody. Raul nodded his head as he listened. He worked in notes where he could find room, he clearly wasn't very familiar with the song, and the two instruments sometimes stepped over each other clumsily, but the audience was no less appreciative. As the song progressed, the two instruments found their roles and by the final notes, were as interlocked as if they were dancing together. I smiled as I thought of how conflicted God had always been about Beethoven.

******

"You really liked those women, huh?" Sophia whispered suddenly.

They hadn't talked as they watched the water and listened to the music, but Billy knew the question had been on Sophia's mind. His heart twisted with guilt.

"I was just surprised to see them," Billy shrugged innocently. "Weren't you?"

"I suppose so," Sophia sighed, her eyes not veering from the waves. "Is that what you like?"

Billy quickly thumbed through possible answers, couldn't find anything he liked, so instead just shrugged again.

"Huh," Sophia replied. "I'm never going to be like that. I'm just not that pretty."

"Don't be silly, you would be gorgeous all grown up," Billy smiled, looking over at her. "But, I like you the way you are, right at this moment."

Sophia chuckled, let her eyes linger on Billy, then looked away. They listened to the music for a few moments before Sophia muttered:

"The brunette did have nice breasts though."

"Um, yeah, if you like that sort of thing," Billy mumbled.

Sophia laughed as she laced her fingers into Billy's hand. Edward and Tommy emerged from the shadows and both walked out into the water. Tommy disappeared under the waves, and was gone for a full minute before emerging several yards away from Edward. Edward paddled over to him.

Billy glanced across the campground and saw Petrov carrying his art case as he walked toward Cabin One.

******

A lone candle sat on the windowsill, casting a warm, yellow light across the cabin. Edward could still hear the music echoing in his head. So much had happened that day that the children hadn't processed it all, further hindered by another day without a proper night's sleep. The impromptu concert had given them something else to concentrate on, a well-timed distraction. Edward's cabinmates were just waiting for Petrov to arrive before putting out the candle and going to sleep.

212

I'd told Edward about the books and he yearned to get a good night sleep so he could wake up fresh and get at the small library. He had always been a ravenous reader and was hungry for something to consume, something that wasn't the Bible.

Edward also wanted to know what the others thought of the volcano — what they'd discussed after making him leave — but the only topic of conversation seemed to center on the women. Edward guessed that he could get Tommy to tell him what the others had said about the volcano, but he didn't want to put Tommy in that position. Edward was terrified of losing him.

He wondered, perhaps for the first time since his childhood on Earth, about the true value of absolute honesty. He knew he should want to tell Tommy the truth about what he saw in the pool on top of the volcano, but he didn't.

A glimmering light appeared outside the window moving toward the cabin. Edward thought it was a candle at first, but as the light approached, it grew larger. The front door of the cabin jerked open and Petrov flew in amid a ball of light and wind.

Petrov dropped to the floor with a thud and the light retreated. Jay and I walked in. I was holding Petrov's art case.

"Go to bed!" Jay growled at Petrov. "We will talk more about this tomorrow!"

Petrov scrambled to his feet and ran to the bed. He quickly curled into a ball and faced the wall.

"Those women will only lead you into temptation!" Jay snarled. "I want all of you in here to steer clear of them. They will be gone tomorrow. Lusting after women is not why we brought you here!"

Jay strode over to Billy's bunk, and Billy sat up to look down at Jay.

"I know that you've been getting close to Sophia," Jay said. "I'm warning you to back off; don't take it any further."

Billy's eyes diverted away from Jay and he laid back down.

"This is Heaven, boys," Jay barked, walking back toward the door. "You are here to focus on God. He gave you paradise, and you need to repay Him."

"This is not paradise," Ossie snipped. The other children held their breaths and watched Jay carefully.

"What?"

"This isn't paradise. You said it yourself — this isn't Heaven." Ossie sat up in his bed and glared at Jay. "We were in paradise, and you pulled us out to come here. Why should we thank you for that?"

"If you ask me," Jay smirked, walking to Ossie. "You shouldn't have been here in the first place."

"What does that mean?" Ossie said, sliding off his bunk and walking toward Jay. I moved between them and held Jay back.

"You know what that means," Jay scoffed. "Everyone in here knows your secrets. Perhaps, next time we tell you not to climb up the volcano, you'll listen."

Ossie took a step back and shook his head, then smacked the bunk.

"What, you didn't think we knew you were up there?" Jay laughed. "We know everything that goes on here. And now you know the dark secrets of all your

cabinmates. I don't think anyone in here deserves
God's love, but He's still giving it to you."

"I don't deserve it?" Ossie growled. "Everything I
went through, I remained faithful to Him. So what, I'm
gay. That's how He created me and I found a way to
live my life morally without denying who I am. Why is
that wrong?"

"Read the Bible," Jay said with a smug grin. "It's
all there."

"You're an asshole," Ossie grumbled, laying back
down. Jay frowned and walked to the bunk. I grabbed
his elbow and held him steady.

"I'm not going to forget you said that," he
grumbled.

"Good," Ossie sneered.

Jay jerked my hand away and stormed toward the
door.

"We didn't find out everyone's secret," Tommy
called to Jay. "Why didn't we see anything about
Edward?"

Edward grimaced and closed his eyes. Jay turned,
looked at Edward and then laughed.

"You did see Edward's sin," Jay said and then
walked out the door.

Tommy leaned over the edge of his bed and looked
down at Edward. Edward covered his face with his
hands.

I walked over to Petrov and handed his art case to
him.

"Hey," I whispered. Petrov rolled away from the
wall to look at me. His eyes were red and frustrated.
"It's okay, you can keep the drawings and the sketch
pad. Just be more careful, okay?"

"Okay," he nodded, taking the case.

I walked to the door and left the cabin. Once the door closed, Simon rolled out of bed and jogged over to Petrov.

"Can I see?" Simon asked as he bent over Petrov's bed.

"No," Petrov mumbled, shoving the case between the wall and his bunk.

"Please," Simon pleaded, hopping up and down like he was having a tantrum.

"No," Petrov repeated, laying down and curling up against the wall.

"Please, Petrov!" Simon said. "Please, please, please, please, please, please …"

"Just show him the damn drawings!" Billy growled.

Petrov sighed, pulled the sketch pad out of the case and handed it to Simon. Simon crossed to the candle and held up the pad. He opened it, flipped through illustrations of the campground, portraits of kids and one of God. He stopped when he came to a picture of himself.

"Is this what I really look like?" Simon asked, holding up the pencil drawing of Simon with a twisted, conniving sneer. Everyone looked at the pad, then nodded.

"Huh," Simon shrugged, then continued flipping. He stopped. "Whoa!"

Billy and Ossie jerked up and ran over to see.

"Wow!" Billy gasped.

It was an ink portrait of the brunette laying on her back nude. She looked straight ahead in clever defiance, her hand cupped slightly over one breast. The drawing was detailed and realistic, but the legs were unfinished.

Petrov had been caught too soon. Simon flipped the page, and there was another nude portrait of the blonde. She was standing with one arm draped over her head and the other hanging at her side.

"Can I keep these?" Simon asked.

"I want one," Billy said.

"No."

"These are really good, Petrov," Ossie said. "Can you draw me sometime?"

"Eww!" Simon scowled.

"Not naked, retard," Ossie said, punching Simon.

"Thanks," Petrov mumbled, then stood and walked over to retrieve the pad.

When he reached for it, Simon held it back.

"Seriously," Simon said. "Can I have one? I'll be you're bestest friend in the whole wide universe."

"No," Petrov chuckled, then grabbed the pad. He wiped the tears from his eyes and smiled.

They all retreated back to their beds as Billy blew out the candle.

"Did they model for you?" Simon asked.

"Yeah," Petrov answered. "I went to God's cabin and He wasn't there. They let me in."

Silence.

"Did they model naked?" Billy asked.

Petrov didn't answer.

"They did, didn't they?" Simon asked, swatting Petrov on the butt. "You're my hero! I need to learn to draw."

"Okay, settle down," Ossie said. "You keep thinking like that, and God's likely to take your pecker away."

The children laughed, except for Tommy and Edward.

"Can you make me a copy at least?" Simon whispered, but to no answer. "Bestest friend in the universe."

"Maybe," Petrov sighed.

"Wahoo!"

Simon chuckled, climbed up to his bed and settled down. Edward stewed in silence, wanting to talk to Tommy, but didn't know what he would say. Tommy saved him the trouble.

"That last vision of me," Tommy whispered. "That was you, wasn't it, the man I undressed for?"

"Yes," Edward replied. "I'm really sorry."

"Why didn't you say anything?"

"I was ashamed. I'm sorry."

"Wait," Billy called, sitting up in his bunk. "You're gay, too?"

"Yes," Edward said, for the first time admitting it out loud. "I should have told everyone sooner."

"Okay, goddamit, for real this time!" Billy growled. "Who else here is gay?"

"Just the three of us, Billy," Ossie said. "I could have told you that on the first day."

"Jesus H. Christ!" Billy grunted.

"Laaanguaage!" Simon sang.

******

Edward rolled restlessly in his bed. He opened his eyes and stared up at the bottom of Tommy's bunk. It was still dark and Edward had no concept of how late it was. He couldn't sleep because he was waiting. He knew Tommy would be leaving tonight. Edward knew it would be because of him.

Tommy's bed creaked, and Tommy dropped off the end. He jerked on his shoes and glared at Edward. Edward mouthed, "I'm sorry." Tommy shook his head and walked to the front door.

Edward leaped off his bed and grabbed his shoes.

"Not this time," Tommy said, emotionless.

Edward laid back down.

"Tommy," Edward whispered, but Tommy disappeared out of the cabin and was gone.

Edward thought about praying. He wasn't sure what would happen if he did, so instead he tried to sleep.

******

Edward's eyes popped open. Edward thought he'd heard something rustle. It was still night and Tommy's bed remained empty.

A dim light glittered from Simon's bunk. Simon was sitting up in his bed with his sheet pulled over his head. The light glowed underneath. Edward rolled off his bed and the light under Simon's sheet blinked out. Simon pulled the sheet off his head and looked over at Edward.

"What are you doing?" Edward whispered as he walked toward Simon's bunk.

"Nothing, why?" Simon replied.

"What was that light?"

"What light?"

"The light under your sheet," Edward said.

Simon smirked and looked around at the other beds. He waved Edward over. Edward climbed up to Simon's bed and it creaked under the weight. Simon pulled the sheet over them.

"Now, don't get all gay and stuff, okay?"

"I won't," Edward sighed.

A faint light appeared between them and it slowly grew. Edward narrowed his eyes as he watched it. The ball of light was growing from the end of a stick that Simon held like a wand.

"How do you do that?" Edward gasped.

"Shh, don't wake everyone."

"How do you do that?" Edward repeated in a whisper, still staring at the twig.

Simon's face glowed—he smiled and his eyes were bright.

"Magic," Simon winked.

"Come on," Edward said. "Seriously, how do you do it?"

"I figured it out earlier tonight," Simon said. "I can do a few things like this, like making small stuff float. I can make other things glow too, but the stick is the easiest."

"How?"

"Well, if I told you, it wouldn't be magic."

Edward shrugged, then noticed Petrov's sketch pad lying beside Simon. It was opened to the nude brunette.

"Simon, put that back," Edward groaned.

"I will, I just want to look at it a little longer," Simon said. "I'll put it back, Mom, promise."

Edward shook his head and took the sketch pad. He glanced at the nude, then turned the page to the other nude.

"Do anything for you?" Simon asked.

"Ehh," Edward shrugged. "They are impressive though."

"The tits or the drawing?"

"Both, I guess."

Edward flipped the pages to the portraits of various kids and stopped when he came to Tommy. He looked it over, noticed Simon smiling and quickly flipped it to the next portrait.

"I kind of knew you were gay all along," Simon said.

"You're only a homosexual if you act on it," Edward muttered like a mantra while he looked over the other portraits.

"Okay," Simon said. "So you gonna act on it?"

Edward glared at Simon and gave him back the pad.

"Hey, it's a fair question."

"We're kids, Simon," Edward replied, pulling the sheet off his head. "And Tommy's gone."

"What?" Simon asked, looking over at Tommy's bunk. "Oh, he'll be back eventually."

"I don't think so," Edward said.

The door creaked open and Tommy walked in.

"See," Simon whispered. "Magic."

Simon fluttered the twig, making the light dim. Tommy saw Edward and Simon sitting on the bunk. Edward smiled; Tommy nodded his head and then walked to his bunk. Simon leaned toward Edward.

"You might not be a kid forever—those women sure weren't kids," Simon whispered. Edward lowered to the ground and then Simon dropped off the other side of the bed. He wedged the pad back between Petrov's bed and the wall.

Tommy rolled toward the wall. Edward watched him with a frown, then turned to look out the window. Simon walked over to him and grinned.

"Don't sweat it," Simon said. "He'll get over it."

Edward nodded, but didn't look away from the water.

"Do you think those women were once like us?" Edward asked.

"No, I don't think they've ever been ten-year-old boys," Simon replied.

Edward chuckled and glanced back at Simon.

"You know what I mean."

Simon shook his head.

"Maybe they grew up and maybe we'll grow up," Simon said. "I like the idea that there is mystery out there, a whole world to explore, you know?"

"I suppose."

Simon glanced up at Tommy and then back at Edward.

"It's kind of amazing, isn't it?" Simon asked.

"What?"

"That even Heaven can't change who we really are inside."

Edward smiled and nodded.

"Yeah, I guess it is."

chapter xviii

The children stirred as the groans grew more frequent and intense. Edward initially dismissed it as Billy and one of his dreams, but then realized the groans were coming from the other side of the room.

Petrov twitched and rolled in his bed, clutching onto his stomach and sweating profusely. Edward stood, walked to Petrov's bunk and watched nervously. Billy and Simon argued in hushed whispers whether they should go find me. They all wondered what was behind Petrov's sudden illness, and all feared that it would soon inflict them as well.

Tommy casually asked Edward how he slept, and Edward knew that the storm in Tommy's mind had passed. He wondered how long it would be until the next one would materialize.

Sunlight seeped in through the windows. Other cabins were showing signs of life; some children had even begun moving toward the mess hall. Edward remembered it was their cabin's turn to work in the dish pit, so they wouldn't be able to skip out on breakfast unnoticed. He knelt down beside Petrov's bunk and placed a hand on his shoulder.

"Petrov," he whispered. "Petrov, what can we get you?"

Petrov grimaced. He turned on the bed, still curled tightly in a fetal position. He looked up at Edward, and Edward could see thin stubble sprouting out of his cheeks and chin.

"I'll be fine," Petrov grunted with a weak smile. "I'm feeling better, I think I ate something bad. Maybe walking around might help."

"Okay," Edward said, backing away from the bunk.

Petrov rolled to his feet and tried to stand, but he couldn't straighten his back without a stabbing pain along his abdomen, so he stayed hunched over. His forearms and legs were sprouting thin brown hairs. Petrov coughed and frowned. He forced his body to straighten and he was suddenly taller than Ossie. Petrov's face was thin, his cheekbones more defined. Acne sprinkled around his chin and neck.

"It's growing pains," Billy whispered to Edward, and Edward nodded.

"Are we washing di—" Petrov's voice screeched and broke.

"Your voice just cracked, didn't it?" Simon asked. Billy elbowed him.

Petrov rubbed his throat, then noticed his arm hair. His fingers brushed against his facial hair.

"What's happening to me?" he gasped.

The others just glanced around at each other. No one knew for sure, but they all had a pretty good idea.

"You can stay here," Edward said. "Wait until you feel better. We'll take care of the dishes and bring you back something to eat, okay?"

"What will you tell the others?" Petrov asked.

"You banged up your knee trying to go to the bathroom last night," Billy answered. "Just lie down and wait for this to pass—you'll be fine."

Petrov nodded and made his way to the bed gingerly as he held his stomach. He curled up under the sheets.

"Why ..." Petrov began, but his voice cracked again. "Why is this happening to me?"

"I don't know," Edward said as his eyes swept to the sketch pad.

When the group emerged from Cabin Five, they found Jay striding toward them.

"Hurry up!" he growled. "Get in there and eat quickly so you can wash dishes."

Billy nodded and waved. They hurried to a jog as they watched Jay turn and head toward God's cabin. They wanted to make sure he wasn't going to Cabin Five to find Petrov.

There were seven other girls already scooping food onto the plates of the lethargic campers. Other kids were trickling in as Edward and his crew quickly ate, then went to the dish pit.

"What are we going to do about Petrov?" Ossie whispered as he pulled on plastic gloves.

"I don't know," Edward answered. "We won't be able to hide him long."

Billy grabbed the small stack of dirty trays and began scraping the remaining bacon and gravy-soaked toast into the trash. He stood a tray, plate and silverware in a plastic rack and reached for the next. Once the rack was filled, Simon slid it into a large dishwasher. He closed the dishwasher doors and the contraption hissed for thirty seconds. When it cut off, Simon opened the doors and Ossie pulled the steaming rack out the other side.

A few kids filed by, dropping off their trays and walking out of the mess hall as others walked in. Billy grabbed the trays and looked around, spotting Jay and me talking quietly at our table.

"Do you think it has anything to do with the volcano?" Billy whispered.

"No," Tommy answered. "I think it has more to do with the drawings of those women. He didn't start feeling bad until after the angel brought him back last night."

"But why?" Simon asked. "What's the big deal? It's just pictures—it's not like he had sex."

Simon grimaced after saying "sex." He looked around to see if angels were going to take him away. None came.

"Well," Tommy finally whispered, "lust is pretty potent, guys. That is kind of what adolescence is all about. Maybe, he jump-started puberty."

"It might also be about defying God," Edward added.

"But Bali said that they couldn't really punish us," Ossie said. "We're in Heaven, right, so what does it …"

Billy shushed them as another group of kids dropped off trays.

"Where's Petrov?" a short, blond girl asked.

"Hurt himself last night trying to go to the restrooms," Billy said.

"We heard he got in trouble," the girl said with a clever smile. "Got caught sneaking in to see those women."

"Who told you that?" Billy asked.

She shrugged. "Is it true?"

"Go read the Bible or something," Billy grunted, taking her tray and turning his back on her.

"Oh come on," the girl chirped. "What difference does it make? Did he do it or not?"

"You really want to know?" Simon asked with a grin. Billy threw him a threatening look, but Simon ignored it. "Are you sure you want to know?"

"Yes," the girl whispered with a greedy grin.

Simon walked over to her, looking around the mess hall.

"Come back here and I'll tell you," Simon said. "You have to keep it a secret."

"Okay," she said, following Simon back into the dish pit.

"Don't, Simon," Ossie warned, but Simon just smiled and nodded at him.

"Okay," Simon said, turning around to her. "This is what happened."

Simon lifted a sprayer and doused the girl. She shrieked and ran out of the dish pit. Simon kept spraying at her as the kids laughed. She finally turned once she was out of range.

"Go to hell, Simon!" she screamed.

"Way ahead of ya," Simon saluted.

Two balls of light burst into the mess hall, one went to Simon, the other to the girl.

"He started it!" she yelled as she began floating into the air.

Simon just dropped the sprayer and allowed himself to be lifted. He gave Edward a thumbs-up and Ossie reached over to give Simon a high five just before he was whisked out of the dish pit by the ball of light.

Both kids floated over to Jay and were gently lowered to the ground. The girl sneered over at Simon, and Simon tried to stifle a smile.

Jay stood and looked both of the kids over.

"Not today," Jay grunted. He then turned toward the rest of the kids. "We've had a really hard couple of days, so I understand that tensions are high. Let's try to have a relaxed day, no fighting, no one getting in trouble. Please, let's just take a break from this."

Jay couldn't hide his exhaustion. He was as close to being defeated as I'd ever seen him.

"I'm sorry, Jay," the girl said, holding out her hand to shake Jay's hand. Jay looked down at the hand, saw that it was wet.

"Just go back to your cabins," he said, sitting back down to finish his breakfast.

Simon gave a grand bow for the girl, motioning for her to go outside first. She huffed, but a smile escaped from her lips. Simon winked at Billy as he followed her out.

After the doors closed, they jerked back open and Simon ran back in.

"Billy!" Simon called. "Come out here!"

Simon disappeared back outside and Billy ran out of the dish pit. The rest of the kids followed them out.

They raced around the mess hall toward the pier where the two women were preparing to get into their canoe. They were now wearing camp T-shirts over their bikinis, but the bottom of the shirts were tied tightly around their waists so their belly buttons showed. Petrov was standing in front of the blonde, who was now shorter than him. They talked quietly, the blonde with a heavy smile. She rubbed her hand over Petrov's thin facial hair and then hugged him. Petrov held her tight.

"We need to go," the brunette said as she climbed down into the canoe.

The blonde peeled away and kissed Petrov on the forehead. Petrov helped her down into the canoe, and the two women paddled away. Petrov continued to watch them as children walked up behind him. He turned and the kids looked at Petrov with a mix of awe and revulsion.

He was over six feet tall. All the baby fat in his face was gone and his eyes were darker, more solemn. His arms and chest were thicker. He now appeared to be a handsome, if gangly, boy of about sixteen.

He began walking through the crowd on his way back to the cabin. The kids moved away from him as if he were a leper.

Billy stepped next to Petrov and reached up awkwardly to pat him on the shoulder. The rest of the cabinmates fell in line with Petrov and they retreated back to Cabin Five. Edward decided the dishes could wait.

******

Petrov sat on his bunk, staring at the nude portrait of the blonde. The others in the cabin remained silent as they traded worried looks and searched for something to say.

"So you can get a boner now, huh?" Simon asked.

The cabin released a collective groan.

"That's really gross, Simon," Edward chided.

"What?" Simon exclaimed. "Like you're not curious."

Edward was grateful when a knock came from the cabin door. He hurried across the cabin and opened the door to find God, wearing a gray hooded sweatshirt and his aviator sunglasses. He reminded Edward of the Unabomber.

"Where is he?" God asked.

Edward stepped back and motioned to Petrov, who closed the sketch pad once he saw God. Petrov looked embarrassed. He didn't stand.

God walked into the cabin. He glanced over the beds at the other campers and then back at Jay who was walking in behind Him.

"Don't they have somewhere they need to be?" God asked Jay.

Jay lifted a clipboard and flipped over a paper.

"Arts and crafts is just about to start," Jay replied.

"Take the others," God said. "I need to talk to Petrov alone."

Jay motioned for the children to leave and began ushering them out of the cabin. Edward and Billy lingered.

"Hurry up," Jay snapped.

Edward patted Petrov on the shoulder and Billy knelt down beside him.

"You're going to be okay," Billy whispered.

Petrov nodded with a weak smile and whispered "go, don't worry about me."

Billy nudged Petrov and gave Petrov a wink. He then allowed Jay to usher him out the door, closing it behind him. God sat down beside Petrov on the bunk and took off his glasses. His eyes were cool blue pools with no irises.

"Can I see?" God asked Petrov.

Petrov hesitated, then flipped open the sketch pad and handed it to God. God glanced over the brunette nude, then the blonde. He studied the blonde, rubbed His finger gently over her eyes. He flipped the pages over to the front and went through the other sketches one by one. He smiled at some, then stopped at His own portrait.

"Huh," He grunted. "Is that what I really look like?"

He sighed, closed the sketch pad and handed it back to Petrov.

"I thought you would be happier here," God said, putting his aviator glasses back on. "After everything you've been through, I thought this would be a welcome break, but it's not, is it?"

Petrov shook his head.

"Can you be happy if you're just creating the art I tell you to?" God asked.

Petrov tried to talk, but his voice cracked and he rubbed at his eyes as a tear sprinkled down. "I'm sorry," he finally managed.

God shook his head and stood.

"It's okay, Petrov," God said, walking to the door. He rubbed the rail of a bunk, checking for dust. He rubbed His fingers together, then wiped the dust on His pants. "Gather your things, I'm going to move you to another cabin."

"I don't want to go," Petrov said, wiping away the tears. Petrov's voice was deeper now. He sounded like an adult and it startled him.

"You have to," God said, not turning from the door. "I can't have your condition affecting the rest of the children."

"You made me this way," Petrov said. "It's not my fault."

"I know," God mumbled, then walked out of the cabin. A glimmering ball of light hovered and waited on Petrov to pack his sheets, clothes and sketch pad.

Outside at the arts and crafts tables, the children lazily traced shapes with red, green and blue fingerpaints. Edward's eyes remained fixed on Cabin Five as he painted randomly on his white paper. When Petrov appeared, following an angel, he was carrying a duffle bag in one hand and his art case in the other.

Edward raised his hand to get my attention and I walked over. He motioned for me to lean closer.

"Where is he going?" Edward whispered.

"He needs to be separated from the others for now," I answered.

"Then what?"

"I don't know," I said, but I did.

"I thought you said we couldn't really be punished since we already made it to Heaven," Tommy growled.

"I said the minor things you can't really get in trouble for," I replied. "His offense wasn't minor."

"Is that what happened to those women?" Tommy asked. "They defied God too, so they got tossed out of the camp?"

I frowned and glanced out at God. He was leading Petrov to an empty cabin close to His.

Cabin Zero.

"Finish your paintings," I told them. "These questions are just going to lead you to the same place Petrov is going."

"Which is?" Edward asked, but I'd already started walking away.

The children glanced at each other, and then at their paintings. Edward wondered what Petrov would have done with the finger paints. He crumpled up his artwork and grabbed another piece of paper. The children stole glances at Petrov as he walked across the campground. When he disappeared into the cabin, they slowly regained focus and stared at their papers and paint.

God closed the door, shutting Petrov inside. God began walking back across the campground to the arts and crafts table.

"Hey, Simon," Ossie whispered, motioning him over.

"Yeah?"

Simon leaned across the table. Ossie swiped his fingers across Simon's upper lip, sending a blue streak under his nose and across his cheek.

"Nice mustache!" Ossie laughed.

Simon stood, poured paint into his hand and jumped across the table, smacking blue and yellow handprints on Ossie's forehead, then rubbing the rest of the paint on Billy's hair. Billy dumped paint on Simon, then flipped it back at Tommy. Within moments, the entire table was consumed in a paint fight. Plastic bottles were tossed across at the girls, who then fired back with a bowl full of red.

I staggered back to avoid getting hit, and watched the arts and crafts devolve into a melee. No angels intervened. God watched with a frown. When Jay walked toward the table, God grabbed his elbow and held him back. Shouts and squeals of rage and laughter overtook the fight. The rainbow of colors covering the children mixed into a uniform brownish gray and the fight moved toward the lake.

From Cabin Zero, Petrov watched through the window and wondered what was next.

234

chapter xix

It is not fair to call God cruel, though the results of His decisions often seem unjust, sometimes even sadistic. If you have the benefit of looking at the totality of the human condition, as I have, then you understand that God's treatment of humanity is not based on cruelty. I am not sure what it is based on, but I do know that it is not cruelty.

Petrov sat cross-legged in Cabin Zero, bent over the sketch pad on the floor. His hands worked quickly, going over pencil sketches with charcoal, working hard to finish as the last shards of daylight lingered in the cabin.

His complexion had cleared aside from rogue pimples on the chin and along the bridge of his nose. His chest was even thicker, his sunken cheeks were now covered by a thin beard. He looked like an adult now, somewhere in his very early twenties.

He knew it would be his last work in the campground. He hadn't been told, but he still knew that it was impossible for him to stay, looking the way he did.

Feet shuffling outside the cabin brought his attention up from the pad. He sighed and then looked down at the paper. Dozens of kids had snuck off to get a peek at him, the freak of the campground. He resented it at first, but learned to block it out and turn his attention to his art.

Charcoal wasn't his favorite medium, but the gloominess of the shadows felt right at that moment.

A tap came from the windowpane. Petrov didn't budge, still studying the sketch, adding details as needed and using his finger to smudge and shade. The image was taking shape and he couldn't stop now.

Another tap.

Petrov glanced up and saw the tops of Barry's and Mary's faces, their eyes just high enough to peer through the glass.

"What?" Petrov called. Their heads poked down for a few moments, then reappeared like prairie dogs.

"Can we talk to you?" Barry called back.

"Hold on!"

The eyes dipped down again and Petrov returned his focus to his work. He stood, leaving the pad on the floor so he could walk around it to examine his creation from all angles. He knelt down, made a few more strokes, and carefully wiped with his pinky finger. He stood, studied the pad again and then put the charcoal back into his supply case. He wiped his hands off on his shirt, tore the sketch off the pad and placed it on the desk.

The sketch was of God—His aviator glasses in His hands, His inhuman eyes turned down and away in shame.

Petrov picked up the pad and sat it on the case, then walked to the door. He opened it and Barry and Mary crept inside. Petrov rolled his eyes and then closed the door behind them.

Barry looked around at the cabin as Mary walked to the desk. She looked at the sketch for a few moments, and then whispered, "oh my."

"What can I do for you?" Petrov asked, his voice deep and gravelly. A faint Russian accent was emerging, one that he'd tried to hide when he moved to America. The accent now felt right to him.

"We were wondering," Barry started, taking Mary's hand. "What's it like?"

"What?"

"What you're going through right now," Mary said. "Do you feel like an adult?"

"I suppose," Petrov shrugged as he turned away and laid down on the bunk. "It happened so suddenly that I'm not really sure yet."

Barry and Mary glanced at each other nervously. Mary nodded at Barry.

"Do you," Barry began, but blushed.

"Do you have urges?" Mary cut in.

Petrov cocked his head and sat up on the bed.

"Why do you ask?"

Barry took a deep breath, chuckling lightly.

"Well, you might know that Mary and I have gotten close," Barry said. "We've both had bad relationships in the past. We believe that we are soul mates, that we were supposed to be together."

"Okay," Petrov smirked.

"What we really want to know," Mary said, "is if you feel …"

Mary sort of did a shrugging gesture with her hands, pleading Petrov to understand where she was going. Petrov smiled and waited, enjoying her torment.

"We would like to be able to—" Barry began, looked over at Mary for help, but she gave none. "We'd like to be able to consummate our relationship."

Petrov chuckled and laid his head back on his pillow.

"In that case," Petrov said. "I do feel like an adult."

Barry and Mary sighed from relief and blushed. Mary squeezed Barry's hand and giggled.

"The question is," Petrov cut in. "Are you sure it's worth it?"

Barry and Mary nodded.

"Because, you don't know what's about to happen to me," Petrov said. "I assume they are taking me across the lake, but what's over there? Have you thought about that?"

"We have," Barry said. "This is really important to us, and I feel this is going to put us at peace with a lot of the pain we had … before."

"Ah," Petrov grunted. He sat up on the bed and walked to the door. He opened it and waited for Barry and Mary.

"Um," Mary said, glancing at Barry, then back at Petrov. "How did you do it?"

Petrov shrugged.

"You don't know at all?" Mary furthered.

"No," Petrov said. "I just woke up one day and everything changed. Maybe I was ready to outgrow this ridiculous place, and my body responded. Maybe if you're ready to move on, your bodies will respond as well."

Barry and Mary nodded and squeezed hands. Mary mouthed "thank you" as they crept back out into the red glow of the sunset.

Petrov looked out along the shoreline and could see Billy and Sophia sitting together. Sophia tilted her head onto Billy's shoulder and looked back as Barry and Mary ran back into the campground. Billy wrapped his arm around Sophia's waist.

"Theeeeyy're back," Sophia sang in a whisper.

"Fabulous," Billy grunted.

"What do you think they were talking about in there?" Sophia asked.

"Not sure, but I have ideas."

Sophia didn't respond at first, but after a few moments giggled and muttered "gross."

She squeezed playfully against Billy, but the smile faded.

"I'm sorry about Petrov," Sophia said, looking up at Billy. He glanced over and shrugged.

She rested her head back on his shoulder and they kept watching the waves. He still had not tried to kiss her, and she felt guilty that they weren't affectionate like Barry and Mary.

But there was a sick feeling still in her stomach that raged when she thought about physical affection, even leaning against Billy was difficult for her. It wasn't as scary now as it had been on Earth, but the feeling was still there.

Maybe one day.

"You hear that?" Billy asked. "Frogs are singing again."

"Yeah," she whispered. "I wish I could hold one."

"Really?"

Sophia nodded her head and nestled closer to him.

"I like the way animals feel," Sophia said. "Frogs, snakes, dogs, even bugs. I just like feeling them move around, seeing how their bodies work and how they are different from mine. I also like letting them go and watching them go back to their lives."

"You would have made a good vet," Billy said.

"Yeah."

"I tell you what," Billy said. "I'll see if I can find you something tomorrow. I'll bring it back to you, let you pet it for a while then I'll take it back before anyone knows."

"You'd do that for me?" Sophia asked, lifting her head to look at Billy. He nodded. "I don't want you to get in trouble."

Billy almost asked "what can they do?" but didn't. Instead he said, "I'll be extra careful."

"You better."

******

The children slept except for five figures that crept behind the cabins. They moved carefully, avoiding angels they couldn't see and hiding from the god they'd been taught to believe was all-knowing and all-seeing. Yet, they still hushed their voices when His house came into view.

Billy led, as always, with Edward, Tommy, Ossie and Simon trailing behind. Petrov's lonely cabin was behind the row of utility sheds.

Billy held up his hand, motioning the others to stop. He looked around the corner of the utility sheds then began moving forward. They crept up to Cabin Zero.

The door swung open suddenly and the kids backed away and then looked for somewhere to hide. They were too far from the utility shed, so Billy fell flat on the ground and the others followed.

From the dark cabin, the blonde woman appeared. She scanned the campground, saw the kids lying on the ground and waved at them. Simon waved back, but Billy pulled his hand down. She laughed and motioned to someone inside. Petrov appeared in the doorway and saw the kids. He laughed and waved them over. The blonde kissed Petrov's cheek and then jogged out across the campground toward the woods on the eastern edge of the lake. She was hiding something under her shirt as she passed Cabin One and disappeared into the treeline.

"There is a way through," Billy whispered to himself.

Billy stood and the others followed. Simon kept his eyes on the woods where the blonde had disappeared. He was too distracted to notice the porch, and banged his shin against the edge.

"Jesus H. Christ!" he hissed.

"Careful," Petrov smirked, helping him up and leading him inside.

The others filed in and Petrov closed the door. Moonlight only lit up small patches of the room. They all sat in silence for a few moments while Petrov watched the trees.

"It's been a while, so I'm not sure," Ossie began. "But does it smell like sex in here?"

"Ossie," Edward sighed.

"That's not a smell you forget," Billy grumbled with a grin.

"No, it doesn't smell like sex," Petrov answered as he turned from the window. "She wanted to see the sketch."

"Did she like it?" Tommy asked.

"She said she did," Petrov answered as he walked to a candle, struck a match and lit the wick. The cabin glowed and the children ducked so they couldn't be seen through the window facing Cabin One.

"I wasn't satisfied with it," Simon sighed, sitting on the bunk. "So I let her keep it."

"Dude, lame!" Simon growled, only to be hushed by the others. "You were supposed to give that to me!"

"Was I?"

"Yes!"

"Sorry," Petrov grinned. "She didn't take the other nude, would you like it?"

"Yes, as a matter of fact, I would."

Petrov walked to his bed and grabbed his sketch pad. He held it to the candlelight, found the nude and pulled it out. Simon emerged from the shadows and snatched it from Petrov's hands.

"Oh, Ossie," Petrov said, flipping the pages. He held up the pad into the light to show a sketch of Ossie's face. He had a big toothy grin, the kind he had when he was teasing Jay or God. "Would you like it?"

"Yes!" Ossie gasped. "Thank you."

242

"It is nothing," Petrov smiled, pulling the sketch out of the pad. "I'm still retraining my fingers. The pencils still don't quite fit my hand."

"I think it's great," Ossie beamed, taking the sketch and admiring it until Billy pulled him down to a crouch.

Petrov looked over the children, who had backed against the walls in the shadows.

"Even here, we're still hiding from God," Petrov mumbled.

Edward frowned, then ducked his face to look at the dark floor of the cabin.

"So how are you?" Tommy whispered.

Petrov grunted absently as he put the pad back on his mattress. He sat down next to it, leaning back into the shadows.

"You look better," Tommy furthered. "All grown up."

Petrov laughed. His voice, Edward thought, sounded satisfied. Edward wasn't sure where Petrov was going to end up, but he began to think that it would be a better fit. He was more confident now than Edward had ever seen him.

"Do you know anything about what's going to happen to you?" Billy asked.

"No, they haven't talked to me since they put me here," Petrov said.

"Well, if there is anything we can do …" Edward said.

Petrov nodded his head and the group settled into an uncomfortable silence.

"So can you have a boner?" Simon asked.

"Simon!" Edward growled.

Simon shrugged and then ducked away as Billy tried to slug him in the shoulder. Simon stuck his tongue out at Billy and settled back against the wall. Billy jerked over and smacked him on the forehead.

"Ow!" Simon winced.

"What about the blonde girl?" Tommy asked. "What does she think will happen to you?"

"I don't know," Petrov said. "I didn't think to ask."

"What?" Tommy blurted. "Are you kidding? How can that not be the only thing on your mind?"

"I've been in much worse places than this," Petrov replied grimly. "Whatever comes, I will find a way to survive, I always have. Perhaps wherever it is that I'm going, there will be no one to tell me what to draw anymore. That is all I really want."

No one replied, but they all agreed.

"We're just worried about you," Billy finally said. "We know that doesn't help you much …"

"No, it helps a lot," Petrov said. "It is good to have friends, and I'm glad that I have them."

They all understood that the conversation had nowhere else left to go, so after a few moments of silence, the kids shook the man's hand. They then filed back out the door and quickly made their way back to bed.

chapter xx

Jay and I ushered the children out of their cabins as the sun peeled away from the horizon. Edward caught sight of a small cloud of gnats near the lake. He wondered how long they would wind around each other, flying in their tight group before God would brush them off the Island. He also thought about what happened to the gnats, frogs, birds and all other manner of life that wandered too close to God.

And what would happen to him if God decided to remove him from the Island as well.

Was there another Heaven after this one, yet another rung of reality that they'd spend eternity slowly climbing until they finally reach nothingness ... nirvana?

God emerged out of Cabin Zero wearing obscenely tight-fitting cutoff jeans and a wifebeater. His long chest hair was thick like shag carpeting.

Petrov followed, still wearing the standard camp uniform, which had apparently grown at the same rate as Petrov. His beard had grown. It was neatly trimmed, with the tip hanging a few inches down from his face. His body had filled out, his shoulders were admirably broad, like a farmer's and his face was mature and stern.

He seemed stronger than he had in the vision on the volcano.

Petrov was still clinging to art supply case as they neared the children. He was quiet and appeared resolved, his head held upright and unafraid.

"Listen, children," God called. "Take a look at Petrov."

Petrov met the children's eyes, unconcerned and unashamed.

"Original sin," God said. "It appears I couldn't keep it out of Heaven, either. Perhaps there is a flaw in the human condition that even the most perfect setting can't correct. I thought that it was My mistake in design, My poorly designed Earth that led to your race's downfall. Now, I'm beginning to believe it was you all along. I was right to judge you as I did."

The children's eyes sank. Edward was furious at the speech and his face blushed as he grit his teeth. Ossie sat on the ground and ripped up grass, blade by blade, tearing each one apart. He glanced back up at God, and God met his glare.

"Do you have something to say?" God asked Ossie.

"You designed us as well," Ossie grumbled.

"I did," God smirked. "But I gave you free will, so your decisions are no longer My responsibility."

"How convenient for you," Ossie replied, finally dropping his head to return his attention to the grass.

God stared at the child for a few moments. The children shifted uncomfortably.

"So what now?" Petrov asked.

God turned to the full-grown man, then motioned to me. I stepped out from behind the group of children and walked to Petrov. I nodded for him to follow me, and we walked toward the pier.

"He's going across the lake?" Tommy asked.

"He's being banished from the campground," God answered while He watched Petrov walk away.

"Why not just send him back to Heaven?" Tommy asked.

"What would that solve?" God responded. He turned away from the children and retreated to His cabin.

Edward ran to the pier.

"Petrov!" Edward called. Petrov was lowering himself into the rowboat, but he paused to turn and wave at Edward.

"Good luck," Edward said.

"I have faith," Petrov called. "I don't need luck."

Petrov sat down next to me in the boat and we began paddling away from the pier. Other children gathered along the shoreline and watched us make our way across the lake. Petrov turned one last time and waved. Many of the children waved back; some of the girls were crying. They were all afraid.

It was a long trip across the lake, and I was thankful for it.

******

"Children, gather!" Jay called as the campers slowly filed into the mess hall. He brought them all over to his table and stood on his seat so he could look down on them. "I know there are many questions, so let's deal with this right now."

"What's on the other side of the lake?" Tommy asked quickly.

"I've never been there," Jay said. "But I do know it is a wilderness—God's protection does not reach into the wilderness. Should you follow Petrov's path and force us to send you across the lake, you will be left on your own."

"How many people are over there?" Simon asked.

"Not many."

"But how many—three, four, twenty?" Simon continued.

Jay frowned, looking over the faces.

"I don't know," he finally said, and the children knew he was lying. "It is a hard place, it is lonely and you will never return to this side of the Island."

The children murmured. A girl began crying and hugged another girl. Barry and Mary were standing toward the back, holding hands.

"What is important is that you can avoid Petrov's fate. If you follow our directions, then there is no reason you will ever be banished," Jay said. "You can stay here, in this paradise for as long as God chooses to keep it here."

"Do you have any idea how long that will be?" Sophia asked.

Jay shook his head. The children began murmuring.

"I want to talk to you about what will get you banished," Jay said. "Perhaps we should have discussed this at the very beginning, but we thought it would be best not to discuss sin."

"Why?" Tommy asked.

"Because discussing it would only get you to think about it," Jay said.

"Jesus," Ossie sighed and walked away to get a tray. Jay shook his head as he watched Ossie.

"Some of you have been developing relationships," Jay said, keeping his eyes on Ossie. "This is a bad idea because it creates temptation. It is also unnecessary, the only object of love should be God. That is why you are here. Your bodies are incapable of reproduction, either here or in the wilderness, so there is no use developing those kinds of attachments. If God feels that your heart is shifting away from Him toward another camper, then He will banish you."

"But we're human," Edward said. "That's what we do; that's what we've always done. It's our primary instinct."

Tommy ducked his head to hide a blushing smile that caught him off guard.

"You aren't human," Jay said. "You are souls. The flesh on your body isn't truly real. There are no real differences between men and women here. There are no pregnancies, there is no real love aside from what God feels for you. And you must do your best to earn His mercy."

"That isn't true," Edward retorted, stepping forward. "Our ability to love is one of the primary ways that God made us in His image."

"Matthew 22:30, 'At the resurrection people will neither marry nor be given in marriage; they will be like the angels in heaven'," Jay growled. "Do not try to use the Bible against me, Edward! I am telling you how to live in this new world, not Earth. You are to do as you are told now, not as you did in that other world."

"And I'm not so sure about the 'no difference between men and women'," Simon grinned. "I saw those women come over from the other side of the lake, and they had some sizable differences that made my flesh feel real."

Simon cupped his hands on his chest as if he were squeezing his own imaginary breasts. The girls averted their eyes and Billy reached up for Simon's imaginary right breast, only for Simon to swat his hand.

"That is what will get you banished!" Jay growled. "Do you want to be the next?"

"Maybe," Simon shrugged. "Certainly does seem more interesting over there, doesn't it?"

Jay glared at Simon. Simon just smirked, turned his back on Jay and walked over to get his breakfast.

"Be very careful," Jay said, returning his focus to the rest of the children. "The wilderness is not a place you want to be. It is empty, lonely and God will not protect you."

Jay stepped down from the chair and stormed out of the mess hall. The children slowly made their way to the breakfast line. No one was sure who was supposed to be serving the food, so Billy brought a few other kids over to help. It was a very quiet breakfast, and no one volunteered at the dish pit. By the time I returned, God and Jay were nowhere to be found, and, as usual, I was left on my own to clean up their mess.

chapter xxi

"Bali!" a child's voice called. I was in the midst of a
conversation with a girl who had found spotting in her
underwear. I looked toward the new voice, which
belonged to Edward. The day was turning into a long
line of questions.

"We really need to talk," Edward urged.

"One moment, please," I said, taking the girl by the
arm and leading her away.

She sniffled and followed. Petrov had accepted his
fate willingly, almost relieved. This girl had once been
a housewife who'd suffered an abusive husband who
gave her chronic gonorrhea. The gonorrhea left her
barren. Most adults would say their life began with
puberty, but that is when her life had ended, and now
she was suffering through it again.

The blooming of her reproductive system would be
as fruitless this time as it had been on Earth.

I took her inside to the dry storage and shut the
door. She sat down on a box of fry oil and buried her
face in her hands.

"How can I stop this?" she asked, her voice muffled
and weak.

"To my knowledge you can't," I said, putting my hand on her shoulder. "You can slow the process, but one day it'll happen."

"How do I slow it?" she asked, craning her head up to look at me. Her eyes were red and her bottom lip trembled.

"Try to clear your thoughts as much as possible," I answered. "Don't think about it, don't think about the hormones, the feelings they are causing. Try to pretend. I'll see if I can get you something for the ..."

I couldn't finish but didn't have to. She nodded and a smile emerged. I knelt down and hugged her.

"When it happens," she asked. "When I grow, and am sent away, will I be happy?"

I sighed and pulled her tight and stroked her hair.

"You can," I answered. "Humans are amazing that way—they can always find a way to be happy, or miserable, it just depends on which you choose for yourself."

"Really?"

"Yeah," I said. "I've met people inside death camps who found a way to normalize and find bits of happiness in the darkest of corners, and I've met kings who couldn't find a reason to smile. It's up to you, especially here on the Island. You can make your life whatever you want it to be."

"But I can't go backwards?" she whispered.

"No. Even God hasn't figured out how to do that yet."

She chuckled and squeezed against me. She stood and wiped the tears from her eyes.

"I'll get you ... um ..."

"Girl Scout supplies?" she offered.

"Um, yeah," I grinned. "I'll get those to you today."

"Thanks," she said, turning to open the door. She paused, but didn't turn around. "Will I be pretty this time?"

I walked up to her and grabbed a plastic spoon from the shelf and a jar of peanut butter. I unscrewed the lid, spooned up the peanut butter. I put it in my mouth and then grabbed another spoon and offered it to her. She shook her head, but I insisted. She took the spoon, sighed and then scooped out a big lump of peanut butter and put it in her mouth.

I licked the spoon clean and swallowed.

"You were pretty back then," I said as I threw the spoon in a trashcan at the side of the room.

"No, I really wasn't," she answered.

I smiled and shook my head. I walked around her and turned out the lights, the storage room went pitch black. I raised my hands, palms up and closed my eyes. Flickers of blue light started popping above my hands. It looked like fireflies buzzing and swarming. The swarm grew thicker and thicker, and the blue light shifted and changed. A woman's face appeared in the light. She had a thick, chubby face. Her brownish-blonde hair draped straight down her face, her eyes were down-turned and sad.

"That was you," I whispered, not opening my eyes.

"Yes, I know," she mumbled. "I wasn't pretty."

"You could have been," I said. "You just gave up on yourself. This is what you could have looked like then, and what you can look like once you go to the wilderness."

The face shifted, grew thinner, her skin brightened, her hair curled. A smile rose from her face, the eyes opened wider.

The girl gasped and tears started dripping down from her eyes.

"I can't look like that," she said. "I can't."

"You can, if you want to," I answered, my eyes still closed. "The Island, of all places God has ever created, is the one place you can truly be whatever you want to be. You just have to really want it."

I opened my eyes, the fireflies faded and disappeared. I turned the light back on and the girl quickly dropped her head and wiped her tears. She didn't look up at me, but reached over and hugged me tightly.

"Can I really be pretty?" she whispered.

"Yes!"

She buried her head into my chest, giggled and then turned toward the door. She opened it and walked out without looking back.

Edward stood on the other side, waiting patiently.

"Okay, Edward," I sighed.

"I have a million questions, but I know you're busy so for now I just wanted to talk to you about the rapture and everything Petrov went through," Edward said, stepping into the storage room. "I hoped to talk to Petrov about it, but the time wasn't ever right and now he's gone."

I took a deep breath and nodded wearily.

"Have a seat," I said, motioning to the box of fry oil. "I suppose this is my new office."

Edward chuckled politely as he sat.

"Bali!" another voice called from outside the mess hall. "Bali, God's asking for you!"

I glanced at Edward. He frowned and motioned for me to go talk to whoever was calling me.

"Sorry, Edward," I said. "We'll talk, I promise."

"Okay," Edward shrugged.

chapter xxii

Campers sat obediently at the arts and crafts table with several piles of multi-colored beads waiting in front of the children. I was relieved to have an activity as an excuse to defer difficult conversations. As long as the children listlessly stared down at the beads, they wouldn't be peppering me with impossible questions. The looming discussion with Edward was a subject I was most dreading and had been ducking him the rest of the day.

Those are days that are best left in the stifled memories of the souls drifting through Heaven.

God thumbed through papers on a clipboard. He looked up at the children and handed the clipboard to Jay. God sucked snot through his nostrils, coughed, cleared His throat and then addressed the children.

"We've got plenty of letter beads here," He said while putting His hand on a box of beads at the front of the table. "I want you to create a necklace that says something about you. This is your chance to express yourself, so be creative and have fun."

God nodded back at Jay and then walked to His cabin. The children let out a collective sigh and began murmuring to each other.

"Okay," Jay called. "We don't have all day—come get your letter beads."

Simon began snickering and stood up. He ran over to the box and dug through the letters. Other children stood and fell in line behind him, none with the same vigor as Simon. Jay watched Simon nervously as he dug through the box. Simon finally found all his letters and took them back to his place.

Billy studied Simon with a curious grin. Billy stood to get in line, with Ossie and Edward following. They all continued watching Simon, waiting to see when the angel would take him away from whatever it was he was doing.

Before the line moved very far, Simon tied off the string of his necklace and put it on. He climbed up onto the table, stood proudly and yelled, "Done!"

Jay walked over and looked at the necklace.

"Porn star?" Jay read.

"Yeah, baby!" Simon chimed, then started dancing on the table. He slithered back and forth like a snake, then pulled off his shirt and waved it over his head like a male stripper. He threw it at a group of girls who scattered like it was on fire. Simon continued to dance, shaking his butt around and swiveling his hips.

He held one arm out in front of him, the other waving above his head as if he were riding a bucking bronco. He pranced around in circles, slapping his butt loudly from time to time.

"Stop that and get down!" Jay growled.

Simon jumped from one table to the next, sending beads bouncing and rolling off the tables. Some girls giggled as they watched him dance, but most averted their eyes and watched Jay nervously. Martha simply sneered.

The divisions were growing wider.

Jay looked up at the balls of light dropping from the sky toward Simon. Simon saw them and jumped off the table. He began running around one end when a light cut him off. Simon rolled under the table and crawled to the other side. He ran toward another table as two lights converged on him. Simon jumped over the table, then rolled back under it. The light lifted the table up and flipped it over, spilling beads across the ground. Simon crawled under another.

"Get him!" Jay shouted.

Edward noticed how intently Tommy watched Simon. He had a broad smile as he watched Simon dart away from the angels. Edward suddenly felt very jealous.

Children hooted and yelled, "Run, Simon, run!"

Simon continued to burrow from table to table. The lights continued to flip the tables over until finally the lights backed him against a tree. Simon laughed and grabbed his necklace as he was lifted into the air and whisked across the campground and thrown into Cabin Five.

Many of the children continued laughing while Jay yelled at them to flip the tables back over and collect beads out of the grass. Other children scowled at Simon's cabinmates while following Jay's commands diligently.

Martha stood and walked over to Billy with a stinging smile.

"When your cabin defied rules," she seethed. "I didn't say anything, but now they are defying God and…"

"Shut up!" Billy growled, sending her back two steps. "Go pick up beads!"

"Martha," Edward added calmly. "Save your sanctimony for God. We're not the least bit interested."

Martha arched her eyebrow, let her eyes pass from Edward to Billy, then swiveled on her heel and marched back to her table.

Edward watched her walk away. He felt fingers lace into his. Edward looked over and saw Tommy watching him with an amused grin. Tommy squeezed Edward's hand, then let go. Edward's chest hummed with a warm burst of nervous energy. He looked away and tried, and failed, to stifle the dumb smile.

Jay growled about how Simon was making the children do extra work. Some kids grunted and sighed in agreement, others chuckled as they picked the beads off the ground.

Once all the beads were collected back into their piles, the kids went back to their necklaces. The children went to work with zeal, and after the first "Slut" and "Pees Standing Up" necklaces showed up, Jay gave up on the arts and crafts project and sent the kids to their cabins.

Edward jogged to catch up with Tommy and began thinking up excuses to get him alone.

******

"Porn star, huh?" Edward asked.

Simon just smiled as he laid on his bed with the necklace still tied around his neck.

"And they let you keep it?" Ossie asked.

"They couldn't get it off me," Simon said, winking at Ossie. "I'll just keep it in the cabin, but it's my war trophy now."

"Good for you," Billy said, patting Simon on the leg.

Edward laid back on his bed and tried not to stare over at Tommy. Instead, he studied Petrov's old bunk bed.

"So, why 'porn star'?" Ossie asked. "Did you actually do a porno?"

Simon didn't answer.

"Simon?" Billy said, leaning up on his bed to look.

Simon sighed and grimaced.

"I was supposed to," Simon said.

"Really?" Ossie asked, standing up out of his bed and looking at him. "When?"

"It was kind of a rough patch in my life and I needed the money," Simon said.

"Was it gay porn?" Billy asked.

"No! No offense, Edward, but no freakin' way!"

"Ossie's gay, too," Edward grumbled, but no one listened.

"So, what was it?" Ossie asked.

"Oh, one of my girlfriends was a stripper and she had this customer," Simon said. "Anyway, he wanted to do a video with her for his web site—offered us money to do it."

"And you did?" Billy asked.

"Um, no," Simon said. "I had, um, issues."

Ossie held up his finger straight, and then let it fall limp. Simon nodded, and the entire cabin erupted in laughter. Simon laughed hardest of all, until his face turned red and tears dripped out of his eyes.

"Okay, okay," Simon gasped. "It wasn't really my fault; the guy was really old and hairy."

"I thought you said it wasn't gay," Billy smirked.

"It wasn't," Simon growled. "But when he came out to film us, he wasn't wearing anything but this leopard-striped thong, which you could barely see 'cause his gut was hanging over it."

They laughed, and once they finally settled, Ossie laid back down in his bed.

"That's pretty horrifying," Billy said. "Can't believe you tell that story."

"It was pretty awful at the time," Simon shrugged. "I like going through weird stuff like that, though, even if it sucks — it's still kind of amazing, you know?"

"No, buddy, I don't know."

"And I hate to tell you this, Simon," Ossie said, "that necklace is a bit misleading—you're performance doesn't actually qualify you as a porn star."

Simon chuckled.

"It's my necklace," Simon replied. "In my mind, I'm a porn star, okay?"

"Okay."

"Still," Simon sighed, rubbing a tear from his eye. "Let's, uh, keep that between us."

Edward kept smiling as he turned to the window and watched the clouds passing over the sky.

"Do you think Petrov is enjoying himself?" Tommy asked.

"I hope so," Ossie answered.

Billy stretched and hopped down from his bed. He walked to the window and looked at the other cabins.

He grunted, shook his head and looked back at the others.

"Anybody wanna bet who is going to be next?"

chapter xxiii

Lines along the breakfast buffet were buzzing early as news surfaced of a kid who had turned up missing. It was a girl and some children were saying she'd been quietly ushered across the lake in the middle of the night. Others said she began menstruating and God considered her unclean.

The girls who shared a cabin with her didn't want to talk about her, but trying to deflect blame, had said that she'd talked to Petrov a couple times before he left. It was a lie, but the children saw puberty as a sickness and no one wanted to appear contagious.

This is why the children kept their distance from Edward and his cabinmates, as if the phenomenon could be blamed on their cabin. Cabin Five was being quarantined. Even the girls who'd been desperately smitten with Tommy began averting their eyes as they neared him.

It didn't particularly trouble Billy, so as long Sophia still talked to him. Edward didn't seem to notice — he spent most of his morning watching me, waiting until I was alone so we could talk.

Fielding questions on history and theology was not why I had been brought to the Island, so I did my best to appear busy all the time.

Ossie and Simon were both annoyed by their status as pariahs and secretly hoped that more kids from other cabins would grow up and be banished across the water so blame would shift somewhere else.

The mess hall grew quiet. God had walked in and was looking over all the children.

"Is He checking us for acne and arm hair?" Ossie whispered.

"Okay, I'm just going to say it," Simon said as he sat across from Ossie. "God creeps me the *F* out."

Simon hunched down and glanced over his shoulder, expecting an angel to grab him. None appeared, so he leaned over the table to further push his luck.

"He looks like some perv you see on *To Catch a Predator*."

"You're right!" Ossie laughed, looking behind him at God, who sat down at my table. "With those '80s aviator glasses, thinking he looks like Tom Cruise."

"Or Jackie Gleason from *Cannonball Run*," Simon smirked.

"I love that movie!" Ossie beamed. "I know I should be ashamed to say that, but I do! I hid a copy of it in my bedroom so my friends wouldn't know."

They laughed and began reenacting scenes. Billy grumbled, stood up and walked away. Simon shrugged and put hashbrowns over his lip to emulate a bushy mustache, then let out his best Burt Reynolds laugh. Edward glanced up and chuckled.

Billy cleared his throat as he neared my table. God looked away from me and turned toward him. He took off His glasses and began buffing them with His shirt. His eyes were silver, almost reflective and Billy had trouble looking directly at them.

"Yes?" He asked impatiently.

"Could I have a word with you?"

God nodded and settled back in His chair. Billy looked around at the other children, not wanting anyone to eavesdrop. He took another step toward the table and waited for children to pass by on their way outside.

"Can you tell me anything about Petrov, how he's doing?" Billy asked.

"Why do you care?" God asked, glancing up at Billy momentarily, then returning His focus to His glasses.

"He's my friend," Billy frowned. "I'm worried about him."

"You know, this is something I don't understand about humans," God said, putting on His glasses. He stood and looked down on Billy. "You come to Me, this is the first time we've talked, and do you ask Me a real question?"

God studied Billy, and Billy kept his eyes fixed on God's.

"No, you ask Me about your friend," God grunted. "Your friend who shrugged off this gift I gave to him."

Billy sighed, then shook his head and walked away from the table.

God huffed and knocked on the table to get my attention while He waved "bye." He scanned the mess hall one more time, then sauntered out the door.

Billy dropped down in his seat.

"What did you talk about?" Tommy asked.

"Petrov."

"What did He say?" Simon asked.

"Jack squat," Billy whispered.

"You shouldn't do that," a female voice called to Billy. He looked up at Martha walking toward them, holding her food tray with three of her friends following close behind.

"Do what?" Billy asked.

"You need to respect your Creator," Martha sneered.

"He's just a man," Billy said. "A man who's going to get just as much respect from me as He deserves."

Billy noticed Sophia watching. She frowned, which made Billy sorry he'd said it. He wasn't going to show it though; he wouldn't give the girls the satisfaction.

"You're going to end up banished just like your disgusting friend," the girl sneered.

"Is that right?" Billy asked, sliding his chair out and facing the girl. "What about you? Gluttony is a sin, and here you are, sixty pounds of beans stuffed into a twenty-pound bean bag."

Martha bristled and her clique bridled.

"You are going to hell," Martha hissed.

"That so?"

"Yes it is," she smirked. "You and all your friends."

Martha took a step toward Billy, smirked, then dumped her tray on Billy's feet. Billy stood up, kicked the tray off his feet and glared at the girl. The mess hall was deathly silent. The other three girls held their trays firm and took a step toward Billy. Billy didn't acknowledge them other than to say, "You'd better rethink that."

They did, and retreated. Their leader's thin smile wavered. She spun away and led the others out of the mess hall. Billy kicked the food off his leg and sat back down to finish his breakfast.

He ate slowly as he fumed. His cabinmates sat silently, waiting for him to finish.

At the next table, Barry stood then made his way over toward Billy and the others.

"Can I talk to you guys?" Barry asked. Tommy motioned for him to sit down.

"You going to throw food at me, too?" Billy asked.

"No."

Barry slid down next to Edward and leaned in over the table, his eyes fixed on me to ensure I wasn't listening.

"Mary and I want to go across," Barry said. "We've been trying to … grow, but haven't been able to."

"So?" Billy asked, not looking up from his food.

"That one girl got her period, but she didn't even want it," Barry said. "We're not sure what we're supposed to do."

Billy glanced up at Barry, and then scanned the mess hall to find Mary three tables down, watching intently.

"You don't have to grow to go over there," Tommy said. "If you want to go, just go."

"Um," Barry mumbled. "I don't think I'd feel comfortable taking Mary over if I wasn't big enough to protect her. We really need to be adults."

Sophia walked by with a group of girls taking their trays to the dish pit. She bent over to pick up the tray Billy had kicked, then gave Billy a sympathetic frown. Billy winked back at her.

After she passed, Edward said, "You don't know what's over there. I don't think you …"

"If you really want to go," Billy interrupted. "I'll help."

"How?" Barry asked.

"I'll tell you, but there's something you need to see first," Billy said.

"Billy," Edward whispered.

"Shut up, Eddie — it's their decision, not yours."

Barry looked back at me. I pretended not to be paying attention. Barry turned back to Billy and nodded, whispering, "We're sure."

"Okay," Billy said. "First things first, have you been up to the volcano?"

"What volcano?" Barry asked. "You mean the mountain?"

"It's a volcano," Billy said. "I assure you. Go up there, then come back and talk to me. If you still want to go to the other side together after that, I'll help."

"Me too," Tommy said.

"Me too," Edward echoed, though he didn't want to.

Barry stood, shook Billy's hand, then Tommy's. He nodded at the others, then turned to look at Mary. She grabbed her tray and stood. They met at the door and hurried out of the mess hall.

"You shouldn't have done that, Billy," Edward whispered.

"They are just wasting their time here, Eddy," Tommy said. "We're doing them a favor."

"You don't know what happens on the other side of the Island."

"That's the point," Billy mumbled.

268

******

Barry and Mary grew into teenage bodies on their way back from the volcano. Mary was a little heavy, with short, brown, curly hair. Barry was stocky with a barrel chest. He became short-sighted, just as he'd been on Earth, so I gave him some glasses. They looked right on him.

They were shaken by what they'd seen, but their devotion to each other only seemed to strengthen. God, to my surprise, decided not to separate them. He did isolate them from the rest of the children.

That wasn't necessary, though, the children would have kept their distance on their own.

I took the couple across the lake after dinner. The children watched and whispered theories. They began to fear that none of them were safe.

Billy decided not to discuss the couple when he met up with Sophia that night. When she arrived, she smiled weakly and they sat together without a word.

Tommy disappeared that night. Edward went to go look for him and was gone most of the evening. They returned together, walking along the shoreline before returning to the cabin.

The girls in Martha's cabin worked all night collecting any extra fabric they could forge, whether extra clothes or sheets. By the time the morning bell sounded, they'd sewed the fabric to their clothes, turning short sleeves into long sleeves and shorts into pants. They used what fabric was left to make headscarves to cover their hair. When they were done, only their hands and faces were uncovered.

Over the course of a week, the girls and boys became progressively more distant, to the point that they barely even spoke to one another.

The camp was as silent as it had been since the children arrived, even Edward and his cabinmates fell in line with the others as all the campers tried to process their new view of the Island.

There were no more banishments, no more periods, no more growth spurts. God felt He had finally brought the children in line.

Simon began disappearing at night and wouldn't allow anyone to come with him. He only said he was practicing and didn't want anyone around.

When Billy and Sophia met at night, he could feel the gap between them widening. He wanted to say something, to salvage what intimacy they'd once had. Most nights, though, they said nothing at all.

Sophia lost her faraway gaze, and spent most of her time staring down at the sand. By the sixth night, she left after only a few minutes and Billy let her go.

chapter xxiv

Billy wasted no time the next morning. As soon as
the children left the mess hall, he returned to his cabin
and told the others his plan. He had snuck some extra
food from breakfast and planned on going to the other
side of the Island. He didn't ask for volunteers to join
him, but they all followed without a word.

Edward knew Billy was doing this for Sophia, but
had no idea what Billy hoped to accomplish.

Jay had forgotten to assign any children to the dish
pit, so it was left to me. Again.

After I'd scrubbed all the dishes and put them away,
I went to talk to the children. I had hoped to finish in
time to catch Billy, but the whole cabin was gone
before I arrived.

Tommy and Billy set the pace for the group,
whispering back and forth as they crossed the
campground. Edward jogged to catch up, and their
voices hushed as he neared.

Jealousy boiled in Edward's stomach when he saw
Tommy whispering to anyone other than him. Edward
knew how ridiculous that was, but knowing it was
senseless didn't make the jealousy burn any less.

Edward eventually fell in line with the others. They crept past Cabin One and then disappeared into the woods behind them. Billy was going to retrace the blonde's path the best he could. If she made it across, so could he.

They stayed close to the lake, always keeping the water within view. Billy wasn't sure if there would be an edge, if there would be a place they could cross the water or if they would have to swim, but if he could just get close enough, he was sure there would be a way. There was always a way.

The group shared a sense of urgency, a need to explore and make sense of the Island. They traveled quickly, creating paths through thick webs of branches and weaving between thorn patches. The forest grew denser as they plunged deeper and deeper.

Edward glanced over the water and noticed that it was flowing like a river, traveling in the same direction they were headed. The waves were no longer lapping at the shore, but were streaming off into the distance.

"Take a look at that," Edward called to Billy. He motioned at the water, and the expedition came to a stop. Billy walked to the shore. As he emerged out of the tree line, he studied the lake, the trees and the shoreline to make sure no one was watching them. He couldn't do anything about an angel, but he didn't want any other kids trying to trail them.

"You were right," Billy said. "Flowing right toward the fog.

"Maybe it's a waterfall?" Tommy ventured. "Water moving this fast is either moving down a mountain or rushing off of something."

"What are we going to do if we can't get across?" Edward asked

"We'll get across," Billy said, putting his hand in the lake. He cupped water in his hand, lifted it to his mouth and took a drink.

"Do you think we'll see Petrov?" Ossie asked.

Billy stood and glanced at the others. He peered into the fog, but it was too dense to see anything. Without answering, they walked back into the tree line.

******

The fog wafted in slow swirls, drifting like waves through the trees. Dense, gray plumes would pass along the woods like small clouds breaking off from a storm system. Just as with the volcano, God used the mist to veil the Island's secrets.

It wasn't a deterrent, Edward thought. It couldn't be—God knew humans too well to think that they could ever ignore the unknown for long. It felt more like a trap, which troubled Edward deeply.

"Stay close," Tommy called, looking back at Edward. Tommy winked, and turned just as the fog enveloped him.

Simon jogged behind, and the rest fell in line. The dense fog veiled the children so that they only saw each other as dim shadows. Edward thought about suggesting they hold hands but wasn't sure if that would come off as too gay. It annoyed him that he had to recalibrate his social instincts.

Billy pulled a branch off a tree, and swung it back and forth in front of him. It clacked against tree trunks and served as Edward's best guide as to which direction to walk. Only tree trunks within a foot were visible, and only the part of the trunk that was eye level. Branches reached out from the fog like claws.

Simon was exhilarated and anxious as he thought back to clichéd horror flicks with long winding trails and sexually charged and naïve teenagers. He often bet with friends which drunk jock, whorish cheerleader or gossipy frat girl would be the next to go. He wondered if someone was watching and had their money riding on him.

"Always bet on the black guy," Simon thought as he looked over to Ossie's silhouette.

Edward heard something like rustling leaves, but there were only pines around them. He listened more intently and realized it was rushing water. It still seemed far off, but as they walked deeper into the blanket of fog, the sound grew distinct. It sounded like a waterfall, but not as loud as ones he'd heard back on Earth. It didn't sound like the water was falling into anything. He could feel water vapor collecting into beads on his face. The pine needles of a nearby branch had droplets of water clinging to the ends. He brushed his fingers along the needles and felt the water drip down his hands. The water was warm, as was the fog.

The rushing water was close. Soon, Billy's branch swung only at air.

"I can't feel any more trees," Billy called over the sound of rushing water.

"Hold on," Simon yelled.

The group stopped. Billy poked his stick on the ground, feeling it give. It was moist like sand or mud.

The fog began swirling, slowly at first. Then the swirls formed into funnels and began lifting the fog into the air. The water ahead of them came into view, the grass and sand along the shoreline. Edward saw Tommy and walked over to his side. The fog continued to lift and they saw the waterfall's edge.

"What's happening?" Ossie asked, then looked at Simon.

Simon's eyes were closed and he had both hands held ahead of him, palms up. He was breathing slowly. His face remained relaxed, but his fingers curled and twitched slightly like he was a puppet master pulling the strings of the funnels ahead of them. The fog now lifted high enough that they could see the other shore. It was about fifty feet from shoreline to shoreline. The water was moving quickly as it streamed to the edge of the Island and fell over.

Billy walked toward the Island's edge and looked over. The water fell down over the edge and plummeted toward the heavens below. It dissipated and turned into fog toward the bottom edge of the Island. That fog then crept back up the edge of the Island.

"What now?" Tommy called to Billy, shouting to be heard over the rushing water.

"We cross!" Billy said as he walked back along the shoreline.

"That water will suck us over the edge," Edward yelled.

"The angels caught Tommy last time that happened," Billy replied. "They'll do it again."

"We don't know if the angels are out here," Edward said. "What if we just fall, what then?"

"Then go back!" Billy growled. "I'm going! Who's going with me?"

Ossie raised his hand, then Tommy. Edward sighed and raised his hand.

"Simon, you coming?" Billy asked.

"Shut up," Simon called without opening his eyes. "You're fucking up my chi."

"Are you coming?"

"Yes!" Simon replied, opening his eyes.

The fog began drifting back over the water. Billy looked across to the other shore. He thought he saw a figure watching them, but the fog quickly overtook the water again.

"Oh, great, you happy?" Simon grunted. "Now I lost my flow."

"Well, it was going to happen eventually," Tommy shrugged, walking to the water.

"Hold on," Billy called to Tommy, grabbing at Tommy's shadow.

"What?"

"I think someone is on the other shore."

Tommy tried to look through the fog.

"How can you tell?" Tommy asked.

"I thought I saw them while the fog was lifted," Billy answered. He cupped his hands over his mouth and shouted, "Hello!"

They listened, but heard nothing.

"Hello!" Billy repeated.

Still no answer.

"Maybe they can't hear you," Tommy said.

"Might have just been my imagination," Billy replied.

"Should we go back and get rope?" Edward asked.

"There is no rope," Billy answered. "I looked this morning, I couldn't find any we could take with us. We'll just have to hold hands."

"Eww, fag," Simon grunted. "No offense, Edward."

"None taken," Edward sighed.

Billy grabbed Simon's hand, Simon grabbed Ossie's. Tommy grabbed for Edward's hand.

"You go ahead of me," Tommy said. "I'll catch you if you slip."

Tommy was close enough that Edward could see him smile. Edward responded with a clumsy smirk. He then reached for Ossie's hand.

Billy waded out into the water slowly, taking careful, steady steps. The sand gave way to large and smooth rocks. The current was strong, but not so strong that Billy thought he couldn't power through it.

Billy took a few more steps, pulling the others behind him. A rock shifted under his feet and he fell into the water, but quickly pushed his way back up to the surface.

"Shit!" Billy gasped.

"Careful!" Simon yelled. "You almost pulled me down."

"What's wrong, can't swim?" Billy grunted.

Billy trudged farther into the water until it rose to his waist. He struggled to keep his footing as the current rushed against him.

"If it gets any deeper than my waist," Billy called back, "we'll turn back, okay?"

The others nodded. Edward could barely make out Billy's silhouette. He turned back to Tommy who was watching the water warily. Edward squeezed his hand, and Tommy glanced up at him.

"It'll be okay," Edward called, trying his best to brave.

Billy pushed farther into the water. It raised a few inches, but leveled off just above his hips. The rocks became smaller and were overtaken by mud. Simon jerked as he felt something brush against his leg.

"What?" Billy asked.

"I think I just felt a fish," Simon said.

Billy smiled and kept on pressing across the water. Edward was now waist deep. He guessed they'd reached the halfway point, and Edward was more confident they could actually make it.

Billy dropped farther into the water, almost to his chest. He quickly rose up to his waist and glanced back at Simon.

"Watch out for that drop down!" he called, but Simon had already begun sliding down into the underwater pit. Ossie tried to pull him up but lost his balance.

"Hold on!" Billy growled.

Edward braced himself and tugged on Ossie, who was beginning to slide and drift toward edge of the waterfall. Ossie jerked and jumped and finally got a foothold. Simon stood up, lifting his head out of the water. He laughed and looked at the others. The smile faded.

"What?" Billy asked.

"Oh no," Simon mumbled, looking out toward the lake.

Through the fog, a wave came barreling down the stream. It pounded into the group. Tommy lost his footing and began tumbling toward the waterfall, yanking Edward's arm. Edward tightened his grip as the line was pulled toward the waterfall. They fought to get their feet under them. When one finally dug his feet into the bottom, he would be pulled on by the weight of the others. They all held on and tumbled toward the edge of the Island.

Tommy was just six feet from the waterfall when Billy, passing a large rock, wedged his feet under it. Simon managed to stand up. The line came to a stop, but Tommy continued whipping forward until he rammed against a large rock at the lip of the waterfall. His face was barely above the water as Edward tried to pull him back.

Tommy looked over the edge and saw the heavens below. He pushed himself up on the rock and tried to move back against the stream. He slipped and fell underwater. His head emerged. He shook the water out of his eyes and braced himself on the rock.

"Déjà vu, huh?" Tommy called to Edward with a weak smile.

Edward frowned and then tried to pull Tommy toward him.

"Here comes another wave!" Simon called.

Edward braced himself. He felt the wave pound against his back. The group lost its footing and tumbled over the edge of the waterfall. Tommy clung to the rock with one hand and tried to hold Edward's weight, but Edward's fingers slipped through his grasp.

Edward rolled and plummeted down the edge of the Island. He grasped through the falling water for the stony face of the Island, but couldn't reach. The water dissipated around him and the blanket of souls appeared beneath him. He could see the other children below him, screaming and groping at the empty air.

Lights appeared all around them, scooping up the other children below him. Edward felt himself slow as light glimmered around him. He came to a stop and then was jerked back up the face of the Island, over the side of the waterfall, and above the water as the others also floated around him. The only one not being carried by an angel was Tommy—he was still clinging to the rock as he watched the others float by and disappear into the fog.

The angels dropped the children on the shoreline and floated away.

"Go get Tommy!" Edward yelled, but the balls of lights faded into the fog.

"Tommy!" Edward yelled, looking into the mist, but not seeing him. Edward could barely make out the blur at the waterfall's edge. "Hang on, we'll get you!"

"Simon, lift this fog again!" Billy yelled.

The fog started swirling again, forming into funnels and lifting. Edward could see Tommy clearly; he was struggling to keep his face above the rushing water.

"Hold on, we'll get you," Edward called. Tommy carefully raised his hand and then clung back on the rock.

"We need a long branch or something," Billy said.

"We need rope, dammit!" Ossie shouted.

"Well, we don't have any, so get some branches!"

"Here comes another wave!" Simon shouted with his eyes still closed.

Edward ran to the shoreline and looked back out at Tommy.

"Here comes another wave!" Edward yelled.

Tommy nodded and braced himself. The water rammed into the rock. It tipped and then tumbled over the side, taking Tommy with it. Edward ran to the edge and watched Tommy fall.

"Where are the angels?" Edward yelled.

Tommy continued to fall. The water started evaporating around him. He was near the bottom edge of the Island. He was reaching for the edge of the Island, trying to grab for something.

His body dissipated like fog and disappeared.

"Tommy!" Edward yelled. He fell to the ground and continued staring over the edge. "Tommy!"

Billy looked over the edge and waited for Tommy to reappear. He began scanning the shoreline. Tommy never appeared. Billy noticed the same hazy figure on the other side of the waterfall. For a brief moment, he thought it was God watching from the other shore. Then the fog quickly fell again and covered the water.

chapter xxv

Distant clangs of the lunch bell woke the children
from their daze. They sat in the mist near the edge of
the waterfall, lonely, confused and reeling from the
regret of losing another friend. Edward cried silently as
Ossie put his arm over Edward's shoulder. Billy
grunted, stood and began leading the others back to the
campground.

Simon lingered and stared at the fog for a few
moments. It swirled and a thin funnel cut through the
mist and revealed the other shore. The funnel veered
left and right, surveying the land like a spotlight. The
funnel spun slower until the fog overtook it. Simon then
jogged to catch up with the others.

The lunch bell clanged again as they approached the
mess hall. I met near the tree line.

"Where's God?" Billy asked as he strode toward
God's house.

"Why?" I asked, trying to jog ahead of him and
slow him down.

"We need to talk," Billy stated, pushing me to the
side and continuing on.

"Not like this, Billy," I said, grabbing at his arm.
Billy jerked it free. "Billy!"

The front door to God's small house opened and Jay stepped out onto the front porch. Jay stood in front of the door like a sentry, watching Billy approach.

"Go eat, Billy," Jay called.

"I need to talk to God," Billy repeated, stepping up onto the porch and reaching for the door handle. Jay grabbed his hand and I stood in front of the door.

"Out of my way!" Billy growled.

"You need to settle down, Billy," I whispered. "Lower your voice, and let's go talk about this."

"I'm tired of talking to God's messenger boys," Billy said. "I'm going straight to the source — now, get out of my way!"

"Billy," I said. "This will be bad for you, and for everyone else in Cabin Five."

I took Billy's hand and eased it off the door handle.

"Now," I whispered, "let's go talk about this. If you can calm down, then I'll talk to God and see if he'll meet with you."

Billy glared at me, but he turned from the door and stepped off the porch. I sighed and glanced at Jay. He shook his head, grunted and followed Billy.

Edward stood in front of Cabin One. I walked to him and tried to lead him away. He jerked his shoulder free.

"Where's Tommy?" he asked, staring at the cabin.

"Edward," I whispered. "Not here, not now. We will talk, I promise."

"I want to talk now!"

I sighed and glanced at the cabin.

"I can't," I whispered. "I can't talk here, okay? Go eat, and we will talk. I promise."

Edward frowned, fixing his eyes on me for several seconds before turning to walk with the others.

"Go ahead and I'll be right there," I called to them. I then turned toward Cabin One.

I should have stayed and made Jay go talk to God. I don't have many regrets from my days on the Island, but I do regret that mistake.

Billy strode quickly toward the mess hall and Jay followed close behind.

"Back off, parasite," Billy growled.

Jay ignored him and even veered closer to Billy. Billy stopped and swiveled around to look at Jay.

"Back off!"

"No," Jay replied smugly. "I'm going to escort you to the mess hall. I don't want you to do anything stupid."

"Like what?"

Jay didn't answer, but held his stare. Ossie walked up and tried to step between them. Billy nudged Ossie back and took another step toward Jay.

"You want to try and stop me?" Billy asked. "Do you really think you can?"

"Don't snap at me because your little friend fell off the side of the Island," Jay smirked. "You led them there — it's your fault, not mine. Certainly not God's."

Billy's nostrils flared. Ossie stepped in again, along with Simon. Billy backed off, turned and continued toward the mess hall.

"Pretty soon, we'll be rid of you and your girlfriend," Jay called.

Billy pushed Ossie and Edward away and sprinted toward Jay. Jay backed up and tried to run, but Billy was on top of him. He pushed Jay to the ground and stood over him.

"Stay away from me!" Jay warned.

Jay tried to get to his feet, but Billy kicked him back down to the ground. Billy grabbed Jay's hand and twisted it around so that Jay's arm was held straight out. Jay rolled to his feet, but couldn't get free. Jay's shoulder was strained and he winced in pain.

Billy forced him forward past the mess hall, toward the lake.

"Stop it!" Jay grimaced. "Bali, help me!"

I emerged from God's house and saw what was happening. I jogged toward the mess hall, but stopped as I neared Billy.

"Be careful, Billy," I warned, but didn't do anything else to intervene.

Edward watched me carefully. I motioned for him to follow Billy as he continued leading Jay toward the lake.

Jay tried to squirm, but couldn't free himself. The closer they got to the pier, the more viciously Jay jerked. Billy swung him to the ground and grabbed his legs.

A dozen children were swimming in the lake, but they stopped playing and watched the scene unfold.

Billy pulled Jay backwards to the pier. Jay grabbed a plank. Billy yanked at his feet but Jay held tightly. Billy glanced up at Edward. Edward looked down at Jay and bent over. Jay looked into Edward's eyes.

"Please," Jay pleaded.

Edward unlatched Jay's fingers and Billy tugged him to the edge of the pier. Billy then dropped onto Jay's back. Billy latched his arms around Jay's head and neck, lifted him up and pushed him to the edge of the pier.

"No, no, don't!" Jay screamed. "You don't know what will happen!"

"You'll either swim or you'll drown," Billy growled.

Jay closed his eyes and took a deep breath just as Billy pushed him over the edge.

Jay fell silently and plunged into the water. He sunk and disappeared below. Edward stepped next to Billy and watched. I began walking to the pier. A series of bubbles hit the surface, but Jay remained below.

Billy stared into the water. Edward and Billy exchanged worried looks. They kicked off their shoes and socks, preparing to jump in after Jay.

"Don't!" I called.

"He's not coming up!" Billy said. "He sank like a stone!"

"He'll surface," I said, taking off my own shoes, then my shirt.

Jay's body finally emerged from the depths. He was facedown as he floated to the surface, like a corpse. He emerged from the water and his body continued to lift. His body rose until he was lying on the surface like it was glass. The water flattened out around him and the waves avoided him.

He lifted his head; his scalp was bleeding profusely. He pushed himself off the water. He stood weakly and looked at Billy and Edward. Blood poured out from his wrists, his shoes were drenched with blood and water. The side of his abdomen began bleeding as well.

The blood seeped through the lake, engulfing all the clear water in dark red. Some of the children began swimming for the shore; others watched in horror as the blood overtook them.

Jay collapsed and blood continued empting out of his body. I lowered down into the water and swam to his body. When I touched it, my body was lifted out of the water as well. I could stand on the surface, which was as solid as concrete.

I lifted Jay's body up in my arms and carried him to the pier. Billy and Edward leaned over and grabbed Jay and helped me sit him on the pier. Jay rolled over and looked up to Billy. He brushed Billy's cheek with his blood-soaked fingers.

"I forgive you," Jay whispered, then passed out.

Billy turned white and looked up at me, his eyes glazed over in panic.

"It's okay," I said, trying to calm Billy as well as the other terrified children. "He'll be okay, but we have to get him to God's cabin. Get his feet."

Billy grabbed Jay's legs and I grabbed his arms — taking great care not to touch the wounds in his wrists. We lifted him up and carried him off the pier. Edward grabbed our shoes and followed as the rest of the children watched.

Light began flickering on the water, just as it had in the volcano. Scenes began appearing around the children still in the water. There were men beating women, children crying, people dying, drugs, screams, moans, sin.

The children gazed at the scenes glittering on the water. The scenes played all together, the sounds drowning each other out, the images and colors running into each other. All together, it was impossible to tell what was happening on the surface of the water, but each individual knew what time of his or her past life was being replayed.

After a few minutes, the scenes faded and the children began trudging through the water to the shoreline. Some went to their cabins to change their blood-stained clothes. Some sat on the shoreline staring at the waves. The blood eventually sank to the bottom of the lake, and the water appeared clear again.

No one went back in.

chapter xxvi

Order amid clutter is the best way to describe Cabin
One. Sketches of planets, stars, animals, plants and
human-like figures cover every inch of wall space.
There are four separate handmade wire and clay solar
systems hanging from the ceiling. The floor has only
slim paths from the couch to the bed and to the door.
The rest is crowded by tables and desks covered with
computers, drawing boards and tiny figurines placed
methodically on role-playing game boards. Tucked in
the corner was an easel with an unfinished painting of
two barrel-chested, cleanly shaven and sweaty Roman
centurions standing victoriously on a battleground filled
with human carnage.

God was crouched over a small table, wearing
reading glasses with magnifying lenses clipped over the
regular lenses. He peered down at a spherical brownish
clay planet in His hands. He glanced at a drawing
hanging next to Him, then back at the planet. He
carefully picked at it with an X-acto knife, tracing small
lines along its surface.

His eye color reflected the detail and hues of the
clay planet, even when he wasn't looking at it.

The door rattled open, slamming into a table. American Civil War figurines on the table rattled and fell over. God didn't look up from the planet as I backed into the cabin, still clinging to Jay's arms. The blood was pouring from his wrists, making it hard for me to grip his arms. As we walked along the slim path in Cabin One, the blood trickled down onto the wooden floor. Billy banged against another table and winced as a grassy, styrofoam mountain tipped over onto a group of chariots, rolled over a legion of foot soldiers and tumbling off the table. Billy kicked it out of his way and we struggled toward a ratty, gray and blue couch pushed against the wall next to the window. We dropped Jay down onto the couch and I knelt down beside him, wiping the blood from his eyes.

"Jay!" I called to him. "Can you hear me?"

God was still carving His little ball of clay as Jay's blood soaked into the couch.

"Sir!" Billy called.

God sighed and looked up at Billy, his eyes magnified through the glasses with the clay planet fading from his eyeballs and a dark blue tide flooding into its place. Billy stared at His eyes until God flipped up the magnifying lenses and His eyes shrank back to normal, or as close to normal as God's eyes ever got.

"Jay needs your help!"

"It can wait," God grumbled, returning his focus to the small planet.

A soft knock on the door drew my attention away from Jay. Edward was standing in the doorframe holding our shoes and my organizer. I motioned for him to leave them by the door.

I pulled off Jay's shirt and Billy helped me take off
his shorts. I took off my own shirt and covered him.
Blood continued streaming down from cuts along his
forehead. I stood and rushed over to God.

"What do you need me to do?" I whispered.

"Leave me alone!" God growled.

I backed away, shook my head, and then walked to
a box shoved under a table. There were white bath
towels folded inside. I grabbed them and tossed one to
Billy and another to Edward.

"Dry him off!"

They rushed over to Jay and began drying off his
skin, his head and hair. Once the towels were soaked
through with water and blood, I threw them new ones.
They tossed the bloodied towels into a pile by the door.
Jay began groaning and jerking as they rubbed the dry
towels into the gaping wounds. Billy wrapped a towel
around his hand and pressed it tightly.

"No!" I called. "He has to bleed. Just get off the
water!"

The process continued, with the pile of bloody
towels growing. By the time the box was empty, Billy
and Edward were covered from chest to feet with Jay's
blood. The wounds had slowed to a trickle, Jay's hair
was wet with blood, but there didn't seem to be much
water left.

God yawned, removed the glasses and stood. He
walked to one of the wire solar systems and pressed the
clay planet onto a wire rod. He studied it, adjusted it
and then wiped His hands off on His shirt. He glanced
down at the pile of bloodied towels.

"I'll get them," I said, rushing over and gathering
them up.

God walked around me toward Jay. He paused and looked over the game boards and the fallen pieces. He shook his head and then knelt down beside Jay. He ran his hand through the boy's blood-soaked hair.

"He always has the hardest time," God whispered to himself. He rubbed His hands over the cuts in Jay's forehead, wrists, abdomen and feet. The bleeding stopped.

"What happened?" God asked, still watching Jay.

"He fell into the lake," I said as I lifted up the towels.

"It was my fault," Billy corrected. "He didn't actually fall—I threw him in."

"I …," Edward mumbled. "I did, too."

God stood and faced Billy.

"Who actually threw him in?"

"I did," Billy said, raising his hand.

God motioned for Edward and me to leave. I cradled the pile of towels that were dripping all over me and led Edward to the door, but he stopped before he stepped outside.

"Why didn't You tell us he was Jesus?" Edward asked.

"What difference would it have made?" God asked, then waved Edward away.

Edward shook his head, took one more look at Jay, then closed the door.

"Sir," Billy started, but God held up his hand. He ducked under a table to fetch the small mountain. He took it back to its game board, sat it down and began standing figurines back up.

"Sorry about that," Billy said. "What can I do to help?'

"You've done enough, thank you."

Billy sighed, dipped his head and waited. God fussed over each figurine, adjusting its position, craning his head down to check the figurine's line of sight. He would then stand and look from above, and if satisfied, move to the next piece. Billy could only stand silent.

When he finished the game board, God walked to one next to Billy. He shooed Billy away, so Billy walked toward the couch and sat down on a patch of floor that didn't have any blood on it. Jay was sleeping on his stomach. His face was still pale; his lips were bluish pink.

Billy looked up from time to time, checking God's progress. Hours seemed to pass as God methodically worked with each figurine, checking its line of sight and its placement in respect to the other figurines.

Billy shifted to different sitting positions as his knees got sore. Jay's face began to warm as God fussed over the last game board we'd bumped into. The dinner bell rang, but Billy stayed still.

"Okay," God mumbled. "Why did you do it?"

"Sir," Billy said as he pushed himself off the ground. "I lost my temper—it was all my fault. I apologize."

"Why did you lose your temper?" God asked, turning to Billy. God's eyes were a light blue. He watched Billy, His expression somewhat detached, like that of a bored supervisor.

"We lost Tommy today," Billy said, dipping his head. "He fell off the side of the Island. It was just a lot to take, and Jay ... I have no good excuse, Sir. I just lost my temper."

"Why did you go to the waterfall?"

Billy didn't answer immediately, taking a few breaths and thinking about Sophia.

"Because I don't understand this place," Billy replied, still averting his eyes. "None of us do, and I just hoped that something over there might give me an answer."

"Why do you think there are any answers for you to have?" God asked, His tone curious. His eyes darkened, almost to a royal blue. He approached Billy and looked down on him. "Why is it not enough just to have faith?"

"I don't know, Sir. I'm trying, but it's hard."

"No," God said dispassionately, turning away and returning to his work table. "It's not hard—you simply don't think about the other side of the lake. Don't think about Petrov, don't think about Tommy, don't think about ... what's that girl you sit with?"

"Sophia, Sir."

"Yes, Sophia," God sighed. "Don't think about the distractions, and they will go away. Okay?"

"Okay."

God examined Billy as he picked up the magnifying glasses and used his shirt to buff the lenses.

"I can send you to the wilderness for this, Billy."

"I know."

"Do you want me to?"

Billy shook his head and looked up at God.

"I want to stay here."

"With Sophia."

Billy's head dropped. He gritted his teeth and his eyes fell on World War II figurines on the game board next to him. There was one that caught his eye, a British Marine figurine. It was molded to look like it had been shot in the stomach. It was laying on the ground, head turned up toward the sky as another figurine, an American Navy Corpsman was bent over him, dressing his wounds. The figurine's anguished face was lifelike.

The figurine's face turned; its eyes met Billy's. It reached its hand up at Billy, asking for help.

Billy jerked back and bumped against another table. The Civil War figurines fell again and God threw up his hands with a growl.

He shooed Billy away as he replaced the figures. He stopped, turned toward Billy and looked down on him.

"Your cabin has been quite the headache for Me; I should send all of you over."

"That wouldn't be fair, Sir. It was my idea. It was my responsibility."

God flipped the magnifying lenses back over his reading glasses and his blue eyeballs blossomed into a dark green.

"Go eat," God mumbled. "I'll give this some thought."

Billy didn't know what to say in response, so he just kept quiet. God turned toward the table and began standing the figurines in their correct locations again. Billy turned and took one last look at Jay.

"Billy," God called. "Give your friends a message for me."

******

"So what does that make Bali?" Ossie whispered.

Ossie, Simon and Edward were huddled together at the table in the mess hall. Everyone was chattering, all about the same thing. Each cabin had become its own insular sect, none of the children trusting their thoughts beyond their small circle. They were all segregated in lumps along the table, whispering back and forth as they tried to fit the new clues into the Island's puzzle.

Martha and her cabinmates were now draped in white bed sheets fashioned like burkas. Simon called them the "Ku Klux Clams" and was annoyed no one else thought it was funny.

The boys in Cabin Three had drawn red crosses on their foreheads and black dots on their wrists where Jay's wounds were. Cabin Four had started a pool on who would be the next to go, and the one who had bet on Billy was gloating. His face quickly sank when Billy walked through the door.

Sophia began to stand but was pulled down by her cabinmates. Billy's kept his head lowered as he retrieved his tray. Edward and the others rushed over to him.

"He's letting you stay?" Simon asked.

"Not sure," Billy shrugged as mashed potatoes dropped onto his plate.

"How's Jay, is he going to be okay?" Edward asked. Billy nodded.

"Go sit down," I called to Billy's cabinmates. "Everyone settle down; we will talk about this in the morning. Hurry up and eat your food and go to your cabins—we're turning in early tonight."

Billy sat down with the others. He motioned for them to huddle in.

"I'm sorry, guys," Billy whispered. "This is my fault."

"Don't worry about it," Ossie replied, patting his shoulder.

"Well, I'm gonna," Billy grumbled. "We all are. God told me that one of us is going over tomorrow, but He won't say who."

chapter xxvii

Billy's eyes fluttered open as he heard the floorboards creak under footsteps. He arched his head up to see over his bunk. Edward was walking toward the door. Through the window, Billy could see the morning sunlight pushing through an ocean of fog that rose off the lake and crawled through the campground. Billy rubbed the sleep out of his eyes and sat up.

The cabin residents had stayed up late, talking and guessing who it would be that left the next morning. Billy felt guilty that he'd hoped Edward would have been full-grown when he saw him that morning.

Edward was still a child.

"Hey," he mumbled to Edward. "Where are you going?"

Edward turned. His eyes were red and he wouldn't lift them up to meet Billy's. Edward just shrugged and turned for the door.

"Hold on," Billy called, slipping down from his bunk. He grabbed his socks and shoes from under Ossie's bed and pulled them on.

Edward paused at the door and waited, not looking back at Billy. Billy threw on an extra T-shirt and then followed Edward outside into the golden fog. The sun

was a dim, blurry disc just above the horizon. It hadn't
started warming the campground yet, and goosebumps
rose on the children's skin. Neither said anything, and
Billy just followed Edward past the cabins and into the
woods.

Billy had already guessed where Edward was
headed.

The cliff came into view, with the plane parked
close to the edge of the Island. Billy wondered what
would happen if they pushed the plane over. Could the
angels catch it? If not, would God be stuck there?
Could He fly? Could the angels carry Him back to
Heaven? Would the children be stuck here? Another
question was more pressing, though.

"Why are we here, Edward?"

Edward shrugged and walked toward the plane. He
raised his hand to touch the nose, wiping off the
morning dew. He kept walking as he dried his hands on
his shorts and stopped just shy of the cliff. He clasped
his hands behind his back and stared over the edge.

Billy stood next to him and watched Heaven below.

"I understand why you are thinking about it," Billy
said. "Believe me, I do. It's not going to do any good,
though."

"Why?"

"The angels will catch you," Billy said.

"They didn't catch Tommy."

There was no answer to that. Billy just stayed close.
He considered what he should do if Edward tried to
jump, and whether it would be for the best to let him
go.

"Have you thought about going over to the other side of the Island?" Billy asked. "Just to see if it's any better?"

"Wasn't that what got Tommy killed?"

Edward's face was blank, drained of emotion. He looked tired, but not in a way that one could simply sleep off. It was an exhaustion that soaked him all the way to his soul.

"Maybe you're not right for this side," Billy began. "Maybe you'd be happier on the other side. Hell, I'm not sure any of us are, and whoever God ends up choosing, it might be the best thing for them."

Edward grunted, but didn't take his eyes off the heavens below.

"If you ever want to …" Billy began, but winced and cut himself off.

"What?" Edward asked.

"If you decide you want to … you know." Billy nodded at the cliff. "I don't think you should, but if you decide to go over, promise you will talk to me first. I won't stop you, but I at least want to know and talk to you first."

"Okay, thank you."

Edward sat on the ground, inched up to the edge of the cliff and dangled his legs off the ledge. Billy sat down next to him and wished Sophia were around. She'd be better at dealing with this sort of thing. He also thought about me, but I knew better than to interfere at this point.

"When I committed suicide," Billy started with a grimace, "I didn't feel that there was anywhere left for me to go. The world seemed closed off to me. War was over, my home was crumbling, I didn't have any real friends around me anymore. The only thing I had were the nightmares and the fear. I can see how you'd feel isolated now, but I think maybe you might explore all your options before you decide to end it all. We've only seen a small part of this place, and maybe the wilderness isn't so bad."

"What would you think of me if I did jump?" Edward asked, for the first time looking over at Billy.

Billy tried to smile, but it came out like a frown.

"I want you to stay here," Billy said. "Our cabin needs you, but if you do jump, I'll support you. I understand the pain, and it's not an easy thing to live with. Hell, if you ask me nicely, I'll push you."

Edward chuckled and looked back over the cliff. He leaned forward and stared straight down to the bottom of the Island.

"I wonder if I'd just sail back into the cliff face, smack into a rock and get stuck?" Edward grinned.

"Like a blob of bird crap?" Billy asked. "They'd send us down to clean you off, or just kick you off like you were stuck in the grill of a car."

Edward smiled wider and leaned back to lay on the ground.

"Here's the real question," Billy said. "Do you really want to die a virgin a second time?"

Edward gave Billy a curious grin.

"Oh, no, not me," Billy said, standing up and backing away, shaking out slightly like he'd fallen in animal feces. "Someone else, boy."

"I know," Edward replied, looking up through the fog. "Um, I don't know. I'm just a kid, those hormones haven't kicked in yet, I guess. What about you?"

"Well, I wasn't a virgin back in the real world," Billy said, still standing uncomfortably. "Sex wasn't ever an issue with me, but I never had any good kind of love, you know? My wife did her best, but…"

The comment just hung and Edward knew better than to pursue it.

"And Sophia?"

"Sophia," Billy echoed. "Yeah, I think I do love her. I'm okay with not ever having sex again, but I don't want to live without her."

"You could go over to the other side of the Island with her, see what it's like."

Billy shook his head and sat back down on the ground. Edward shrugged and looked back up at the fog.

"Is sex really worth it?" Edward asked. "Is that really enough to justify living?"

"Son," Billy chuckled. "When I was at the loneliest in my life, one good lay gave me a hundred times the hope that any sermon ever did. I don't know nothing about your kind of sex, but our kind is just about the greatest thing God ever came up with."

"Huh," Edward grunted with a smile. He sat up and stood, then glanced over the edge. "Angels would probably catch me anyway."

Edward turned to Billy and motioned back to the campground. Billy stood and followed.

"Thanks for talking with me," Edward said.

"No problem."

"So, if I do decide to go over to the other side of the Island," Edward said, "any idea how to get started on that?"

Billy took a hard breath. He glanced over at Edward, but only shrugged.

"I guess it's between me and God then."

They walked silently down the path. Edward stopped and grabbed Billy, pulling him into a hug. Billy grimaced.

"You're all right, Marine."

"Uh, thanks," Billy cringed. "Just don't let anyone see us like this, okay?

******

The first growth spurt started just before breakfast, and they continued throughout the morning. Around 11 p.m., Edward was a full-grown man. The others in the cabin hid their relief, instead giving Edward sympathetic frowns, patting him on the back and talking about their time in camp.

Edward seemed more relaxed. Somber, but resolved.

I offered to let Edward eat his lunch at the campground, but he was ready to leave. The children had gathered at the shore. Jay emerged from Cabin One and watched from behind the mess hall. Sophia and Billy stood together on the pier. Edward walked up to Billy and bent to hug him. Ossie reached in and hugged Edward. Simon ran up and jumped on Edward's back. He wrapped his arms around Edward's neck and squeezed tightly.

"Okay," Edward gasped, peeling Simon off his back. "I have to go."

"Thank you, Edward," Sophia whispered. She believed that Edward had chosen to go so Billy didn't have to—perhaps she was right.

Edward smiled and walked down the pier where I waited near the boat. Edward turned one last time as he stepped down into the boat. He waved and his cabinmates waved back.

"Tell Petrov 'hello'!" Ossie called.

"I will," Edward smiled.

I sat down in the rowboat and grabbed one oar, and motioned for Edward to take the other. We began rowing away from the pier.

"Bali?" Edward asked.

"Yes."

"Am I going to be happy over there?"

"If you choose to be."

We continued rowing. The sun bore straight down on us. Edward looked back to the shore; some of the children still watched us drift away. The airplane engine growled and revved up. It soon soared up from the Island and zoomed across the lake. It disappeared into the clouds.

"Is He going to find another soul to replace me?" Edward asked.

"Don't worry about that," I replied. "Just worry about finding your place in the wilderness."

"How many people are over there?"

"You won't be alone," I answered. "Unless you choose to be. It's not an easy place to live, but you will have more freedom. Probably more freedom than you ever had on Earth."

Edward glanced back at the campground one last time, and the remaining children were just small dots on the pier. Edward waved his arm high above his head, but couldn't tell if they waved back.

When turned to look at the far shore. It was long and there were no piers anywhere. There were no signs of civilization at all. We were passing the waterfall and the currents tugged at us but didn't alter our route.

Edward looked down into the water as we paddled, watching thick, big-mouth bass race alongside and under the boat.

God would sometimes row out and feed them, which no one knew but me. I think He missed the wildlife, too, but they caused Jay too many problems.

"I guess I'll have to learn to hunt and fish," Edward chuckled.

White birds flew out from the other shore and were circling above us. They were all sizes—some seagulls, some doves and even a crane.

"Looks like someone came out to meet you," I called to Edward.

He looked around to the shore to see a lone figure standing near the water.

"Who is it?"

"Do you really have to ask?"

Edward smiled.

"No, I guess I don't."

With that, he began rowing anxiously. I struggled to match his pace, but we started veering off course. When the figure waved from the shore, Edward rolled out of the boat and dropped into the lake. The figure ran out into the water and the two swam to meet each other and to, together, face the next phase of God's experiment on that lonely Island.

CPSIA information can be obtained at www.ICGtesting.com
Printed in the USA
LVOW10s2325230815

451270LV00001B/12/P